Day of the Accident

NUALA ELLWOOD

PENGUIN BOOKS

PENGUIN BOOKS

UK | USA | Canada | Ireland | Australia
India | New Zealand | South Africa

Penguin Books is part of the Penguin Random House group of companies
whose addresses can be found at global.penguinrandomhouse.com.

First published 2019

003

Set in 13/15.25 pt Garamond MT Std
Typeset by Jouve (UK), Milton Keynes
Printed and bound in Great Britain by Clays Ltd, Elcograf S.p.A.

A CIP catalogue record for this book is available from the British Library

ISBN: 978-0-241-97734-7

www.greenpenguin.co.uk

Penguin Random House is committed to a
sustainable future for our business, our readers
and our planet. This book is made from Forest
Stewardship Council® certified paper.

For Nerina

'When it hurts, we return to the
banks of certain rivers'

Czesław Miłosz

What readers are saying about

Day of the Accident

★ ★ ★ ★ ★

'Hang on to your seats'
Sue, *Netgalley*

★ ★ ★ ★ ★

'Intriguing and compelling . . . it kept me awake for hours'
Christina, *Netgalley*

★ ★ ★ ★ ★

'A brilliant read. Highly recommended'
Joanna, *Netgalley*

★ ★ ★ ★ ★

'Clever. Original. Inventive. Exhilarating. 5/5'
Natalie, *Netgalley*

★ ★ ★ ★ ★

'I really didn't see the ending coming'
Matthew, *Netgalley*

★ ★ ★ ★ ★

'Oh, this is a fabulous book!'
Valerie, *Netgalley*

★ ★ ★ ★ ★

'Wow, what an incredibly well-written book. I loved it'
Melita, *Netgalley*

★ ★ ★ ★ ★

'WOW and WOW again. This is definitely going
to be one of my favourite reads of this year'
Nicki, *Netgalley*

★ ★ ★ ★ ★

'A brilliantly fascinating, multi-layered mystery that
kept me hooked and guessing'
Jennifer, *Netgalley*

★ ★ ★ ★ ★

'Highly recommended'
Pauline, *Netgalley*

ABOUT THE AUTHOR

Nuala Ellwood was chosen as one of the *Observer*'s 'New Faces of Fiction 2017' for her first thriller, the bestselling *My Sister's Bones*. Nuala teaches Creative Writing at York St John University, and lives in the city with her young son.

Prologue

Now that I'm finally here I realize that what I feel, more than anything, is a sense of unburdening. I always knew deep down inside me that it would have to come out in the end; that someone would have to pay.

The two officers flanking me stare straight ahead, though my eyes are drawn to the ceiling. Its honeycomb design seems to shift and bend as we walk, like the ripples on the surface of a river. Somewhere up there they will be taking their seats, the strangers with whom my fate now rests. They will be issuing polite greetings, shuffling papers, reading notes. All in a day's work for them, this case, an open and shut one according to my lawyer, though not to me; not to me.

Elspeth is with me as we come to a halt by an ornate wooden door. I can feel her presence like a second skin as the first officer steps forward to open it, then with a tilt of the head ushers his colleague and myself through.

The officers lead me to my spot and though my

lawyer has prepared me for this moment, rehearsed it until I'm pitch-perfect, it is still a shock to be in this room. I look up to a sea of black-robed figures all on their feet and I'm reminded of Elspeth's charcoal drawing of the crows that used to litter the meadow at Larkfields. When she'd finished it we hung it on the wall in the kitchen so everyone could admire it. Yet, though Elspeth had been very proud of the drawing, I had always found it chilling, as though it were alluding to something much darker, something rotten that lay hidden at the heart of our family. And now, in this moment, when my mind should be focused on the proceedings at hand, all I can think of is the collective noun for a group of crows.

A murder.

I swallow the thought as the judge begins to speak. As he reads out the list of charges I lower my eyes and try to summon Elspeth to my side again. But all I can see is the river and that secret spot where the two alder trees, leafless and bone clean, bend their heads towards each other. I recall the pain, the eerie silence. The panic. The fear. I hear the words I told myself over and over. This is for the best; this way I can wipe the slate clean and make it all better.

'Margaret Rose Allan.'

The judge is addressing me. I stand up. I try to appear calm though my left leg is shaking violently.

The judge continues to speak. I hear the word

'manslaughter' and though I have prepared for this, the enormity of it suddenly hits.

'How do you plead? Guilty or not guilty?'

'Forgive me, Elspeth,' I think as I enter my plea. 'Please forgive me.'

PART ONE

I

I wake to a liquid world. Orbs of yellow light hang in front of me. I try to blink them away but they grow bigger and bigger until their bloated shape is all I can see.

I close my eyes and the pain begins; faint at first then raw, excruciating, splitting my head into tiny pieces that fall into the dead space around me as I lie here unable to move. I hear movement in the room and voices low and muffled. A hand touches my arm and I feel something sharp penetrate my skin.

'She's stirring.'

A male voice. He sounds like he is under water. I stay still, my breath rising and falling alongside the pain in a twisted tandem. Up and down, up and down.

'Have we managed to contact her husband?'

The aquatic voice gurgles somewhere on the margins of the room. I can only hear in waves. Another voice answers but I can't make out the words. Then the man speaks again. This time he sounds clearer, like his face is pressed right next to mine.

I recognize his voice now. It's the man from my dream. I want to see him but my eyes won't focus properly. Everything is blurred.

'Maggie, can you hear me?'

I go to speak but my mouth is full of water. River water. The milky taste of the Ouse. I hear it rushing in my ears, into my nose. I try to breathe but the water is consuming me.

'Maggie,' he repeats, the name a rock thudding against my head. 'Can you hear me?'

The answer is, yes, I can. And not only at this moment but for some time now. I've lived with his voice, all their voices, in my dream world, the world I'm reluctantly leaving. The lure of sleep is over-whelming. It entices me with its velvet embrace, tempting me to lose myself in its folds.

'Maggie,' says the man firmly. 'I need to know if you can hear me.'

I turn my head then and look straight at him. The fog begins to clear and he comes into focus, a man in his early forties with cropped greying hair and thick blue-rimmed glasses.

'Yes,' I whisper, finally, hearing the collective sigh of relief trickle through the room. Then more loudly: 'Yes.'

2

Wednesday 19 July

Something is shifting. I become aware, slowly, of noise, chatter. My eyes are the first to respond, flicking open like a switch taking me from darkness into light. I see a glass window in front of me. There's a blur of colour behind it; movement, figures. I try to focus on the figures but they bleed out like street lights reflected in a puddle. I blink, once, twice, three times, then I turn my head. The movement brings about a sensation akin to travel sickness. I'm aware of a tightening in my throat. I go to touch it but my arm won't move. I look down and see wires. They are attached to my hands and chest.

'Hello,' I say, my voice a croak. 'Hello?' Louder this time.

I hear the door open. A man appears at the end of the bed.

'Maggie?' he says, his voice loud and deliberate.

I recognize his voice.

'My name's Dr Elms.'

Dr Elms. I last heard the name in my coma dream.

'Wheremi?' I say, pushing the words out. 'Wheremi?'

My mouth feels twisted. The words aren't forming properly. My lips feel numb.

'You're in Lewes Victoria Hospital.'

He is speaking very slowly, like a warped record.

I look beyond him and see two women, one in a blue uniform, the other in pink. The one in pink smiles at me then comes over and sits by the bed. I feel her hand on my hand. It's warm.

'You're doing really well, Maggie,' she says, gently.

I turn to look at her. She's middle-aged with short mousy hair and a soft, kind face.

'I'm Claire,' she says. 'I'm your nurse.'

When she says that word a sharp pain engulfs my chest and I ball my fists, willing the pain to subside.

'Let me get you some water,' says Claire.

She pours a cup from the jug by the bed then brings it to my mouth. I take a long sip. The water is cool and refreshing but the pain remains. Panicky pain.

'Whatsss,' I say as Claire takes the cup away. 'Whatsshappened?'

My brain feels like it's turned to liquid and my words are drowning in it.

Dr Elms walks over and sits down on the chair next to the bed.

'I'm afraid you were involved in an accident,' he says, emphasizing that final word with a nod of his head. 'You lost consciousness and have been in a coma for nearly ten weeks.'

Claire rubs my hand. It sends a shiver up my spine and I jolt up in the bed.

'Accssdent?' I say, my mouth twitching as I try to take hold of the word. 'Accssdent?'

'Yes, an accident,' says Dr Elms. 'A car accident.'

As he speaks, I'm suddenly gripped with panic. I look around the room. There's Dr Elms, Claire and the other woman in a blue uniform. There's a room with a window looking out on to a corridor. I look back at the three people. Elms, Claire, uniform. Elms, Claire, uniform. Someone is missing. Someone should be here.

Elspeth.

'Essh,' I cry, throwing back the sheet. 'Essh . . .'

Claire puts her hand out to hold me back.

'It's okay, Maggie,' she says. 'Try to keep calm.'

The name is in my head but it won't form on my lips. The most important name, the most important person in my life, and I can't get it out.

'Daaaa . . .' I begin, ripping through the film that separates my thoughts from my speech. 'Dauu . . . Esssh?'

'What is she saying?' says Elms, turning to Claire.

'I'm not sure,' says Claire.

'Esssssh,' I cry, pounding my fists on the bed in frustration.

'Maggie, it's okay,' says Dr Elms, coming towards me with his palms raised. 'You're safe now. It's all okay.'

I shake my head as he approaches. He puts his hand on my hand.

'Whesh,' I gasp, but I can feel my voice getting weaker. 'Wheshe?'

'I didn't quite get that, Maggie,' he says gently. 'But don't worry, just try to rest for now.'

Raw terror rips through me. Why won't they answer my question? I need to get out of here. I need to find her.

'Maggie, no,' cries Elms as I launch myself forward.

I feel his arms on mine.

'Claire, get the midazolam.'

I try to fight him but he's too strong. Claire's face appears in front of me. I feel a sharp sting in my arm and then the room starts to melt. I put my head back on the pillow. The panic dissipates. I try to remember what I wanted to ask but I can't grasp it . . . it's slipping . . . I fall.

3

Elspeth is sitting on the end of the bed. Her hair is sopping wet and the purple fleece dressing gown I bought her last winter is caked with mud. She pulls her knees to her chest. Her feet are bare and filthy.

'Oh my darling, thank goodness,' I say, sitting up. 'Where have you been? Mummy was so worried.'

She doesn't answer me. Her eyes look strange, almost glassy.

'Elspeth, what is it?' I say, wishing I could take out the wires that anchor me to the bed. 'What happened to your dressing gown?'

She opens her mouth to speak but the voice that comes out isn't hers. It is a woman's.

'Maggie.'

My eyes flicker and I feel myself rising up.

'Maggie.'

'Elspeth,' I cry.

My eyes open. Elspeth is gone. Instead I see a nurse. I'm sure I've seen her before. Then I remember. Her name is Claire.

'Good morning, Maggie,' she says. 'You're looking a little brighter.'

I look around the room, my chest tightening with fear.

'Wherishi?' I say, my words still not forming properly. 'Where . . . whereishi? Sh – she – wazere. She . . .'

The effort of trying to get my words out exhausts me and I lie back on the pillow, defeated.

'Maggie, I'm just going to get Dr Elms,' says Claire, her voice calm and steady. 'I won't be a moment.'

The memory of Elspeth sitting on the bed stills my nerves a little. She's in another room of course. She'll be in the children's ward. That's why Claire's gone to get the doctor. He'll be able to take these wires off me so I can go and see her. I whisper this to myself over and over, trying to keep the fear at bay. But the room feels like it's closing in on me. The smell of antiseptic and boiled vegetables hangs heavy in the air and it reminds me of another place; a place I have spent my life trying to block out. Don't think about that, I tell myself, as I lie here waiting for them to return, don't let the dark thoughts in. Everything is going to be okay. They're going to tell you where she is.

The door opens and I look up with a start.

'Hi there, Maggie.'

Dr Elms walks in, followed by Claire.

'How are you feeling this morning?' he says, sitting down on the plastic chair by my bed.

'Where's . . .' I say, willing myself to get the word. 'Where's . . . my . . . girl?'

A look passes between Claire and Dr Elms. A look that says something is wrong, something is terribly wrong.

'Tell,' I say, terrified now. 'Please . . . you got tell . . . me.'

Claire sits down on the other side of the bed and puts her hand on my arm. I don't like the way she is looking at me. It scares me.

'What?' I say. 'What . . . is it?'

Dr Elms takes off his glasses and rubs his eyes. Then, replacing them, he leans forward and speaks slowly, gently.

'Maggie, do you remember I told you that you were involved in a car accident?'

I nod my head.

'Well, your vehicle was found submerged in water on the banks of the river.'

The river. I see a canopy of trees, their branches bending in the wind.

'You were lying face down on the riverbank,' he continues, his eyes boring into mine as he speaks. 'Unconscious with some head and hand wounds.'

I look down at my hands for the first time. I have no fingernails.

'It seems you made contact with the vehicle as you tried to stop it rolling into the water,' says Dr Elms.

I look down again at my mutilated hands. There is only one reason why I would try to stop a rolling car and that would be because there was someone inside it.

'Whereishi?' I say, my whole body seizing up with fear. 'Elspeth?'

I try to grab the doctor's arm, but the effort almost knocks me sideways. The pain in my chest intensifies and I flop back on to the pillow.

'This might be too soon, Dr Elms,' says Claire. 'Perhaps we should wait a little longer.'

'In my experience it will be worse if we leave it,' says Dr Elms, his voice muffled as he turns away from me. 'She is asking the question. I am obliged to answer truthfully.'

They are talking as though I'm not here.

'Worse?' I say. 'Tell . . . what . . . happened.'

He sits up straight and clears his throat. His eyes can barely meet mine.

'Okay,' he says. 'We think you were trying to free her when you were knocked unconscious.'

'Her,' I say as the room folds in on me. 'Wh– what?'

'Your daughter,' says Dr Elms. 'The fire crew reported that she was still in the car when the car rolled into the water. The door was locked.'

I shake my head; try to take in what he is saying.

'No,' I say. 'I'd never . . .'

16

Dr Elms goes to speak then stops.

He looks across at Claire. She shakes her head.

'But they . . . they got her out, didn't they?' I say, my body pulsating with terror. 'They got her out . . . of the car . . .'

They don't answer.

'Elsp,' I scream, yanking at the wires. 'Please . . . you have to . . . tell me she's . . .'

Claire puts her hand on my arm. Her skin feels clammy on mine. I push her away.

'I'm begging you,' I cry, tears clouding my eyes. 'She's my . . . baby . . . She's my . . . she's my life.'

Elms pushes his glasses up with the tip of his index finger, then fixes his eye on me.

'I'm very sorry, Maggie,' he says, his voice as spare as a telegram. 'But I'm afraid your daughter died at the scene.'

A high-pitched sound, like the air being released from a balloon, fills the air. Only after a couple of minutes do I realize that the noise is coming from me.

'I'm so sorry, Maggie,' says Claire.

'She wouldn't have felt anything,' Elms says. 'It would have been like going to sleep.' But his eyes don't meet mine.

I start to rock, forwards and backwards; as though movement will suspend the horror.

'We realize this is the worst possible news,' says Elms. 'And we are so terribly, terribly sorry.'

I look up at him but all I see is Elspeth. My beautiful girl.

'No,' I say, shaking my head. 'No. You're wrong. She wazere, just . . . just on bed. Wet hair. She's cold. She . . . she needs me.'

Elms shakes his head.

I look across at Claire. Her eyes are full of tears.

'Help,' I whimper. 'Help . . . me . . . find her.'

'Maggie, she's not here, love,' says Claire, wiping her eye with the back of her hand. 'She's not here.'

And then something rises up inside me. A hot burst of anger.

'This is crazy,' I cry. 'I saw her. She was here. Going to go find her.'

I throw the covers back and try to get out of the bed.

'Maggie, don't,' says Claire.

I try to jump down but the wires hold me back. I grab at the drip in my arm, try to yank it out, but Elms grabs my arms tightly.

'Let me go,' I cry. 'Please just let me go.'

'Oh God,' whispers Claire, beside me.

Elms holds me down as Claire adjusts the drip. I catch his eye. And something about his expression confirms it all. My Elspeth, my beautiful Elspeth. I start to scream. My body jerks. Elms shouts something to Claire but I don't hear what he says.

'No,' I cry as they try to guide me back on to the pillow. 'Not Elspeth. Not my baby. No, no, no.'

'Quickly, Claire,' hisses Elms, still holding me down.

I look up into Claire's face as she prepares to administer the sedative. Her eyes are swollen with tears and her bottom lip is quivering.

'I'm so sorry,' she says as she leans forward and pushes the needle into my skin.

I look at her blankly. Then I let my head drop back on the pillow. As the door closes I feel something snap inside me. I put my hand to my heart. It is still beating steadily though it has broken into a thousand pieces.

4

The room is quiet save for the soft beeping noise of the bedside monitor where my blood pressure is displayed in stark green letters. Outside the door I can hear the nurses chatting at their station. One of them lets out a shriek of laughter and the noise cuts through me like a blade.

It has been twelve hours since I received the news. Twelve hours of lying on my back, unable to move. I want to scream and yell but my body is numb and when I try to talk the words won't come. Claire came in earlier and administered more pain relief. It's so strong it feels like I'm floating above myself.

A moment ago Dr Elms came and sat by my bed and told me about my injuries. I sustained some lung damage while in the river. Most likely it was my attempts to call for help while submerged in water that did it. He talked about the risks of developing inflammation of the lungs and how they are monitoring me for this; he spoke of his relief that the CT scans, taken when I was in the coma, showed healthy brain activity; no sign of damage.

Yet all the while he sat there, talking, as doctors do, in that cold, matter-of-fact way, about recovery and rehabilitation and physiotherapy sessions, I could only think of Elspeth, my beautiful ten-year-old girl.

I can't accept what they are telling me. I would know if she were dead. I would feel it in my bones. There would be a sense of finality, a full stop. No, they are wrong. Elspeth got out of that car. She wandered off and now she is out there somewhere, lost and afraid. I can feel it.

It's the same feeling I used to get if I lost sight of her in the supermarket, a raw, knee-buckling panic. But she would always reappear; I can see her little face now, peeking out from behind the shelves. 'Did I scare you, Mummy?'

She would always reappear.

That is why I know she is still alive, and that, wherever she is, she needs me. She needs her mummy.

5

Dear Mummy,

I'm so scared. I don't know why I have been sent away. Did I do something wrong? If I was naughty then I can make up for it. I promise I won't be naughty again. This place is very cold and dark. The walls are bare and white and nobody smiles. I miss my old room. I miss the smell of the countryside. All I see when I look out of the window is concrete and glass. It's like a prison. When can I come home? They have told me that you and Daddy are not coming back but that can't be true, you love me more than anything in this world, I know you do. I think about you all the time and wonder what you are doing. There are some books here. They're old and the pages are ripped but I don't want to read them anyway because stories and books just remind me of you and then I get upset. Mummy you can't forget about me, even if you're angry with me I'm still your daughter.

Please don't leave me here. I need to be with you.
I promise I'll be a good girl and I won't make you cross.
I love you Mummy and I just want to come home.

Your lovely daughter xxx

6

It's Christmas morning. I'm sitting on the sofa, knees tucked underneath me, watching as Elspeth opens her presents. The living room is a sea of brightly coloured wrapping paper and ribbon. It's her second Christmas, and her little face is beaming with happiness. The toy drum we bought her lies discarded on the floor. She's more interested in the glittery box which she has placed on her head.

'Hat,' she says, looking up at me. 'Baba got hat.'

'Yes,' I say, my heart surging. 'And it's a very lovely hat.'

'Is it too early for one of these?'

I look up. Sean is standing in the doorway holding a box of mince pies. He's wearing a Santa hat and a bright red Christmas jumper. He looks so silly I can't help but burst out laughing. When Elspeth sees me she starts laughing too.

'Daddy silly,' she says, clapping her hands.

'What did you say?' cries Sean, sticking his bottom lip out. 'Did you say your daddy was silly? Why, I'm going to gobble you up for breakfast.'

He lifts Elspeth up from the paper-strewn floor and blows a raspberry on her tummy. She beams with delight.

'Again, again,' she cries.

I watch as the two of them play. My family, my beautiful family, warm and cosy and happy all under one roof. And then something happens. The room seems to fold in on itself. I can still hear Elspeth and Sean laughing but I can't see them any more.

'Sean,' I say. 'Where have you gone? I can't see you. Where have you taken her?'

I hear a noise and my eyes open. I see the end of my hospital bed and Claire coming in the door. Then it hits me. Why I'm here. What I've done.

'How are we doing, Maggie?' says Claire, smiling as she comes towards me.

I don't answer her. My head is still in the dream. If I focus on it enough, perhaps I can go back there. To Elspeth. And Sean.

'I'm just going to check your blood pressure,' she says, moving to the monitor by the side of the bed.

I listen to her muttering numbers that don't make sense to me. She says it's 'all good'.

'Could you tell me where Sean is?' I ask. 'My husband?'

'I should really go and get Dr Elms, he –'

'No,' I say. 'You don't need Dr Elms, just tell me where Sean is.'

The colour drains from her face as she pulls the chair out from beside the bed and sits down.

'What is it?' I say, dread rising up from my stomach to my chest.

Claire grasps my hand. 'Shh, Maggie, it's okay. He's fine.'

'Oh, thank God,' I gasp, lying back on the pillow. 'Thank God for that. So, where is he? Can I see him?'

I look to Claire for some sort of reassurance but she just shakes her head.

'What do you mean?' I cry. 'Where is he?'

'We don't know,' says Claire. 'What we do know is that six weeks ago Sean left the unit to collect some things from home. He returned a couple of hours later, left something at the reception desk then walked out.'

'Walked out? What do you mean?'

Claire looks at me sadly.

'It's horrible to have to tell you this, Maggie, what with everything else you're having to deal with,' she says. 'But he hasn't been back since that night. It seems that your husband . . . Sean has disappeared.'

7

Monday 24 July

I have been transferred from the ICU to a ward. They tell me I'm recovering well. My speech is improving and my blood pressure has gone down, my heart rate is sound and the threat of my lungs becoming infected has lessened. 'All good,' said Claire, repeating her favourite mantra, as the porters wheeled me down here.

All good.

How can she say that?

My child is dead. My husband has disappeared. There is nothing good any more.

The woman beside me has pulled the curtains round her bed. The other two patients in the ward, an elderly woman and a teenage girl, have had a steady stream of visitors all morning. It's the girl's birthday and her family are gathered round the bed, clutching balloons and toasting her with plastic cups of fizzy pop.

I turn on my side and close my eyes, try to block out their cheery voices, but they grow louder.

People often talk about emptiness but I don't think I have ever truly felt it, not really. Before, emptiness was an abstract concept, a throwaway phrase that fitted everything from the state of the fridge to the silence of the house on a weekday morning. Nothing could prepare me for this kind of emptiness, the raw, exposed state I'm living through now.

I have nothing. I am nothing. I would doubt I even exist, if it weren't for the sensation of warm breath escaping in and out of my mouth. I remember the reading Sean and I had at our wedding: 'Love is what makes us real'. I chose it because I liked the way the words sounded, the romantic, youthful undertones. I never really thought about what it truly meant, when you strip it down to its bare bones, though now I'm coming close.

Elspeth and Sean made me real. They were the hands that held me aloft, the air that transformed me from a loose bit of plastic into a buoyant balloon. Without them I don't exist.

As I lie here, pressing my hands to my ears to block out the visitors' happy chatter, I think back to the moment I gave birth to Elspeth. The midwife said it would feel like an expulsion. 'You'll never forget that sensation,' she'd said afterwards. 'That emptiness.'

I know what she meant but that wasn't emptiness, nothing close to it. The vacant space in my womb had been replaced with an eight-pound-six-ounce bundle of baby who took up permanent residence in my arms. The muscles of my right arm became firm and taut with the weight of her head resting on it. My breasts were full to the brim with milk, so heavy that sometimes I feared I would topple over. The house, that had seemed too big at first, sprang to life, each room stuffed with Moses baskets, changing stations, Bumbo chairs, cuddly toys and nappies. Elspeth filled Larkfields to the rafters. With her arrival it transformed from house to home. Life was so busy there was no spare time to think. Sean left the house at seven each morning, kissing me on the cheek as I gave Elspeth her first feed of the day. When he came home we were both so shattered from our respective labours we'd eat dinner on our laps in the living room, sometimes even in bed. My brain was baby shaped, every inch of it consumed with Elspeth, her feeding times, her temperature, her targets. There was no room for any other concern. My life was a well-fed stomach, full and fat and sated.

How can she have just stopped being here? I ask myself as I turn on my back and look up at the strip-lit ceiling. My beautiful baby. How can she be gone? It's inconceivable.

'She's just through here.'

I don't look up when I hear the nurse ushering yet another visitor into the ward but then the footsteps stop at my bed. I sit up and see a police officer standing there. She's about my age, tall and rosy-cheeked with thick auburn hair tied back in a ponytail. She is wearing an ill-fitting black trouser suit and a pale-blue blouse. As she draws closer I can smell her perfume: a bitter citrus scent.

'Hello, Maggie,' she says. 'My name is Detective Sergeant Grayling. I'm part of the team investigating the accident. Do you mind if I sit down?'

She's got a Yorkshire accent and it reminds me of a girl from Leeds I knew when I was young.

'No, I don't mind,' I reply.

She pulls the chair towards me and sits.

'I was wondering if I might be able to ask you some questions,' she says, bringing her chair closer. 'Nothing too gruelling, it's just regarding the accident.'

'The accident?' I repeat, flinching as one of the girl's visitors lets out a roar of laughter.

Grayling looks over at him and frowns then she turns to me, her face softening a little.

'Would that be okay?'

I nod my head.

'Right, well, I know Dr Elms talked through the rough details of what happened,' she continues. 'But there are a few things I'd like to clarify.'

Suddenly my heart starts to pound.

'Is there something . . .'

'Maggie, please don't worry,' says Grayling, placing her hand on my arm. 'These are just routine questions.'

I pull the covers up to my chest, my hands trembling with nerves.

'I just need you to tell me anything you can about the evening of the twelfth of May,' says Grayling. 'Why you were in the car. Where you were going. Any little detail you can possibly remember will be helpful.'

I look at her blankly. She might as well be speaking a foreign language. In my jumbled head the 12th of May is an abstract concept; as removed and alien as the disembodied voices that are bleeding into the room from the corridor.

'You were outside the Plough Inn,' she continues. 'In the car park by the bridge. Can you remember what you were doing there?'

I know the Plough Inn. It's the gastro pub just outside Lewes. I've been there once, years ago when Sean and I first moved into Larkfields. We didn't really like it. The food was awful and the regulars were rather cliquey. I have no idea why I would have headed there that night. I shake my head.

'So you don't remember parking the car?' says Grayling, narrowing her eyes.

'No,' I whisper. 'I don't remember anything. Please, tell me what happened.'

'Well,' says Grayling, hesitating for a second. 'It seems you got out of the car for some reason, leaving your daughter in the back seat. The fire officer's report showed that the handbrake . . . it was only partially engaged.'

'You mean I . . . it was my fault?' I say. 'I caused it?'

'That's not what I'm saying,' says Grayling. 'It appears from the misapplication of the handbrake that it was just an accident. The car rolled and you couldn't stop it. And judging from the injuries to your hands, it seems you did everything you could to save your little girl.'

I look up at her. We both know what that means. I did everything, but it wasn't enough.

'The coroner was satisfied with that,' she says, nodding her head. 'Enough to have returned a verdict of accidental death.'

My head is fizzing with facts. Coroner. Accidental death. Handbrake. None of it makes any sense. Why can't I remember anything?

'There's just one thing that's bothering me,' she says, her tone changing.

'Oh,' I say, my throat tightening.

'It's the fact that the car doors were locked,' she says, fixing me with a cold stare. 'Is there a reason you would have locked your daughter into the car?'

'No,' I reply. 'I've never locked her in, ever. I don't understand that. Are you sure it was locked?'

'Yes, the fire officer's report was definite. Could you have been going into the pub?'

'No,' I cry. 'Why would I go into a pub on my own? I don't really drink. And there's no way I would have left Elspeth alone in the car like that.'

'Could you have been meeting someone?'

'No,' I say.

'But how can you be certain if you have no memory of that night?'

'I just know,' I reply, my voice trembling. 'I don't socialize much, hardly ever in fact. My whole life revolves around my family; Sean and Elspeth. Look, she –' I stop, my throat feeling like it's closing up.

'Take your time, Maggie.'

'Elspeth was scared of locked doors,' I say. 'When she was about seven Sean took her with him to collect his suit from the dry-cleaner's. She fell asleep in the back of the car so he locked it and ran in to get his suit. The car was parked right outside and he was only in there a few minutes. When he came out she was banging on the windows, terrified that he'd . . .'

'That he'd what?'

'That he'd abandoned her.'

Grayling nods her head and writes something in her notebook.

'After that she was scared of being in the car,' I continue. 'It took years for her to get over it. So there is no way I would have locked that door.'

'And Sean?'

'What about him?'

'He never locked her in the car again after that incident?'

'Of course not,' I reply. 'He knew how scared she'd been.'

'Well, that leads me on to my next set of questions,' she says, looking down at her notepad. 'And these are regarding your husband.'

'Sean,' I say. 'Have you found him?'

'No,' says Grayling. 'Though to be honest, he's not officially missing. Our investigations have pointed to him leaving of his own accord. We just wanted to get your side of the story. Can you think of any reason why he would leave? Were you having problems?'

I think back to that last conversation, the anger in his voice. Things were not good between us, no. But it's none of her business.

'Maggie?'

I can't. Instead I shake my head.

'No,' I say. 'There were no problems. We were just . . . normal.'

Grayling narrows her eyes.

'That's quite rare, don't you think?' she presses. 'To be married all those years and have no arguments? And with a young child as well?'

'I'm not saying we didn't argue,' I say, trying to keep my voice steady. 'Of course we did. But it was just over silly things. Nothing that would give him grounds for leaving.'

She nods her head but I can tell she doesn't believe me.

'Claire said he left just after . . . after the funeral,' I say, my voice trembling. 'And I have no idea why. The police must have spoken to him after the accident. Did he give any hint that he was going to do this?'

'I did meet Mr Allan,' says Grayling. 'I spoke to him in the immediate aftermath and then he came to the station to collect your phone which we'd recovered from the riverbank.'

My phone. It's the first time I've given it a thought.

'Your husband was in a very bad state,' continues Grayling. 'He was grieving for his child. But, no, he didn't mention leaving, not at that point.'

'He will come back, won't he?' I say, searching her face for some element of reassurance. 'He can't have just left for good?'

'I can't give you an answer to that, Maggie,' says Grayling. 'Though what we know so far doesn't point to any kind of foul play. If what you say is true and you weren't having any marital problems then it's most likely that the shock of your daughter's death may have prompted him to leave. Grief does strange things to people.'

She stops and stares at me with an odd look on her face. Almost as though there's something else she wants to say.

'Anyway, I'll leave you to get some rest now,' she says, with a sudden smile. 'Thanks for answering my questions.'

She stands up and slips the notepad into her pocket.

'Is that it?' I say, watching as she walks to the door. 'My husband is missing. You need to try and find him.'

'As I said, Maggie, the results of our investigation point to your husband leaving of his own free will,' she says, with the same strange expression on her face. 'There's not much more we can do. But if you do remember anything, however small, that you think might be important, get in touch, yeah? I'll leave my details with Dr Elms.'

She opens the door then, letting in a scent of over-cooked food from the corridor. When she closes it I lie there for a moment, trying to take it all in. Sure, things were fraught between us, but Sean would never leave me, knowing that I would wake up and have to face the horror of Elspeth's death alone.

And then I remember that last conversation, the thinly veiled anger in his voice. *I can't take much more of this, Maggie.*

I lie back on the pillow and as I close my eyes a deep sense of unease ripples down my spine.

8

Dear Mummy,

Why have I been sent to this place? I'm trying my best to understand but all I can think is that I did something terrible, something I need to be punished for.

I don't like it here. The people are so mean. They tell me to toughen up and stop crying but I can't. I cry all the time, particularly when we have to sit round the table and have dinner. Last night we had lamb chops. They were a weird purple colour and had lumps of fat all round them. I almost threw up just looking at them but the woman said if I didn't eat them I'd be sent outside. So I tried and they actually tasted better than they smelled but I've got this sadness lump in my throat and the food won't get past it; nothing will. I started to cough then and all the other kids were looking at me and laughing. The woman rolled her eyes then gave me a glass of water. She's so horrible. Her face is all pointy and sharp, like a weasel, and she never smiles. I make myself better by imagining she's a real weasel, like the ones in the Wind in the Willows.

I'm sharing a bedroom with a girl called Zoe. She's much older than me, about fourteen. She's got black hair that's cut really short and her eyes have purple circles under them, like she hasn't slept in months. She spends most of the time just sitting on her bed listening to music on her headphones.

We've got bunk beds. I'm on the bottom bunk, she's on the top. The bed is really uncomfortable and the sheets make me itch. Last night Zoe told me to 'shut the fuck up' because I was crying in my sleep. (Sorry for that word, but that is what she said.) The next morning she said I'd kept her awake and if I carried on crying she'd give me a slap. So now, I'm training myself to stop crying and if I do I make sure I do it silently.

I don't belong here Mummy. There's been some terrible mistake, I know there has. You and Daddy wouldn't just leave me here.

Please come and find me Mummy.

I miss you.

I love you.
Your lovely daughter xxx

9

Monday 31 July

I sit in the corner of the hospital day room, an item of lost property waiting to be claimed. From the newspapers and magazines that are scattered across the coffee table beside me I see that it is July 2017. Two weeks ago I woke up in a hospital bed with no memory of how or why I had got there. Today I will be discharged. I look down at the wedge of prescriptions that Dr Elms gave me this morning: four weeks' worth of strong painkillers, enough to numb the physical and mental pain, if only for a few hours at a time; antiseptic skin cream that I must rub into my hands twice a day to encourage my nails to grow back; and finally, two sets of inhalers, one to strengthen my lungs, the other to help when I'm breathless. It seems I have everything I need to set me on the road to recovery – everything except my husband and child.

The door opens with a creak. An old woman walks in. She looks around the room, her face etched with confusion. Then she notices me and flinches, almost imperceptibly. She had thought the room was empty. And she might have been right. After all, I am no more than a ghost.

According to Claire, Elspeth's funeral took place three weeks after the accident, once the coroner's report had been returned. At that point they didn't think I was going to come through and if I did they were certain that I would be in a permanent vegetative state. Elspeth's body was released and then Sean organized a service at St Peter's Church in Rodmell. Her friends from school attended. Everyone wore violet, Elspeth's favourite colour. It was a beautiful sight, the vicar told Claire when he came to sit by my bed. A very fitting send-off.

But I never got the chance to say goodbye.

Elspeth was buried in the churchyard, in a peaceful spot away from the road. I know this detail because, according to Claire, after the funeral Sean returned to my bedside and told me all about it.

Then he left and never came back.

I try to imagine what was going through his head that night. Did he feel like I do now? Raw, exposed, sick with grief and pain? I still can't remember anything, though I've tried and tried. I just have these recurring nightmares of water and Elspeth crying. I must find Sean. It's the only thing keeping me going, the only thing stopping me from taking the pills they have given me all in one go and ending it. I have to find him. I have to find out what happened that night and whether I am to blame.

They asked me yesterday if there was anybody they could call to come and help me. Did I have any friends or family members? And the answer was no. My parents died before Elspeth was born, and as for friends, well, I've never needed anybody but Sean and Elspeth. As I said to Grayling, they were my life.

And now they're gone.

The elderly woman has chosen a comfy armchair on the other side of the room. I watch as she fiddles with her handbag. She reminds me of my mother, neat and solid. A woman who had a fresh handkerchief every day though she would rather have died than use it to dry her tears. Emotions were troublesome, according to my mother, they ought to be controlled or else everything fell apart. The woman catches me looking at her and smiles awkwardly. I look away, saving her from the embarrassment of having to initiate small talk. Though my speech has improved, I still find it hard to get my words out properly. The doctors have told me that this is normal and will improve with time and therapy but it still unnerves me.

I can feel the old woman's eyes on me as I pick up a magazine and pretend to flick through it. Photographs of celebrities blur in front of me along with advertisements for expensive face creams and beach-body diets. I think of Elspeth on our last holiday to Whitstable, delighted because she got to wear her new Hello Kitty sunglasses, and my eyes fill with tears. How is it possible that I will never see her beautiful little face again; feel the warmth of her skin as she presses her face next to mine. 'Night night, Mummy. Love you all the world and sixpence.'

That was my father's old saying, passed down to me and then to Elspeth. All the world and sixpence. Oh, my darling girl, I loved you more than that; I loved you more than you will ever know.

I put the magazine down and clasp my hands together, trying to hold it all in.

'Hello, Maggie.'

I look up and see Claire.

'Sorry to keep you waiting,' she says, lifting a fleshy arm to usher me out. 'Dr Elms was just putting together your discharge papers.'

I stand up and make my way towards her reassuring voice, remembering how it always made me feel better when I heard it in the coma dream. She would talk about the weather, about her two teenage sons and what was happening on her favourite television programme. When I heard her voice I knew that I was safe.

'Oh, and the team from Lewes Social Services have just arrived too.'

'Social Services?' I say. 'Why are they here?'

'They're here to help you with your next steps.'

'Do you mean a carer?' I say, my chest tightening. 'You mentioned yesterday that I might need a carer to help me around the house. Is that why they're here?'

'Why don't we go and see what they have to say,' says Claire gently. 'And then we can take it from there.'

I nod my head and let her guide me along the corridor. There are children's paintings pinned to the wall, potato prints in bright primary colours, oversized butterflies and fat, smiling caterpillars. As we walk past them my eyes prickle with tears.

Elspeth loved to draw. It was how she made sense of the world. If she'd had a new experience or been somewhere unfamiliar she would run upstairs to her desk when she got home and draw it in precise detail. She could sit there for hours, lost in the new worlds she had just experienced – a train journey, a seaside holiday, moving to a different classroom at the beginning of a new term – and try to situate herself into it. That was the hallmark of Elspeth's drawings: she always placed herself in the middle of them. She was there on that train, on that beach, in that classroom, so therefore those experiences became real to her. Those new things were not scary any more and she felt safe.

And then my thoughts turn to the riverbank. Why the hell couldn't I have kept her safe that day? I was her mother, that was my job. And I failed. I failed.

10

Dear Mummy,

I'm trying to be strong and trying not to cry too much, though it's very very hard.

I'm writing this in an exercise book that Weasel Face gave me. I told her I wanted it to practise my spelling. She doesn't know that I'm writing you letters. I think she'd be angry if she knew. Zoe is sitting on the bunk above me smoking a cigarette. The smell is getting into my throat and I really want to cough but I'm trying to keep it in. I've realized that the slightest thing annoys Zoe and I don't want to end up getting slapped.

I've found a way to stop myself crying. Whenever I feel sad I write down my thoughts. It's a bit like a word soup, out they all pour on to the paper. Yesterday when Weasel Face took me into town I thought I saw you on the street. I always look out for you. I got all sad and panicky and wanted to cry but I stopped myself by thinking happy thoughts. I kept the happy thoughts in my head until I came home then I wrote them down in this notebook. This is what I wrote:

Mummy and Daddy

Animals and birds
Hot buttered toast
Sweet tea
Running through snow
The feel of wool
C. S. Lewis
Summer holidays
Numbers and counting
Dipping my toes in the sea
Hugs
Mint ice cream
Mummy coming to take me home
Going to sleep in my own bed
Mummy's face
Mummy's voice
Mummy

Please come soon.
Your lovely daughter xxx

I sit trembling in the front seat of Amanda's Nissan Micra. Though we've only been driving for a few minutes it feels like an eternity.

Amanda is my social worker; a stranger in whose hands my future now lies.

I close my eyes and recall the events of this morning. When I got to Dr Elms's office I was met by Amanda and her colleague, a thin, bug-eyed young man called Mike Saunders. As I sat there, half listening to them discussing my care plan and discharge forms, all I could think about was getting back to Larkfields, lying down in the big iron bed, pulling the covers over my head and blocking out the world. But then Mike Saunders said something that made me sit up rigid in my seat: 'The priority is to get Mrs Allan into emergency accommodation.' At first I thought I'd misheard him but then Amanda had intercepted and explained that she had found a place for me at a nice bed and breakfast in Lewes. I had no idea what they were talking about. Why would I need to be placed in emergency accommodation? Why wasn't I going home?

I know the answer to that question now but I still can't comprehend it. As I sat in the office with Claire's hand on my shoulder I was told that when Sean left he terminated his tenancy agreement on the house. I told them there must be some mistake; we owned Larkfields and had done for ten years. Then came the first bomb-shell. Mike Saunders, reading from a piece of paper, leaned forward and calmly told me that Sean had sold the house seven years ago to a property company called BH2 Properties. He had rented Larkfields from them ever since.

None of it made any sense. If Sean had sold the house I would have known. Of course I would have known. But then came the next bombshell: after terminating the contract Sean had emptied his bank account. He was the main breadwinner, this money was our sole income source. As I tried to take in the deluge of information I could hear them asking me questions: 'Do you have any other source of income, Mrs Allan?' 'Do you have any savings, pension, ISAs?' 'How about inheritance?' I knew the answer to all of these and it was 'No, no, no.' I have nothing. Abso-lutely nothing.

'Okay, Maggie,' says Amanda as she stops the car and takes off her seat belt. 'Here we are.'

I look out of the window. I recognize this street. It's a few blocks from the leisure centre. My heart hurts as I remember little Elspeth standing outside waiting for me to collect her after Sophie Bailey's birthday party. It was a few weeks before the accident. She didn't normally like big noisy events, but she always loved going to Sophie's parties. They were best friends and they both loved music. Elspeth had been so excited because this was a disco-themed party with a DJ and glitterball. I had been excited too because the party meant that I would have a couple of hours to myself once I'd dropped her off. It was the anniversary of my mother's death, and I knew that the only thing that would make me feel better would be to sit at my desk and lose myself in words.

I'd been writing a novel for years, and never thought anything would come of it, but this year, high on New Year's resolutions, I had got it into my head that I would finish it. Most people would have said it was a waste of time, particularly as I don't have a qualification to my name. But once I started taking it seriously, I found I couldn't stop. Writing was the only way I could keep the dark feelings at bay. The novel was a fictionalized account of Virginia Woolf's time in Rodmell. It explored her hopes, dreams and fears which, strangely enough, were similar to my own. I found that pouring the emotions I'd always kept hidden into the novel made me feel better; lighter even. And soon, getting to my desk and writing the next chapter became an addiction. If I couldn't do it I became irritable and depressed.

So on the day of the party I told myself that I'd only write for a couple of hours. But, as usual, I got too caught up in the story and before I knew it the clock was telling me it was 4.30. The party had finished at 4.00. I jumped in the car and drove like a maniac all the way to Lewes. When I got there Elspeth was standing on the steps with Sophie's mum. Her face was swollen with tears and she was clutching her party bag to her chest. I'd apologized profusely to Sophie's mum and when we got in the car I promised Elspeth that I would make it up to her, that we'd have fish and chips in town or go and see a movie, but she just sat beside me in silence, gulping down her tears, all the excitement of the party evaporated.

I'd failed her again. Let her down when she needed me. Why did I need anything other than her? In the darkness that had been my life up to that point, having Elspeth was like the sun finally coming out. If I could do it all over again, I would take her hand and march into Sophie Bailey's party with her. I would laugh and whoop as she danced with her friends. I'd eat cake and chat with the other mums. And when it was all over I would look at the happiness on her face as we drove home and I would be content. There are so many things I'd have done differently. But it's too late now. There will be no more parties; no more sunshine.

'We're a bit early but I'm sure they'll have your room ready,' says Amanda, opening her door. 'Maggie?'

I can't move. The seat feels like it's clamped tight around me. My whole body is shaking.

'I understand this is difficult,' says Amanda, placing her hand on mine. 'But we are all here for you. This is just a temporary measure. Think of it as a rest home, a place to spend a few days finding your feet.'

My heart feels like it will burst out of my chest. The memory of Elspeth fills my head. I need to talk to Sean. I can't get through this without him.

'Let's just take one step at a time, eh?' Amanda says, noticing my panic. 'Now you wait there and I'll come round and help you out of the car.'

As she shuts her door I am tempted to lock mine. I could sit here in Amanda's little car for ever and never have to face the outside world again. Just sink into those memories.

The car door opens and I jump. The air outside is cool and brings me out of my thoughts.

'Right then, love,' Amanda says. 'Let's get you out.'

As I unfasten the seat belt I get a strange sensation up my spine. I see Elspeth looking at me instead of Amanda, her face quizzical.

Where are we going, Mummy?

Elspeth.

I don't want to, Mummy.

'Easy does it.'

Amanda is guiding me out of the car, and Elspeth is gone. Every movement hurts. Pain slices through my lungs as I step on to the pavement. Dr Elms says that there is no sign of inflammation, but I will need to use inhalers to build my lungs back up.

'Now wait here a moment, love,' says Amanda. 'I'll just get your things from the boot.'

'My things?' I say. 'What things? You mean . . . from home?'

'I'm afraid not,' says Amanda, making her way to the boot. 'It's just some new clothes we cobbled together for you.'

'Do you know what's happened to all my stuff from Larkfields – from my house?' I say. 'When can I get it back?'

Amanda pauses then turns to face me.

'We tried to get it for you,' she says, putting her hand on my arm. 'I went over to Larkfields myself but the new tenant said that everything had been thrown away by the landlords.'

'What?' I exclaim. 'But they can't do that. Surely it's against the law?'

I think about Elspeth's bedroom; her books and toys, her beautiful craft creations; all our photographs.

'I'm ever so sorry,' says Amanda. 'I really am. Look, let me just get these bags out and then we'll go inside and make a nice cup of tea.'

I wait on the pavement while she retrieves the

clothes. I feel so fragile; as though the slightest touch could send me flying from this spot. I see myself landing in the middle of the road and shattering into a thousand pieces. It's a tempting thought. How nice it would be to simply stop existing.

Amanda slams the boot shut and I fold my arms across my chest protectively as she comes towards me. She's holding a large carrier bag with the name of a discount shop on it.

'As I said, it's nothing fancy,' says Amanda. 'But it will set you up for now until you get yourself sorted.'

I look down at the clothes I'm wearing. A pair of ill-fitting polyester trousers, a sky-blue hooded sweatshirt with the words 'LA Living' printed across the chest and a pair of black plimsolls. All courtesy of Claire, who had raided the hospital lost-property room for me.

'Right, let's get you inside,' says Amanda, putting her arm round me.

I nod my head. My mouth has gone dry and my legs feel leaden. It's like I'm fourteen years old again. I shudder as the memory of that time resurfaces: the smell of antiseptic, the walls that felt like they were closing in on me, the horror of knowing that my fate was in someone else's hands. And now it's happening again.

I grip Amanda's hand as we walk up the short path that leads from the street to the front door. There are two stone lions on either side of the door. One of them has a chipped nose.

'Quite nice, isn't it?' says Amanda as she raps three times on the door.

I don't have a chance to answer because at that moment the door opens and a thin man with ginger hair and a blotchy face stands in front of us.

'Mr Hutchinson?' says Amanda, extending her hand. 'I'm Amanda Jones from Lewes Housing Support Service. This is Maggie Allan.'

The man sighs and nods his head.

'You'd better come in,' he says, looking at me like something he's just trodden in. 'And please wipe your feet.'

We follow him into a circular hallway. It's clean, pleasant even, though the air stinks of cooking fat mixed with cheap air freshener. I scrape my trainers against the brittle entrance mat. Amanda removes her sandals.

'It's through here,' mutters Mr Hutchinson, pointing at a door to the left of the staircase. 'You said she couldn't do stairs.'

'That's right,' says Amanda, smiling warmly at me. 'Mrs Allan has just been discharged from hospital and is still quite fragile. She was in a coma for almost ten weeks.'

The man looks me up and down then shrugs.

'As I told your colleagues, I don't normally do

DSS,' he says. 'You sure she's not going to be any trouble?'

I stand impotently as Amanda reassures Hutchinson that I am no threat to him or his establishment; that I am in a fragile state; a 'priority need' case. I want to run away, as far away as possible from here. Back to my home and my family. At this time of evening I would be preparing dinner in the kitchen. Elspeth would be drawing at the table. My eyes fill with tears as I remember the simple happiness of those moments and how I never truly appreciated them; or her.

'Right,' says Hutchinson, nodding at Amanda. 'Well, I'll know who to bill if anything goes wrong. I'll show you the room.'

He steps towards the door. Amanda hangs back and squeezes my arm.

'Please try not to worry,' she whispers. 'It's all going to be fine.'

I nod my head though I know that it is far from fine. It is as bad as it can possibly be.

'Okay,' says Hutchinson as he unlocks the door. 'After you.'

He stands back to let us through. Amanda enters the room first.

'This is lovely,' I hear her say. 'Really light.'

I take a deep breath then step inside.

'Oh, there's a kitchenette,' Amanda cries, clapping her hands together. 'That's good.'

I follow her to the other side of the room where a microwave sits on a small metal counter. There's a white jug kettle and two mugs, a metal bowl with sachets of sugar and four tiny cartons of UHT milk.

'Crockery's in that cupboard under the sink,' says Hutchinson. 'I've made an inventory of it so I'll know if any of it goes missing.'

I want to speak. I want to tell him that I have no intention of stealing his crappy stuff. That nothing is worth anything to me any more. Instead I just nod, like a dumb animal, and listen as he explains how the microwave works.

'TV's over there by the bed,' he says, pointing to a flat screen that is wedged on a table. 'We just ask you be respectful to the other guests when you're watching it. Keep the volume low.'

I nod my head though I'm not really taking in what he's saying. I can feel my heart speeding up as panic grips me. This can't be happening.

'Oh, and no visitors after seven p.m.,' says Hutchinson, tapping his fingers on the door frame. 'That's a strict rule.'

I look up at him and the room starts to spin. *No visitors.* I thought the darkness was gone for ever but now as I stand here in this strange room, it hits me. I'm back where I started.

'Elspeth,' I whisper.

'Who's Elspeth?' says Hutchinson, his eyes widening.

'No,' I cry, my tears making a blur of Hutchinson. 'I can't. Not again. I need to find my baby, my beautiful baby girl. I need to get her back.'

Amanda grabs my arms before I fall to the ground and I let her hold me; let her carry for just one moment the weight of my despair.

'It's okay, love,' she whispers as she pushes my hair out of my eyes. 'You let it all out. Have a good cry.'

In the background I hear Hutchinson walk to the door.

'I'll leave you in peace,' he says. 'If you need anything just ring zero from the phone on the desk.'

'Thanks, Mr Hutchinson,' says Amanda, lifting her head.

He closes the door behind him and I wriggle free from Amanda's embrace.

'I'm sorry,' I mutter, aware suddenly that I've exposed my vulnerability to a complete stranger.

'You have nothing to feel sorry about, Maggie,' says Amanda. 'This is a huge ordeal for you in every way. But we're here for you.'

I rub my chest. The pain is starting up again.

'I need my inhaler. Could you get it for me?' I say, sitting on the bed.

'Yes, of course,' says Amanda, standing up and taking the small blue inhaler from my bag. 'My house is cluttered with these. My son has asthma but he's always losing his bloody inhalers. Which isn't surprising considering the state of his bedroom. Still, that's teenagers for you. Oh, I'm sorry, I didn't mean to . . .'

'It's fine,' I say, putting the inhaler to my mouth and taking a sharp breath.

'Here's some water,' says Amanda, handing me a yellow plastic beaker.

I take it and sip slowly.

'Does that feel better?' she asks, smiling at me as though I'm a small child.

'Yes,' I reply.

I drain the cup then put it down on the floor beside me.

'I saw you have a box of painkillers in your medicine bag,' says Amanda, picking up the beaker and taking it to the sink. 'How many do you have to take a day?'

'Six,' I reply. 'They're for the muscle pains.'

Amanda nods her head.

'Well, I think it's probably best if I leave you enough for tonight and then I'll give the box to your carer, who'll be visiting each day from tomorrow. It's a good idea if she administers them, just for the time being.'

She smiles but I can detect an underlying wariness. She doesn't trust me with them.

'Anyway,' she says, rubbing her hands together,

'I think it's time for a cuppa. It's just this crappy UHT milk, I'm afraid. Are you happy to have it black?'

I nod my head though I really don't want a cup of tea. I'm so tired. I slip off my shoes and climb on to the bed, my eyes suddenly heavy with sleep. In the background I can hear Amanda filling the kettle. I close my eyes. I see Elspeth paddling in the sea at Whitstable. Sean is holding her above the water and she's kicking her little feet. The water splashes in Sean's face and he looks over at me and laughs. I am sitting on the beach, watching them. They look so happy. But then I see it. The huge wave. It's coming up behind them. I jump to my feet and throw my arms in the air. 'Sean,' I cry. 'Look behind you.' But they can't hear me. I start to run but the shingle slows me down. The wave is getting higher. It's almost upon them. I scream Elspeth's name and at the very last minute, just before the wave consumes them, she looks back.

I wake with a start. Amanda is standing by the side of the bed holding a mug with faded flowers on the front.

'Here's your tea, love,' she says gently. 'I'll pop it here on the side table then I'll leave you to get some rest. I've popped some basics in the cupboard for you if you're hungry later. Then I'll be back tomorrow with your carer and we can discuss what's next.'

She walks towards the door and I suddenly feel afraid.

'You promise you'll come back tomorrow?' I say, sitting up. 'You won't leave me here?'

'Maggie,' says Amanda soothingly, 'I told you. We are all here for you. We're going to help you get through this. I promise.'

She closes the door behind her and I curl on my side, tucking my knees into my chest. Upstairs someone slams a door and I hear Hutchinson talking to Amanda in the corridor outside. I put my hands over my ears to drown out his voice then close my eyes, willing myself to sleep. But all I can see is that giant wave enveloping Elspeth's tiny body.

It's no use. I have to do something, I tell myself, as I throw the covers back. I can't just lie here. I need to start looking for Sean.

12

Dear Mummy,

It's the middle of the night and I can't sleep. Every time I close my eyes I see horrible shapes, like big sea creatures with tentacles coming at me. Last night I dreamed I was drowning. I was sinking in brown muddy water and I couldn't breathe. When I woke up, Zoe was standing by the side of the bed. She said I'd disturbed her with my screaming. I thought she'd be angry but she was quite nice. She went and got me a cup of hot chocolate then came and sat on the edge of my bed while I drank it. She said that she had nightmares when she first arrived too but then once she got used to it they stopped.

Zoe is snoring now but it's not an annoying sound. It's actually quite nice because I know she's there. Weasel Face doesn't talk to me much. She just tells me what I should be doing, what time I should be up in the morning, what she wants me to help her with. On my second day here she handed me a piece of paper which she said was the rota and told me to stick it on my wall so I wouldn't forget what jobs I need to do.

Today I had to empty the bins in all the bedrooms, wash the bathroom sink and then scrape the vegetables before dinner. It was hard work but that didn't bother me so much because being busy takes my mind off things.

The worst part of the day is now when everything's quiet and all I can hear are my thoughts. That's when I think of you. I wonder where you are. Maybe you're looking for me and any minute now you'll hammer on the door and say, 'It's okay, we've found her.'

I wish that would happen. I wish it more than anything in the world.

Anyway, I'm going to stop now because my eyes are closing.

Goodnight Mummy.

I love you.

I miss you.
Your lovely daughter xxx

13

I get out of bed and search the room for a pen. There's a pencil by the kettle that Amanda must have left behind. I pick it up and look around for something to write on. Then I see a red plastic ring binder on the little table by the window. The words IVY HOUSE INFORMATION PACK have been neatly written on the front in black permanent marker. I open it, flicking past the laminated pages outlining the fire drill, the visiting hours and the correct way to work the shower. I pull out a page that says 'Useful numbers' and see that it is only printed on one side.

That will have to do, I think to myself as I take the paper and pencil over to the bed and sit down. Turning to the blank side, I make a list of people who may know where Sean could be. My hands feel shaky at first, and the first few lines are barely legible.

I start with Rob Daniels, Sean's desk partner at work. They got on well enough though I wouldn't say they were the best of friends. He lives in Surrey but has a flat in London. Maybe he let Sean stay there?

Number two: Colin Greaves, Saffy and Alexandra's dad. Of all the parents at the school, Colin was the one Sean made time to chat to at parties and parents' evenings. He worked for a recruitment consultancy in Brighton and was a huge Spurs fan. I remember he once gave Sean a spare ticket to accompany him to a match at White Hart Lane. Sean had been so busy work-wise this last year that he let the friendship drift. Just like he was letting everything drift, I think.

I pause to give my hand a rest before going on to number three: Alan Hamilton, Sean's friend from university. They had shared a house in his final year, and though they lost touch after graduating, Sean had bumped into him on the tube a couple of years ago and they'd met up for drinks a few times since. The last I heard he was working for Lambeth Council. I write the words 'long shot' in capital letters next to his name.

Then, finally, Hester Trueman: Sean's aunt. She lives in Portsmouth and must be in her eighties now. As his only living relative, maybe he contacted her to tell her about Elspeth's death? I jot down the name of the village where she lives. I have no idea what her address is but Google may be able to help.

But then I remember. I can't google because I don't have a phone or a laptop. I throw the paper and pencil at the wall in frustration. This is hopeless, I think to myself as I flop back on the bed.

I close my eyes and try, desperately, to think back

to the afternoon of 12th May but there's nothing. It's like my brain has been wiped. I can remember snippets of detail from earlier in the month. The May procession. The school spring fair. And I remember Elspeth had a new interest: Native Americans. She'd borrowed a book from the school library all about them. And she had wanted to make a dream catcher. Yes, I remember that. I went into town, to the craft shop, and bought willow sticks and wool and netting, and Elspeth had sat at the kitchen table and got started on it. Was that the day before the accident or the previous weekend? I'm not sure. I sit up in the bed, my heart pounding.

I think hard about that dream catcher. The wool was purple and blue: Elspeth's favourite colours. I see myself sitting at the kitchen table weaving strands of blue wool across the surface of the willow circles and Elspeth's voice, loud and insistent: 'No, Mummy, you're doing it wrong. The feathers have to be next to the pine cones.'

My heart sank as I looked up at her. I was useless at crafting, always had been. Unlike the other mums at the school who could knock up a knitted jumper or a batch of muffins effortlessly, I was seriously lacking on the domestic skills front.

'You can't put two feathers next to each other, Mummy, or it won't look right. Sophie's mum showed us how to do it.'

'Okay, okay,' I snapped, slamming the feathers on to the table. 'Well why don't you ask Sophie's bloody mum to do it.'

And then, right on cue, Sean had walked in. Home from work early for once. I remember the look he gave me, as if to say, *Honestly, Maggie, arguing with a ten-year-old?*

'Do you want me to help, Elspeth?' he said, putting his briefcase down and loosening his tie. 'I'm sure I'll be able to work it out. Even after a full day at the office and a six a.m. start.'

He'd addressed this last point to me.

I decided not to retaliate. We'd done nothing but argue for months and I couldn't face another row.

'Right, what have we got here then?' he said, settling in next to Elspeth.

'It's a dream catcher,' she replied, not looking up from the piece of twisted willow that she was busy threading feathers round. 'And it has to be exactly like the one in this book.'

'Okay,' said Sean, picking up the book that Elspeth had propped up in front of her. '*Native American Crafting.* Sounds great.'

I busied myself preparing dinner, listening as Elspeth explained the intricacies of weaving to Sean who, despite his frostiness with me, was at least spending time with Elspeth. He'd been doing a lot of late nights at the office recently, sometimes going days without seeing her. But I couldn't really complain.

He never said it but I knew it irked him that I still hadn't gone back to work. Though he knew that what I'd been through when I was younger had damaged me and he knew that I just wanted to be there for Elspeth, to give her the childhood I hadn't had. He also knew how clingy Elspeth was. We used to call her the little shadow because that's what she was like, particularly with me. Wherever I went, she would go too. When she was very small she wouldn't let me out of her sight. It wasn't until she was about seven that I was finally able to go to the loo on my own. We thought school would make her more independent but the moment she arrived home she would come and sit by my side and cuddle into me. When I dropped her off at the school gates she would ask what I was going to be doing that day. 'You won't be late to collect me, will you, Mummy? Promise me you'll be there?' So the thought of returning to work, particularly to the soulless reception jobs, which were all I was qualified for, just seemed out of the question. But there was another reason now, one I never told anyone, one I barely even admitted to myself, and that was if I did go back there would be no time to work on the novel. Writing that book had become my lifeline, my sanity, though I made sure I worked on it in secret when Sean was out. Whenever he was home I would busy myself with Elspeth, take her on nature walks, sit with her while she did her crafting, made it look like she was a full-time occupation. And Sean believed the lie.

I think back to that evening. I had stood chopping carrots at the kitchen counter while Elspeth and Sean chatted about feathers and wire. But after that there's nothing, just a deep sense that I was waiting for something – or was it someone? I don't know because the next thing I remember is waking up in hospital with Dr Elms repeating my name.

14

Tuesday 1 August

I am in bed in a strange room. As my eyes begin to focus I see a dark wooden wardrobe, a kitchen counter, a white kettle, and I start to panic. This is real. My little girl is gone and I am trapped here.

Instinctively I put my hand out to reach for my phone to call Sean, forgetting that I don't have one any more. I need to find him. Only he can help me make sense of all this. Then I remember Claire saying how she had tried to call him and his number had been disconnected. So even if I had a phone I still wouldn't be able to contact him.

'Sean,' I cry, slamming my fists down on the stiff bedcovers. 'Where are you?'

I see a piece of paper on the other side of the bed. It's the list that I made last night. I reach over and hold it in my hands. I turn the paper over and see the names I'd written down, the friends and acquaintances who may know where Sean is. But as I read through my jumbled handwriting I realize that the chances of Sean being with any of these people are remarkably slim. The truth is, Sean and I were quite private people. Like me, he was an only child. He never knew his dad and his mum had died from breast cancer just before we met. We used to say we were two lost orphans who had found each other. We had friends, people from the village, parents from the school, but we kept them at a distance. We only needed each other.

I turn over in the bed and as a sliver of golden light trickles through the gap in the curtains I think back to the day I met him.

I was thirty-one years old and working as a receptionist for an asset management company in London, just by Waterloo Station. My days were spent sitting behind a giant glass desk, doling out visitor passes to grey-faced suits, booking meeting rooms and making coffee. It was soul-destroying but it paid reasonably well and for someone like me, who had thrown any chance of a decent career away over a decade earlier, it was a solid job.

It was mid-afternoon and I was sitting behind the reception desk ignoring the rolling news on the TV screen that the boss insisted should be on at all times and reading *Night and Day* by Virginia Woolf. Growing up in Rodmell, Woolf had been a constant presence, a relic whose death had cast a shadow over the village, and because of that I'd avoided reading any of her work. I imagined the novels would be rather snobbish, full of dull descriptions of high tea and London society, but after I was sent away I found a big pile of them in the library. There wasn't much choice. It was either Woolf or a stack of romance novels, so I picked up *Mrs Dalloway* and when I started to read I realized how wrong my assumptions about Woolf had been. There was something in her voice that made it feel like she was speaking directly to me. The writer who I'd thought of as dusty and as irrelevant as a museum relic slowly became my confidante. After that, whenever I was feeling tense or anxious I would pick up one of her books and the darkness would recede. The day I met Sean was one of those days.

I heard someone clear their throat. I quickly hid the book under a file then looked up and saw a man smiling at me.

'Sorry to disturb,' he said, a faint trace of Irish in his accent. 'My name's Sean Allan. I'm here for an interview with Stewart Jacob.'

He smiled warmly and I felt myself begin to blush. He had the most captivating blue eyes with thick, dark lashes. The navy-blue pin-stripe suit he was wearing was beautifully tailored and his light-brown hair was cut in an Edwardian style, long on the top and short at the sides. I found myself getting flustered as I arranged a visitor badge for him and put in the call to Stewart Jacob's office to let them know he'd arrived. I hadn't had this reaction to a man for a long time, not since Ben. In fact, I hadn't even *looked* at a man properly. Never let myself.

'If you'd like to take a seat, Stewart will be with you in a moment,' I said, my face reddening under his gaze.

'If it's all right with you I'll just stand here,' he said, adjusting his tie. 'I've been sitting on the tube for an age. Need to stretch my back.'

He laughed and I smiled at him awkwardly.

'What are you reading?' he said after a moment of silence.

'Sorry?'

'When I came in you were reading a book,' he said. 'Just wondered what it was. I'm always after a good recommendation.'

'Oh, that,' I said, taking the book from under the file. 'It's er . . . just a Virginia Woolf novel.'

I held the book up so he could see. He nodded his head.

'Virginia Woolf? Don't think I've read any of hers. Is it any good?'

'I'm not sure yet,' I said, flicking through the pages nervously. 'I've only just started it.'

'What's it about?'

'Erm, well, it's —'

But before I could tell him, Stewart Jacob strode into the reception area. He was a broad, imposing man, with steel-grey eyes and a hawkish expression. He dressed impeccably in expensive suits and silk ties. I always became tongue-tied in his presence. There was something about the way he looked at me, as though he was waiting for me to trip up. But thankfully, that day, he completely ignored me and went towards Sean, his hand outstretched.

'You must be Sean Allan,' he said, a rare smile appearing on his face. 'Stewart Jacob. Good to meet you. Do come through.'

He turned on his heels. Sean followed. And as he passed my desk he turned to me with a smile that looked halfway excited, halfway terrified, and crossed his fingers.

'Good luck,' I mouthed.

'Thank you,' he mouthed back.

Then he was gone and I spent the rest of the afternoon sitting at my desk, casting furtive glances towards the door that led to Stewart Jacob's office. At 5 p.m. I took the huge sack of post down to the mailroom to be franked. When I came back I saw Sean's visitor badge on the desk. I'd missed him. I felt a strange, empty feeling in the pit of my stomach as I closed down the computer and put my coat on. I couldn't stop thinking about Sean; I'd liked the way he'd asked about my book, the way he'd smiled nervously and crossed his fingers. I'd liked the fact that, for just a few moments, I'd stopped being invisible.

As I made my way out I was mentally preparing myself for another night sitting on the sofa with a mug of tea and a book when I saw him standing by the lifts.

'Hi,' I said as I approached him, trying to appear nonchalant although inside my stomach was doing somersaults.

'Hello again,' he said, smiling. 'Sorry, I didn't catch your name before.'

'It's Maggie.'

'Maggie,' he said, looking at me so intently I felt exposed.

'So how did the interview go?' I said, trying to draw the attention away from me.

'Really well,' he said. 'I am, as of ten minutes ago, the new Marketing Manager for Jacob & Stanley.'

'That's wonderful news,' I said. 'Congratulations.'

'Thanks,' he said. 'Though to be honest it was a tough interview. Old man Jacob doesn't take any prisoners.'

The lift doors opened then and as we stepped inside he turned to me.

'Where are you headed?'

'Now? Just home I guess. Why?'

'Well,' he said, his eyes twinkling, 'I've just landed the job of my dreams and met this intriguing woman all in the space of an afternoon and I was wondering if she'd fancy joining me for a celebratory drink.'

I could feel myself blushing. Nobody had ever called me intriguing before. I didn't know what to say.

'So, are you up for it?' he said as the lift doors opened and we stepped outside. 'I know this great pub just behind Waterloo.'

'That would be lovely,' I said, and as we made our way towards the pub I knew deep down inside me that this beautiful man with eyes the colour of the night sky was going to become a big part of my life.

How could it have gone so wrong? How could Sean have changed so much? I think back over the last few years, the late nights at the office, the constant checking of his phone, the almost involuntary turn of his cheek if I tried to kiss him. Our marriage had been in trouble for years but as usual I ignored it. I became absorbed in writing the novel, tried to pretend that the growing chasm between us would somehow rectify itself, but it just got worse.

As I lie here I try to remember the good times, try to focus on that image of us walking out of the offices of Jacob & Stanley towards our future, but it's replaced with a flash of memory. I'm pulling into the car park outside the Plough Inn. As I slow the car down, Elspeth asks why we're there. I turn round in my seat to answer and then everything goes blank.

I take the heel of my hand and hit the side of my head once, twice, three times, as though I can somehow dislodge the memory and the answers will come down like the winnings from a slot machine. But there is nothing, just a black void. What were we doing that night? Where were we going?

As I try to order my thoughts I'm startled by a loud knock at the door.

I lie there not daring to move, my body cold with fear. I don't feel safe in this place. I think back to the ICU, the security, the nurses there for me twenty-four-seven. What if it's Hutchinson? I pull the covers up to my face. If I stay quiet, maybe whoever it is will go away.

But there's another knock, harder this time.

'Maggie,' a voice calls through the door. 'Are you there, love?'

Relief floods through me as I recognize Amanda's raspy voice.

I get out of the bed and make my way across the bedroom. My back has seized up after a night on a sagging mattress and I wince as I undo the latch and open the door.

'Morning,' says Amanda. 'Sorry to wake you.'

She has a young woman with her who stands looking at me quizzically. She has short, spiky hair, dark at the roots, bleached blonde at the tips, and elaborate piercings in her nose and lower lip. In her oversized baseball sweater and long shorts she looks like a punky American high-school student.

'Maggie, this is Sonia, your designated carer,' she says, squeezing the young girl's arm. 'May we come in?'

'Er, yes,' I say, gesturing to the room. 'Please do. Sorry I'm not dressed. I didn't realize the time. I must have overslept.'

'Don't worry about that,' says Amanda as they come inside. 'I'm just glad to hear you got a good night's sleep. Sometimes it can be difficult when you transition from hospital to –'

She's about to say 'home' but stops herself.

Sonia gives a half-smile as Amanda sets about opening the curtains and making the bed.

'Nice to meet you, Maggie,' she says. 'Shall I make us a cup of tea? I don't know about you but I'm parched.'

Her accent is Scottish and it hurtles me back to childhood. My parents were from Edinburgh but they moved down south before I was born when my dad got a job at an insurance firm in the City. From then on my mother set about transforming herself from working-class Scottish girl to Home Counties clone. By the time I came along the transformation was complete but her accent would creep in from time to time, if she was excited or upset, and she would blush with the shame. I could never understand why she wanted to hide her true self. As far as I was concerned her Scottish accent was what made her special, it was

76

genuine and warm. Yet my mother spent her entire adult life trying to be the exact opposite.

'Maggie, do sit down,' says Amanda, pulling out a wooden stool from beneath the kitchen counter. 'You look a bit unsteady there.'

'It's okay,' I say. 'I was just . . .'

'Do you need your inhaler?'

I shake my head.

'Right, well, let's get your medication sorted first and then we can chat. Sonia, you've got Maggie's pills, haven't you? Why don't you deal with that and I'll fix the tea.'

I sit on the stool while Sonia goes to her rucksack and takes out a box of pills and a bottle of mineral water.

'Here you are, Maggie,' she says, popping two oblong tablets out of the foil wrapper and handing them to me.

I swallow them down with a long sip of water.

'That's great,' says Sonia, smiling, as she takes the bottle from me and puts it on the counter.

'Here,' says Amanda, handing me a mug of tea.

I take the warm mug and hold it in my hands. The tea smells sour.

'Okay,' says Amanda, sitting on the stool opposite me. 'Now, Maggie, I realize you've got loads to deal with right now, and I don't want to add to the pressure, but we need to discuss where you stand in terms of benefits.'

Behind me I hear Sonia sip her tea.

'The reason being,' continues Amanda, 'that the damned things take such a long time to come through so we need to act fast.'

I watch as she brings out a handful of leaflets from her bag. The letters DWP are stamped in red at the top of them: Department for Work and Pensions.

'So, we've been addressing your situation,' says Amanda, handing me one of the leaflets. 'And, because of your health issues, you are entitled to what is known as Universal Credit.'

I look down at the leaflet. There's a line drawing of a man in a wheelchair with a grimace on his face.

'You will also qualify for Housing Benefit and, subject to a health assessment in six weeks' time, Job Seeker's Allowance.'

I look up at Amanda. Doesn't she understand? None of this matters.

'Now if we break it all down,' she says, her voice a drawl, 'you'll be entitled to Housing Benefit . . .'

I can't focus on what she is saying. My head is full of Elspeth. I see her terrified little face, her fists pounding on the car window. I hear her screaming for me to help, begging me to get her out.

'Enough,' I cry, my hands shaking so much I almost drop the tea.

Amanda stops speaking and looks up at me, startled.

'I don't care about the money,' I say. 'What I need is to find out how this happened, why my little girl was locked in that car, where my husband is. Can you please help me find him?'

Sonia grabs my cup of tea before it falls to the floor.

'Maggie, please,' says Amanda, putting her arms out towards me. 'You mustn't upset yourself. As I said, we are here to help.'

'Here to help?' I yell. 'Can you help me bring my daughter back? You know she drowned, trapped in a car seat.' I start sobbing again, unable to help myself. 'I never had a chance to say goodbye to her. My husband, he buried her, and now they can't find him. I can't . . .'

Sonia looks down at her feet while Amanda shifts awkwardly in her seat. I'm making them uncomfortable but I don't care.

'So I don't need Housing Benefit forms,' I cry. 'We need . . . we need the police. They have to do a proper search. Oh God . . . do you understand? I have to find him. You've got to . . . you've got to help me.'

'I'm so sorry, Maggie,' says Amanda. 'Much as I wish I could, I have no way of finding your husband. But what I can do is make sure you're looked after properly.'

I sit back down on the bed, deflated. My lungs are sore from shouting. I rub my chest but it only makes the pain worse.

'Let me get your inhaler,' says Amanda.

She goes to the counter and opens the blue medical bag.

'Here you are, love,' she says, passing it to me.

I take two big gulps. The action makes me feel dizzy. I put my head in my hands to steady myself.

'You're not alone, Maggie,' says Amanda, leaning across and placing her hand on my knee. 'And I realize that this is about so much more than the money and the house. You've lost your little girl. You need to be able to come to terms with that and we can help there too as much as we can. There's a wonderful grief counselling service running in Lewes. I can arrange for you to go along to one of their sessions. It might help to meet people who are going through the same experience as you.'

I'm not even close to being ready for that. How can I be? How can I talk about my grief when I can't even remember how I came to be in that car in the first place?

'No,' I say, sitting up. 'Thank you but that won't be necessary.'

'I understand,' says Amanda, glancing across at Sonia, 'I really do, but then I've also found that in times of hurt being around other people can be an enormous tonic.'

'I'm afraid I've always found the opposite to be true.' I know I sound rude, but I don't know how to explain to her. 'People make me anxious at the best of times.'

I catch Sonia's eye and she nods her head. Perhaps she feels the same way too.

'Maybe we leave the counselling sessions for a wee while, Amanda,' says Sonia. 'It's still early days.'

'Of course,' says Amanda, her voice a little more brittle than before.

Behind me, Sonia starts picking up clothes from the floor and folding them into neat piles.

'Here, Maggie,' she says, handing me a piece of paper. 'You must have dropped this.'

I take the paper and press it to my chest.

'I started writing a list,' I say to Amanda. 'Of people who might know where Sean is. But . . . well, I have no way of contacting them or looking them up because my phone was lost in the accident.'

'I'm sure we can organize a phone for you,' says Amanda. 'Perhaps when you go into town later, Sonia?'

'Sure,' says Sonia. 'It'll probably have to be a cheap pay-as-you-go but it's something I guess.'

'Thank you,' I say, tears brimming in my eyes. 'That would be so helpful.'

'Hey, it's no bother,' she says gently.

'Thank you, Sonia,' says Amanda. 'Now I'm afraid I'm going to have to leave you as my next appointment is in five minutes. Oh, before I forget, here's a list of emergency numbers. Mine is at the top. If you need me at all please do call from the landline here.'

She hands me the list and I put it on the bed.

'I'll leave you with Sonia. She's going to take you to the bank to check your account. You said you had a small savings account, separate from your joint account, is that right?'

I nod my head.

'Well, the contents of that account could help you until the benefits come through,' says Amanda. 'Which usually take around six weeks.'

I smile politely, though I know there's just under two hundred pounds in that account. I have no idea if that will last me six weeks.

'Then once you've sorted everything out at the bank it's on to the Job Centre to register,' says Amanda. 'I know it's not the nicest thing in the world but every little bit counts at this stage. Oh, and I almost forgot.'

She opens her bag and pulls out a book.

'You left this behind when they discharged you,' she says, handing it to me. 'Your ICU nurse gave it to Mike to pass on.'

'What is it?' I say, taking the book from her out-stretched hand.

'They call it your ICU diary,' says Amanda. 'Every patient who has been in the unit long-term is given one of these.'

'A diary?'

I touch the shiny plastic cover, see my name written at the top in black biro.

'Well, they say diary,' says Amanda. 'It's actually more a record of your time in the unit. They wrote in it each day, giving little updates on your progress.'

'They?'

'The ICU staff,' says Amanda. 'Mainly Claire and Dr Elms I guess.'

'But why would I need it now?' I say, placing the book on the bed.

'I think some patients find it helpful to look back and read what happened while they were in the coma,' says Amanda. 'Others don't. It's entirely up to you, Maggie. But it's there if you feel you want to find out more.'

'Thanks,' I say, though I know I won't be reading it. The last thing I need is to be reminded of that place.

'Right, well I'll be off then,' says Amanda. 'See you soon, Maggie.'

While Sonia sees Amanda out I sit and look at the list of names I've compiled. Might any of these people know where Sean is or am I just wasting my time? I don't know the answer but what I do know is that, no matter how hard it gets or how long it takes, I have to find him.

15

My heart is racing as we step out on to the street. It's almost lunchtime and Lewes high street is packed with shoppers and tourists. Sonia leads the way while I trail behind her, a nervous child following her mother.

Ten minutes later I'm sitting on a chair in an open-plan office while a stocky pimple-faced young man called Neil outlines my 'Back to Work' plan. I watch as he types something into his computer. Sonia is waiting in the reception area so I'm going it alone.

'Right, so what would you say are your key skills?' says Neil, looking up momentarily from his keyboard. 'What sort of work should we be looking for?'

'I used to work in admin,' I say, speaking slowly so my brain keeps up.

'Okay,' says Neil, resuming his typing. 'What level?'

'Level?' I say, imagining myself standing in the lift of the Waterloo office as it rose up to the sixth floor. 'Er, well, it was mostly reception work.'

'Basic then,' says Neil, nodding his head. 'Reason for leaving?'

He's reading the questions from a screen.

'I had a baby,' I say. 'And I . . . I gave up work to look after her full-time.'

Although this young man has been informed at the beginning of the interview that my child is dead, he shows no hint of emotion as he types in my answer.

'You see, my husband, he was the main bread-winner once Elspeth was born.'

'So how long have you been out of employment?' he says.

'Ten years,' I reply.

'You haven't worked for ten years?'

I can feel him judging me.

'Not officially, no,' I say, sweat beginning to gather on my forehead. 'Though I've been writing a book and I was hoping . . .' I trail off when I see the look on his face.

'What sort of work are you looking for?' he says, with a sigh.

I look at him blankly. I can't even begin to think about work. What I'm looking for is my husband and my daughter.

'Reception? Front of house?'

I nod my head and he types something into his computer. Then his phone starts to buzz on the desk. He grabs it swiftly and turns it off. As I watch him I remember something. I'm sitting at my desk in the study, staring at the screen just like this young man is,

86

and then my phone buzzes. I know it's the day of the dream catcher because some of the wool is on the desk in front of me. I feel my heart leap in my chest.

'Mrs Allan?'

I look up. Neil has freed his hands from the keyboard and sits with them folded on the desk in front of him.

'Sorry,' I say. 'I'm still finding it hard to concentrate.'

'Yeah, I can see that,' he says. 'Now due to your health issues it may be a while before you're declared fit for work. I'll organize an assessment for six weeks' time but in the meantime here's a breakdown of what you're entitled to.'

He hands me a piece of paper with various boxes printed on it.

'You'll need to come in to sign every two weeks,' he says. 'We'll count today as your first signing day and then it will be every other Tuesday. Now if you could just sign the two boxes at the bottom of the form, we're all done.'

I hastily scribble my name then hand the forms back to Neil.

'Thanks,' he says. 'See you in two weeks.'

I scramble to my feet, trying to keep my composure as I make my way through the open-plan room as fast as I can. But I can feel Neil's eyes on me, judging me, a woman who hasn't worked for ten years, a flaky idiot who couldn't even keep her daughter safe. And the worst thing is, I know he's right.

'Okay, this is it,' says Sonia a few minutes later, stopping outside the bank.

I'm not really listening to her. I'm trying to remember more about that phone call, the one I remembered when I was sitting in the job centre. Who was it?

'Ready, Maggie?'

I look up at the familiar building, a sinking feeling in my stomach. I have banked with this branch almost all my life. I know many of the cashiers by name. There is Sue, who organized a loan for us when we were renovating the house; Val, the red-haired Welsh woman who always gave Elspeth a barley sugar sweet whenever we came in; Ashley, the manager. The thought of going back in there in this state, having to answer questions, having them look at me with pity in their eyes, I just can't bear it.

'It's okay,' says Sonia. 'It's just a bank. We'll be in and out in moments.'

There's a short queue and while we wait I scan the desks to see if any of the cashiers I know are working today. I see Val through a glass screen in the back office but she is having a meeting and doesn't look up. I'm pleased. I couldn't bear having to explain to her what has happened.

'Our turn,' says Sonia.

I look up and see a green light flashing above the glass-protected screen. A young woman with her hair piled up in a messy bun sits behind it.

'Hi there. How can I help you today?' she says languidly.

'Er, I'd like to check my balance,' I say, gripping hold of the counter as a wave of dizziness comes over me.

'You can do that at the cash points,' says the girl, gesturing to the row of blinking machines on the far wall. 'There's no need to queue up here if you just want a balance.'

Sweat starts to gather on my forehead. I'm burning up despite the cool temperature in here. The girl looks at me warily.

'Sorry,' I say. 'I'm just a bit . . .'

'Are you okay, Maggie?' says Sonia, who is standing next to me. 'Do you need to sit down?'

I shake my head.

'No, I'm fine,' I say. 'I just want to get this done.'

'Mrs Allan's just come out of hospital,' says Sonia, picking up on the girl's bemused expression. 'She's been in intensive care and she's still a little fragile.'

'Oh, I'm sorry,' says the girl. 'Listen, how about I get one of my colleagues to come and talk to you? There's a customer services suite with plenty of seats. Maybe that would be better if she's still having difficulty on her feet.'

She addresses all of this to Sonia. I no longer exist.

'I'll go and get my colleague, Val, and she'll come out and help you,' says the girl, standing up.

'No,' I cry, putting my hands on to the counter, 'No, that won't be necessary. I don't want to make a fuss.'

'It's no trouble,' says the girl.

'No, please. It's fine.'

'Okay,' she says, sighing heavily. 'Well, if you're happy to use the cashpoints, they're just over there.'

'I can't,' I say, my head spinning. 'I don't have the . . . I mean, my memory was affected after the accident. I don't remember my pin.'

'Oh,' says the girl, looking at me with narrowed eyes as though I'm a criminal. 'Well, do you have any ID? A passport? Birth certificate.'

'No,' I say. 'My husband got rid of them.'

The girl's eyes widen.

'I'm afraid I can't help you then,' says the girl. 'For security reasons we need some ID.'

It all becomes too much for me then and I slump forward. Sonia catches me just in time. I hear the girl call for assistance and then a familiar voice.

'Maggie. Is that you?'

I turn and see Val coming towards me. Sean used to say that Val and I looked alike, though she is much more polished than me. Unlike my wild mane, her auburn hair is cut in a neat, glossy bob, her eyes shaded by smart black-framed spectacles. I look down at my borrowed clothes but I don't feel ashamed any more. I just feel numb.

'Is everything okay?' says Val, putting her hand on my shoulder.

'I need to check my balance,' I say, rather more abruptly than intended. 'I didn't want to make a fuss but all my stuff has –'

'Hey, hey, don't worry,' says Val, sensing my agitation. 'Let's go somewhere quieter and we can sort this out.'

She gestures to the girl behind the counter then leads Sonia and me towards a small, glass-fronted room.

'Do take a seat,' she says as we enter.

Sonia helps me into the stiff plastic chair.

'Right,' says Val, sitting down opposite. 'First, Maggie, can I say how truly sorry I am – we all are – to hear about little Elspeth.'

I nod my head, tears clouding my eyes. Elspeth loved the bank. She would skip around the room while I queued up to see a cashier, lost in her own little world. If Val was here she'd pop a barley sugar sweet into Elspeth's hands and ask her how school was going.

'She was a lovely child,' says Val, interrupting my thoughts. 'I can't begin to imagine how you must be feeling.'

'Can we . . . can we just sort out the account, please,' I say, wiping my eyes. 'It's just . . . I find it very hard to talk about her still.'

'Of course,' says Val gently. 'If you pass your card over I'll have it sorted in moments.'

Sonia and I sit in silence as Val types something into her computer. After a couple of minutes she looks up.

'Okay, so the balance of your account is £198.54.'

'Right,' I say. 'Thank you.'

Val smiles awkwardly. 'We, er, we had the police visit us,' she says, folding her hands on the desk. 'They were asking questions about your husband.'

Of course, I think to myself. This will have been one of the last places he visited. I sit up straight in my chair and try to compose myself.

'They said he took all the money from his account,' I say.

'Yes.'

'Did he say why he was doing that? Or where he was going?'

'I'm afraid I don't know,' says Val, looking pained. 'It was our deputy manager, Jamie, who dealt with the closing of the account. He told the police all he knew. I guess if your husband had given any explanation then Jamie would have said.'

'He . . . he lied to me,' I say, tears welling up. 'He said we owned our house but we were just tenants.

And then . . . when I was in . . . in the hospital he moved out of the house and threw away all our things . . . all Elspeth's things. I've lost everything.'

'Oh my goodness, that's terrible,' says Val. 'You poor thing.'

I put my face in my hands, trying to hide my tears.

'How about we go and get some air, Maggie?' says Sonia.

I nod, allowing her to help me out of my seat.

Behind her, Val stands watching us, her eyes have filled with tears. I can't bear it.

'That must have been tough,' says Sonia as we walk out of the bank. 'But you did really well. Now, how about we find somewhere to sit and catch a breath before we walk back?'

I am about to answer when something catches my eye. There's a woman standing on the other side of the street. She's staring right at me. My skin prickles. It's Barbara. Ben's mother. She has aged considerably since I last saw her but her hair is still blonde and swept up into a bun; her make-up is immaculate, her clothes expensive and chic. I want to run but it's too late, she's heading this way.

'I don't believe it,' she says as she approaches. 'They let you out then, did they?'

'Hello, Barbara,' I say, my voice quivering. 'How are you?'

'Never mind that,' she says, her face twisted with

hatred. 'I want to know why you're out walking the streets. They should have locked you up years ago.'

'Maggie? Is everything okay?' asks Sonia, stepping in between Barbara and me.

'Who are you?' says Barbara, her eyes widening as she takes in Sonia's outfit.

'I'm Maggie's carer,' says Sonia, puffing her chest out defiantly. 'And I don't think you should be talking to her like that when she's just come out of hospital. She's not well.'

'I know she's not well,' says Barbara, her cheeks reddening. 'She's not well in the head.'

'Barbara, please . . .' I say, my head thudding with the tension.

'A carer?' she says, rolling her eyes. 'Gosh, I've heard it all. Well, you always did need someone to hide behind, didn't you? When I think back to what you got away with, it makes me sick. And now you've done it again by all accounts. That poor little girl. You're dangerous, that's what you are, and dangerous people ought to be locked up.'

Her eyes flash with hatred. I go to speak, to defend myself, but no words will come. Instead I let Sonia guide me away, Barbara's venom ringing in my ears.

16

Dear Mummy,

They've told me that I'm starting a new school tomorrow and I'm scared. I won't know anybody.

Zoe goes to the school next door to mine. It's a school for bad kids she said. I asked her if she liked it but she just shrugged her shoulders and turned her music up.

Now I'm lying in bed writing this and my hands are shaking I feel so nervous. I've tried to think of my happy thoughts but Zoe's music is drowning them out. My uniform is hanging up on the back of the door. It smells all musty and damp because Weasel Face got it from a charity shop. This one is all grey except the tie, which is blue with yellow stripes. Even my shoes are old. They used to belong to one of the other girls but she's grown out of them. Weasel Face said they had 'plenty of wear in them yet'.

I wish I could read something to take my mind off things. There are books here but they're not good ones, just annuals and ones with glitter and puppies on the cover.

Zoe's smoking again. She must have gone through a whole pack tonight. I told Weasel Face about it and she just laughed and said Zoe was a law unto herself, whatever that means.

Anyway, I'm going to try to sleep now. I'll dream of you and Daddy and our cosy home and I'll wish with all my heart that when I wake up I'm back there with you.

I love you.
Your lovely daughter xxx

17

'Here, drink this.'

Sonia passes me a bottle of mineral water. We're sitting on a bench in a little side street, off the main thoroughfare.

'Thank you,' I say, taking the bottle. 'I just need a minute to gather myself.'

'Sure,' says Sonia. 'Take your time. Look, I know it's none of my business but who was that woman?'

'She's the mother of my . . . of a man I used to know,' I say, pausing to regulate my shallow breathing. 'His name was Ben.'

'She was pretty pissed off with you,' says Sonia. 'What happened?'

'Ben and I got into some trouble when we were younger,' I say, looking up the street in case Barbara is heading this way. 'It ended badly. I can't really . . . It's too painful.'

'That's fine,' says Sonia. 'You don't need to talk about it. You've been through enough these past few months. I mean, I don't know the ins and outs but Amanda told me a little about what happened. Jeez, to lose your little girl like that; it must be hell.'

I look at Sonia. She seems like a good person. A kind person. As we sit here I suddenly get the urge to unburden everything, tell this stranger every little detail of what has happened in my life to get me to this point: Ben, the bad place, my mum, me and Sean. But before I can speak, Sonia gets to her feet.

'Come on,' she says, holding out her hand to me. 'Let's get you home.'

I lie down on the bed and pull the covers tightly round me. The room smells of pasta sauce and detergent. Sonia warmed up a ready meal in the microwave for me before she left but the thought of food made me feel sick, so I threw it away and washed the bowl. But though the food has gone the smell remains.

I hear the lock being turned in next-door's room and Hutchinson's now-muffled voice filters through the wall.

'Here it is, your twin bedroom. I fully understand, mate. Once you get to our age it's separate beds all the way.'

He laughs manically and I flinch. It reminds me of that place. No privacy, raised voices coming through the walls, people everywhere, but no one I knew. Trapped. Alone.

Although I eventually escaped, the feeling of entrapment stayed with me for years. After everything that had happened, my parents couldn't face living in the village any more so they had left Sussex and bought a small bungalow in Croydon. When I got myself straight I went to live with them and spent my early twenties working in a variety of retail jobs. From a sandwich shop in Sutton to the lingerie department of Croydon M&S, none of them lasted long and then my parents' health deteriorated and the darkness reared its head again.

Dad died first. A heart attack when I was twenty-six. There were no big goodbyes, no dramatic last speeches like you see in the movies; he just collapsed at his desk. His boss called us but by the time we got to the hospital he was gone.

Mum was never the same after Dad died. She was already heartbroken from having to leave Larkfields and Sussex, and no matter how much poor Dad tried to put a gloss on things, the Croydon bungalow in an unassuming cul-de-sac could never compete with beautiful Larkfields; with the Sussex country set, with Barbara and her dazzling parties. But while Dad was alive, Mum still had a role, however outdated it might seem. She would still cook elaborate dinners and get dressed up to greet him from work. When he died, she shrivelled. Her whole world collapsed around her and the only person left was the daughter she had spent years trying to avoid. We may have lived under the same roof but Mum could barely bring herself to look at me. I had destroyed her life and here I was, a twenty-something burden floating from one dead-end job to the next. For my mother, Dad's death only served to magnify my presence. If I walked into a room she would find an excuse to leave it. Sometimes at night I would hear her crying through the wall that divided my bedroom from hers, thick, heaving sobs that sounded like they were coming from the depths of her soul. It was unbearable.

Still, nothing could have prepared me for what she did. I'd just started a new job, a temping role at an insurance company in London. It was better money than I'd ever made and I enjoyed being in the city, commuting from grey Croydon into the heart of the West End. The office was based on Shaftesbury Avenue and I would spend my lunch hour walking through Chinatown, people-watching. After the silence of the countryside, the noise of London was a welcome relief. For the first time in years I felt like I could breathe easily; that I wasn't being judged. Sometimes the girls from the office would invite me to join them for drinks after work. I went along a couple of times but I never really felt comfortable. Having to make small talk and mingle made me feel anxious so I would usually make my excuses after one drink and head out into Soho or Covent Garden, bustling places where I could lose myself in the crowd. Most people would say it was a sad, lonely existence but back then I needed to be alone like other people need air. It was the only way I could make sense of everything that had happened to me. As the months went by I found myself spending less and less time at home. Mum's moods were getting worse and the thought of having to spend night after night sitting on the sofa while she watched some mind-numbing TV show was too much. So on weekends I would travel back to the West End. Sometimes I'd watch a matinee performance at the theatre; other times I just wandered round the shops; anything rather than have to face Mum and that depressing house. For a short period in my life, the dark thoughts that had festered inside my head since I was a child began to lighten, and I allowed myself to believe in the possibility that I could actually get better. Maybe Mum picked up on this; maybe, because I was always out of the house, she could sense me slipping away from her. I don't know. I will never know because she never gave a reason. There was no note next to the body when I found her slumped over the kitchen table one Saturday evening, no 'I love you', no goodbyes; just my mother, cold and lifeless, next to an empty box of pills.

When the house was sold, I was left with a small sum, after debts and other fees had been accounted for. I should have bought a modest property, invested in my future, but nobody had ever taught me how to handle money properly and in many ways I was still a naive fourteen-year-old girl, locked in a state of arrested development. So instead of getting on the property ladder I spent the last few years of my twenties on a mad spending spree. I got expensive haircuts and shopped on Bond Street. I started to wear make-up and would think nothing of buying a scented candle for two hundred quid. I moved to London and spent a fortune renting a tiny flat in Battersea. It would have been cheaper to flat-share but my past experiences had left me distrustful of others. Home was my refuge, a place I could go back to each night, close the door and shut out the world. I worked in a series of admin jobs, usually front of house, where I could sit and read novels in between having to answer phones and make coffee. It was like I was a teenager again, only instead of lying on my bed, reading books and blocking out the world, I was sitting behind a desk doing the same. One of my bosses, a woman called Helen, once caught me reading a novel when I should have been preparing a meeting room for an important conference. I thought she would go ballistic and sack me for neglecting my duties but she sat down and asked a bit about me, about my past, where I'd grown up, where I'd gone to school. When I told her about my lack of education, she urged me to go back to college, perhaps enrol on a literature course and put the reading to good use. But I was too scared. Doing that would mean facing up to everything that had happened, opening up hopes and aspirations that I'd long since buried. No, I was happier to block it all out by sitting behind one dreary reception desk after the other. Better to be numb than to have my heart broken again. But then I met Sean and everything changed. He gave my life meaning. He gave me Elspeth.

And now they are gone.

The piece of paper with the list of names I compiled yesterday sits redundantly on the bedside table, my search for Sean put on hold until I get a new phone. We were supposed to go and buy one today but the encounter with Barbara left me so shaken I couldn't face staying in town. Sonia said she would pick one up for me tomorrow. She promised she'd get the cheapest model she could find. But even then, the £198 I have in my account is not going to last long.

Thoughts of the past have left me feeling restless and panicky. I need to distract myself. I toy with the idea of turning on the TV but I know that will only make me feel worse. Then I see the diary Amanda brought back. It's sitting on the counter, by the sink. I get out of bed and go over to the kitchen. Pouring myself a glass of water, I pick up the diary. Do I read it? It's tempting. But then I ask myself what good will come from revisiting the horrors of what happened? So I put it down and take my glass of water back to bed.

I lie there for a couple of moments, the silence of

the room seeping into my skin. I close my eyes and try to sleep but it won't come. I sit up and look over at the diary. I'll just read a bit of it, I tell myself, as I get out of bed, then if it gets too much I'll stop. I take the diary over to the chair by the window. A silver beam of moonlight filters through the curtains and lights a wavering path across the room. I open the book and read the unfamiliar writing on the first page.

> Hello. We hope this diary will help you to make sense of the time you spent in Intensive Care.
> You were admitted to Lewes Victoria Hospital at 21.47 p.m. on 12th May 2017 suffering the effects of Near Drowning. At this stage you were unconscious as a result of hypoxia.

I look up at the wall, trying to take in the details. 21.47 p.m. Elspeth was already dead by then. 'Dead at the scene' is how Elms put it. Dead at the scene. I try not to let the images come but I can't stop them: my little girl trapped in the back of that car, unable to breathe, unable to escape. She will have screamed my name and I couldn't save her. Her mum, the person she trusted more than anyone in the world, couldn't save her. Not only that but I had locked her in the car. The guilt presses down on my chest. I can't bear it.

I remember how furious I had been when Sean

told me what happened outside the dry-cleaner's when Elspeth was seven. 'How could you?' I'd screamed at him. 'How could you lock our child in the car like that? She was terrified.' And yet, Sean's actions that day were nothing compared to what I did at the river. And not one bit of it makes sense. I was always the overprotective one, the one who made sure Elspeth wore a helmet when she went bike riding, who panicked if I lost sight of her in the supermarket.

My paranoia was a constant source of conflict between Sean and me. He used to say that I was doing Elspeth no favours by being so overprotective, that she wouldn't thank me for it in the future.

Well, now there is no future.

The diary is still open in front of me but as I skim through the rest of the page all I can think of is Elspeth. I look again at those words, 'Near Drowning', and then I read on as they describe their attempts to prevent further damage to my lungs, about the CT scans carried out without my knowledge but with 'your husband's permission'.

I read about the tracheostomy I was given and touch the small scar on my neck where they made the incision before fitting the tube into my windpipe, and I want to scream and shout.

While those doctors and nurses were battling to save my life, Elspeth was lying in a cold morgue.

Her life ended by a decision I can't even remember making.

I can't read any further. I let the book fall to the floor, the room momentarily erased by my tears.

The B & B is silent now. Light filters through the curtains. The digital clock by the bed reads 5.37. Morning has come. I lie back on the pillow wishing that my brain would be like Elspeth's dream catcher and clasp my memories in a woven net. But as I close my eyes I see the river. Elspeth paddling in the water, wading out further and further until it reaches her shoulders. She stops and turns to me, her face beaming with happiness.

'Come back, Elspeth,' I call. 'Please, angel, it's too deep.'

She starts to speak but I can't make out the words. It sounds like she is underwater though she is right here in front of me.

'What is it?' I call. 'I can't hear you.'

And then she disappears underneath the water but at the very moment her head submerges I hear her voice whispering in my ear, so close I can feel the warmth of her breath.

'Go home, Mummy,' she says. 'Go home.'

I wake up gasping for air. I climb out of bed and go to the kitchenette for a drink. As I stand by the sink gulping mouthfuls of icy water I run the dream over and over in my head. I think of the flashback I had in the job centre, sitting at my desk and my phone buzzing beside me. Could that be a memory of the day of the accident? I don't know. But then I hear Elspeth's words again and it all makes sense. She is right. I can't expect to recall the events of 12th May by hiding out in this room. If I want to find the answers I need to go home.

18

Wednesday 2 August

Thirty minutes later I'm washed and dressed and on my way to Lewes bus station. I left a note for Sonia with Mr Hutchinson, who was manning the reception desk. In it I told her that I was going for a walk; that I needed to be alone to gather my thoughts. I thanked her for leaving the two codeine tablets on the kitchen counter last night and said that I would be back at the B & B no later than 3 p.m.

Thankfully the streets are quiet as I head into the town centre. I still feel weak and confused and the thought of bumping into someone from the village or the school or, worse still, Barbara, fills me with dread. I pull the hood of my coat up, put my head down, and don't look up until I reach the bus station.

At the concourse I stand for a moment to read the timetable. I haven't caught a bus in years and with my limited brain function the timetable reads like a complex mathematical equation.

'You all right there, love?' says a male voice from behind.

I turn to see a man in his late sixties. He's got a newspaper under his arm and a polystyrene cup of tea in his hand.

'I'm fine, thank you,' I reply, turning back to the timetable. 'Just looking.'

I hope the tone of my voice deters him from pursuing a conversation. My speech still isn't fully recovered. I can think of words in my head, and they sound right, but when I try to say more than a sentence or two they come out all jumbled. I really don't need the embarrassment of having this stranger pity me. But I can sense him still standing behind me.

'Which bus are you after?' he says, tapping me on the shoulder.

His touch makes me flinch and I jump backwards, clutching my chest.

'Hey, it's okay,' he says, his eyes widening. 'I'm not going to hurt you, just thought you needed a hand making sense of that blooming timetable. It's as clear as mud.'

He smiles warmly and I suddenly feel bad for acting so jumpy. He's just a chatty pensioner, not some serial killer.

'I need to get to . . .'

I look at him blankly. What is the name of the village? It's completely gone.

'Yes, dear?' says the man gently.

'Erm . . . sorry, I . . . my mind's gone blank,' I say.

'I need to get to . . . the village . . . the village where Virginia Woolf lived.'

'Ah, Rodmell,' says the man.

'Yes,' I cry, clapping my hands together. 'Rodmell.'

I mutter the name under my breath several times, terrified in case I forget it again.

'Well, that's easy,' he says, jabbing his finger at the timetable. 'I live just near there. It's the 123 towards Newhaven you want. Rodmell's the sixth stop. Next one's due any minute now.'

'Thank you,' I say. 'I really appreciate your help.'

'Not a bother, dear,' he says. 'You like her, do you?'

'Sorry?'

'Mrs Woolf,' he says. 'I'm guessing that's why you're off to Rodmell. To see Monk's House? Where she used to live?'

'Er . . . yes . . . yes, that's right,' I reply, looking over his head to see if the bus is coming yet.

'Oh, we get a lot of fans here, making the pilgrimage to Monk's House, particularly on the anniversary of her suicide,' he says, taking a sip of tea. 'When I was a taxi driver I used to get loads of them. They'd start off here in Lewes, get off at Rodmell to see the house then they'd go to the spot where her body was found in the river at Southease and lay flowers. Funny lot they were. All dressed in black with pale faces. Most of them looked like they could have done with a good meal. You look pretty normal to me.'

I smile politely. I just want the bus to arrive so I can get on with what I need to do.

'Thank you,' I say, moving away from him. 'You've been really kind.'

'Once a taxi driver, eh?' he says, raising his newspaper in farewell. 'Anyway, dear, I'll go and wait for my bus. I'm off to Haywards Heath to see my daughter. Cheerio now. Safe journey.'

He walks over to the bench by the station cafe, sits down and opens his newspaper, leaving me to wait for the 123 alone. The station is pretty grim and hasn't altered much since Ben and I used to come here to get the bus to Brighton when we were kids.

As the bus pulls up I catch a glimpse of myself in the window and think about the beautiful, carefree fourteen-year-old I had once been, before the dark thing happened. Now I look like a hollowed-out shell, a ghost woman trapped between worlds.

When the bus pulls up I wait while two schoolboys clamber on. Once they've got their tickets I climb the steps.

'Yes, love?' says the driver, a young man with a goatee beard.

I open my mouth to say the name of the village, the name I've just spent the last few minutes reciting under my breath, but I can't remember it.

'Where would you like to go?' says the driver, drumming his fingers on the steering wheel impatiently.

'I'm sorry,' I say, laughing nervously. 'I've completely forgotten the name of the village. I think it begins with "D".'

The driver shakes his head then presses some buttons on his machine.

'I'll do you a day return,' he says as a long white ticket snakes towards me. 'You can get off at any stop along this route with this ticket then back again.'

'Oh, thank you,' I say, pulling the ticket out of the machine. 'That's great.'

I go to walk away but the driver calls me back.

'Hey, you haven't paid.'

In a panic I pat my pockets. I left the B & B in such a rush and I can't remember picking up my purse. I can hear the two young schoolboys laughing behind me as I make my way back to the driver.

'I'm sorry,' I say as I feel the reassuring bulk of my purse in the back pocket of my jeans. 'I wasn't thinking.'

'Four pounds,' says the driver, his voice impatient now.

I unzip my purse. There are two five-pound notes and a ten.

'There you go,' I say, thrusting a fiver into the driver's hand.

He nods then pushes a button on his machine and hands me my change.

'Thanks,' I say, taking the coin and putting it into my back pocket.

As the engine starts I go to find a seat. The two teenage boys snigger again as I trip over a folded pushchair that's been left in the aisle. I curse under my breath, then, steadying myself, head for the back of the bus, away from them and the crying baby who is sitting up front with its mother.

I look out of the window as we leave Lewes. A small white building comes into view: Elspeth's school. I crane my neck to see if I can spot any of her friends but it's still early, another few hours yet until the morning bell. I imagine the children sitting at their desks later, all safe and sound. All safe and sound, except Elspeth. Then a thought comes into my head unbidden: if only it was one of them instead.

As we leave the school behind and head out into open countryside I try to think clearly. Surely seeing her school and travelling through this landscape should trigger something but there is nothing.

I look out of the window as a familiar road sign looms into view. Ketton House Farm: Ben's house. My chest tightens as I recall the evening of Barbara's party all those years ago; the night that changed my life for ever. I see myself, fourteen years old, all dolled up in a tight black dress, walking down that narrow lane with my parents. I see the playhouse and Ben standing at the door. I can hear the loud music, smell the sickly scent of dope in the air and the sweat of hot bodies. Then I remember Barbara's words, 'Dangerous people should be locked up,' and I start to tremble. Maybe this was a bad idea. Maybe I should just turn back.

But I've come this far. I can't lose my nerve now. The bus starts to slow. We must be getting close. I look out of the window and see the village. This is it. I'm home. I stand up and make my way down the aisle, my head fizzing with a mixture of adrenaline and fear.

'Thank you,' I say to the driver when I get to the doors.

'No bother,' he says. 'Oh and just so you know. The name of this place is Rodmell. Is that what you were wanting?'

'Yes,' I say. 'Yes, it is.'

'Here,' he says, handing me a leaflet. 'Have this. It's got all the return times on.'

It's a timetable with every village name clearly printed. I am so grateful it's like he's just handed me a million pounds.

'Thank you,' I say, tears prickling my eyes. 'Thank you so much.'

'No worries,' he says, with a laugh. 'It's only a timetable.'

Then he presses a button and the bus doors open. I turn and walk down the steps, like a hesitant child. I hear the doors close then the bus pulls away.

I stand for a moment taking it all in. Everything is as it was three months ago: the pretty flint cottages, the narrow country lane and the pub where Sean and

I used to take Elspeth for Sunday lunch. She loved their ice cream sundaes and the fact they had a resident cat, a fat ginger tom called Archie. The last time we were there the landlord told us that Archie had got into a fight with a fox and had needed stitches. He'd pointed to a bench on the far side of the bar where the poor old cat was curled up asleep. He was wearing one of those plastic ruffs round his neck to stop him picking at the stitches. Elspeth was distraught and asked if she could take her meal over to where Archie was. She spent the entire afternoon cuddled up next to him, feeding him bits of fish finger.

I turn away from the pub and start to walk, the ground bumpy and uneven under my feet, and then I see it up ahead: the church. As I draw closer I see the gate to the churchyard. Someone has left it open and it swings back and forth in the breeze. I walk towards it in a daze, my eyes stinging with dried tears, but when I get to the gate I pause. There, on the other side, conspicuous amongst the lichen-covered stones, is a fresh grave. The stone is white and though I can't see the lettering I know from the mounds of purple flowers, teddy bears and balloons who it belongs to.

'No,' I cry, clasping my hand to my mouth. 'Oh God, no.'

I turn from the gate and stumble back towards the main road, tears blurring my vision. I can't do it. I can't go and stand at that grave. I can't say goodbye to my beautiful child without knowing what happened that night. I have to get home – if I go home then I can think straight and maybe the fog in my head will clear.

It's just a few hundred metres from here yet every step I take feels leaden, like my body is trying to stop me from getting there.

At the top of the hill the Downs spread out across the horizon and I force myself onwards until I reach the dip in the road and turn left into an expanse of ash trees. I can't see the river yet but I can sense it. The air changes the closer you get to the water, it becomes damp and ripe. As I walk through the wooded copse I hear voices behind me, whispering, but when I turn round there is no one there, just the trees swaying in the breeze.

I quicken my pace and head towards the stones, Elspeth's stones. I can see them up ahead, the final resting place of Sir Edwin Chatto, gallant Knight of Sussex, and his beautiful Lady Vivien. At least, that was what Elspeth said they were. In reality the stones were just the remains of old millstones from the nineteenth century but Elspeth wasn't satisfied with that. The stones had to be special, they had to have a deeper meaning, and so the story of Sir Edwin and Lady Vivien was born.

When I reach the stones I stop for a moment to catch my breath, remembering the days when I would stand here for hours waiting for Elspeth to finish talking to her long-dead friends. Sometimes she would bring flowers and place them on the stones for Lady Vivien's birthday or the anniversary of her death. Other times we'd bring a picnic and she'd leave an offering of cake or fruit. It would seem strange to most people, but Elspeth had always been that way.

I carry on walking and then, after a few moments, I see it, peeking out from between the trees. A Gothic lodge house with a sloping roof and long diamond-shaped windows that only ever let in a fraction of light. As I follow the curve of the lane the house is momentarily hidden from view. The hawthorn bushes that line the path seem to get higher and higher so that it feels like I'm stepping into the centre of a maze. My breath grows shallow. I stop, take the inhaler out of my bag and take two long drags. As my lungs ease I carry on walking. This path is so familiar I could walk it blindfold and yet it feels strangely altered, like it's become another, more complex, version of itself. A hundred yards further the lane opens up and I find myself standing at the edge of the sweeping sycamore-lined driveway looking at a rickety wooden sign nailed to the gate. In spidery metal letters it spells out a name:

LARKFIELDS.

19

I push the gate open and make my way down the drive. When I reach the front door my hands instinctively go to my pockets to retrieve my keys. It's a natural reflex. I must have stood at this door a thousand times. If I close my eyes I can imagine that I've just dropped Elspeth off at school and this is an ordinary day. I'd go inside and load the breakfast dishes into the dishwasher, then make myself a pot of coffee and head upstairs to my study. I'd sit at my desk, secure in the knowledge that Elspeth is safe at school, working in her classroom and playing with her friends. She isn't lying in the ground in St Peter's churchyard. She is alive and well and waiting for her mummy to come and collect her at 3.30.

I put my hand on the wooden door frame to steady myself. My lungs feel like they are on fire. I peer through the window. The house looks empty. I turn the handle, praying for it to give, but it is locked. When I was a teenager my mum would leave a spare key underneath the bay tree pot that stood outside the door. I take a look around but there are no pots, no keys. Obviously, the real owners –

B-something-or-other from what I remember – are more security conscious than that.

I step back from the door and make my way round to the back of the house. The living-room curtains are closed and there is no light coming from behind them. At the far end of the house there is a stone archway that leads to a small patio. Elspeth and I used to sunbathe out here in the summertime. It was so quiet and peaceful. But now it is overgrown with weeds and dead leaves. I crunch through them as I make my way across the patio to the back of the house.

I gasp when I see the garden. Like the patio, it is a tangle of weeds. The vegetable trenches where Elspeth and I planted carrots and green beans have been ripped out. The roots lie discarded on the path. The air smells of rotten vegetables and something else, a dusty decaying smell that I can't quite place. It is eerily quiet; the only noise the crunch of my boots on the gravel path. Then I see the greenhouse and my heart sinks. Its windows are filthy and cracked. I walk towards it, aware that something is missing. No, I whisper, surely not. The beautiful wooden summerhouse Sean built for Elspeth when she was three years old has been removed; the only trace left of it a square of scorched dead grass.

I turn on my heels, unable to take it all in. Despite seeing it with my own eyes it still doesn't seem real.

As I make my way round the side of the house to the kitchen I half expect Sean to appear and hand me a mug of tea, tell me this has all been a terrible nightmare. But when I reach the kitchen door there is no Sean, there is just a thick, foreboding silence. I put my hand on the familiar metal latch and click it up. To my surprise, the door yields. I push it open.

I step inside my kitchen. It all looks the same – the Rayburn stove, the black beams, the York stone floor – and yet I can feel a great absence. Everything that was us, the Allan family, has departed. The air is different. It smells stale and oppressive, like the trapped air in the vaults of museums and old churches. Then slowly, as my eyes adjust, I start to see more solid changes. Elspeth's collage of paintings that hung proudly on the wall by the dresser has been removed and replaced with a white rectangular clock; the kitchen table, where Elspeth and Sean had sat to work on the dream catcher, has gone and a small round one put in its place. The dresser, which once was laden with all our mess and miscellany, now houses a neat collection of blue-and-white-striped chinaware.

I walk over to the dresser and pull out a drawer, expecting to see Elspeth's craft materials, but it's empty. I pull out another and another, my body trembling with pain and grief. Who could have done this? Who could have come into my house and swept away all trace of my little girl? Why would Sean let this happen?

And then I hear footsteps on the stone floor behind me, a sharp intake of breath.

'What the hell do you think you're doing?'

I turn round and see a tall, blonde woman standing with her hands on her hips. She has a round, pale face, the skin almost translucent, and large green eyes that she fixes on me.

'Are you going to answer me?'

'I . . . I was . . .'

My brain has shut down. I desperately try to scramble some words together but they won't come.

'I'm calling the police,' she says, putting her hand in her pocket and pulling out her phone.

'No,' I say, holding my hand out. 'Please don't do that. I used to live in this house. The door was open and . . . look, I'm sorry. I'll go now.'

I feel her eyes on me as I stagger to the back door.

'Just because you used to live here doesn't mean you have the right to bloody break in,' she calls after me.

I don't answer but unclick the latch on the door and step out as quickly as I can. She is right. What the hell was I thinking? The pain in my chest intensifies as I hurry round the side of the house. All I can think about is my little Elspeth and those empty drawers in the kitchen. Every trace of her has been scraped away; it's like she never existed, like our whole family life was just a figment of my imagination.

As I reach the driveway I see the woman's car parked outside the house. It is a red sporty one with a soft-top roof. She mustn't have children, I think to myself, those kind of cars are not made for families. And as I look at the car I hear Elspeth crying. I feel the softness of her dressing gown on my fingertips as I push her into the seat. 'I don't want to, Mummy, please can we just stay at home?' I can smell the toothpaste on her breath and the soft lavender scent of her shampoo. She's had a bath and is ready for bed and I am forcing her into the car. I hear her screaming: *No, Mummy, no.*

20

Dear Mummy,

I've cried so much tonight it hurts.

I don't want to be here.

I started at the new school today and it was just horrid. I kept on getting lost because it's a big building with lots of winding corridors and stairs.

When I got to the classroom the teacher told me to go and sit on a table with three other girls. They were all really neat and pretty with glittery hairbands and expensive shoes. When I sat down one of them said, 'Yuk, what's that smell?' The other girls started laughing then the rest of the class started sniffing and pulling faces. This boy, who is much taller than all the others, got out of his seat and came over to me. He put his face right next to mine and said, in a really mean, hissy voice, 'Skank.' Then the teacher came over and told him to go back to his desk but for the rest of the morning I could hear him muttering it under his breath: 'Skank. Skank.' I tried to focus on the lesson, which luckily was maths, which I love, but my eyes were so full of tears it made the numbers dance across the page and I couldn't catch them.

At break I walked around by myself for a bit. I thought about all my friends at my old school and what they would be doing. Probably playing dragons and fairies. I was always the dragon because I liked dragons best. The others would be fairies and I would chase them and cast spells. I wonder who'll be the dragon now. The girls at the new school don't play games like that. They just stand in groups, plaiting each other's hair and doing handstands against the wall. I stood for a bit watching them but they just ignored me so I went and sat at the edge of the playground. There was a ladybird on the ground. I put my hand right next to it and it crawled on to my finger. It tickled but I got to see her beautiful spotty skin. It was glossy and smooth. And then I remembered the song we learned at nursery, 'Ladybird, Ladybird, fly away home. Your house is on fire and your children all gone.' I started to sing it. Then something hit me in the head. I looked up and saw the tall boy from my class. He was standing there staring at me. 'Look,' he said to his friends. 'The skank's talking to herself.' I was scared he was going to throw another pebble at me but then the bell went and I jumped up and ran inside.

At home time all the mums were standing round the school gate and for a second I imagined you standing there with them. But you weren't. Then I heard someone call my name and saw Zoe. Weasel Face must have told her to walk me home. She didn't speak, just nodded her head *then lit up a cigarette. As we walked I could feel tears in my eyes. I didn't want Zoe to see me cry so I stared down at the ground and thought about my happy things.*

I love you.
Your lovely daughter xxx

21

Elspeth's voice burns in my ears as I walk out of the gate and make my way down the narrow lane that runs by the side of the house. The memory had been brief but brutal. She was begging me to stop. She was scared. Her hair was wet and she was wearing her dressing gown. As I walk I try to imagine what kind of circumstances, what major emergency could have made me bundle my half-dressed daughter into the car and head for a pub at that time of night. I try to piece together the information I have: my phone buzzing on the desk; Sean and Elspeth sitting at the kitchen table making a dream catcher and Elspeth telling me not to strap her into the car, begging me not to make her go out. Are these memories linked? Do they all stem from the day of the accident? I don't know and it's killing me that I can't remember.

A chill flutters down my spine as I reach the end of the lane and see the field up ahead. This stretch of land links Ketton House Farm to Larkfields. It was where I used to meet Ben after school and later we would walk across the field to reach the river. I shudder as I remember: two alder trees bending towards each other, the river trickling away.

Most people would think I was crazy to return to the place that held so many bad memories but Lark-fields had always exerted a strange hold over me. When I lived in London the house would return to me in my dreams, like an unfinished puzzle I had to solve. When I saw that it was for sale it felt like fate. We could go back and make everything right again. And for a few years it seemed like we had. Elspeth's presence at Lark-fields turned the bad memories into good. She loved the land around it and claimed it as her own. It was where she felt safest.

The wind rushes into my face as I reach the field and I take great gulps of it, the tightness in my chest easing slightly. I brush my hair out of my eyes and then I see them again: Elspeth's stones.

I crouch down next to the biggest one, running my hand along its rough surface.

'Hello, Edwin,' I whisper as I settle myself on the grass. 'What have you been up to today?'

And then I hear her voice fluttering across the breeze.

'Here lies the body of Sir Edwin Chatto, Gallant Knight of Sussex.'

My heart freezes as I recognize the line. It was what she would always declare as she reached the meadow and saw the stones. It was as normal to her as saluting the magpie. She's quiet now, waiting for my response.

'And here,' I say, wincing as I get to my feet and step across to the smaller stone, 'is his beloved Lady Vivien, the fairest maiden in all of –'

I don't manage to get the word out because there, sitting on top of Lady Vivien's stone, is Elspeth.

'The fairest maiden in all of Sussex,' she says, expanding her arms towards the sky. Her purple dress is a wash of colour against the mottled grey stone.

I step towards her, my hands shaking.

'Elspeth,' I whisper. 'What are you doing here?'

'I want to play hide and seek,' she says, jumping down from the stone. 'Try and find me.'

'No, Elspeth, come back,' I call, but she is already making her way down the hill. 'Please, darling, come back.'

I go after her, keeping my eyes fixed on the flash of purple as she darts left and right looking for a hiding place, but my legs are too weak, I can't keep up. When I reach the narrow lane that leads back to Larkfields, I call her name.

'Elspeth. I don't want to play any more. Please come out.'

And then I hear it. A scream. Cutting through the air.

'Elspeth, what is it? What's happened?'

I pause and listen. The noise comes again, sharper this time.

'Elspeth,' I cry. 'It's okay, darling, Mummy's here. I'm coming to find you.'

And then I look up and see a straggly crow perched on a branch in the oak tree above me. It opens its beak and lets out a caw so high-pitched and pitiful it could be mistaken for a child's cry.

'No,' I scream up at the bird. 'No, no, no.'

22

There's a screech of brakes. A door slams and footsteps crunch on gravel. Then I feel a hand on my shoulder.

'Hello?'

Elspeth.

'Can you hear me? Are you okay?'

I open my eyes, pain ripping through my head and spine.

'Elspeth?' I whisper. But as the face comes into focus I see that it is not Elspeth, it is a woman; the woman from the house.

'Are you hurt?' she asks, her voice firm and brusque.

I shake my head and try to get to my feet.

'Hold on,' she says, keeping her hand on my arm. 'I need to check that you're not injured. Goodness, what's happened to your fingernails?'

I yank my hand back.

'I was in a car accident. Sorry, I have to go.'

She stands back as I stagger to my feet. Flashes of white light dance in front of my eyes and I put my hand out to try and steady myself. The woman rushes to my side and takes my arm.

'Come on,' she says. 'I'm taking you back into the house. You need to sit down and have a glass of water and I need to check you're okay.'

'No,' I say, pushing her hand away. 'I can't . . .'

'Well then, at least let me drive you home,' she says, gesturing to her car, which is poking out of the driveway, the driver's door wide open. 'Where do you live?'

'Look, I'm fine,' I say. 'Give me a couple of minutes to catch my breath and then I'll walk back.'

'I can't let you do that,' she says firmly. 'I'm a doctor and I can clearly see that you are in no fit state to walk anywhere. I insist.'

I glance at the long country lane that leads back to the village. She's right. I'd never make it, not the way I'm feeling right now. I hate being like this, unable even to help myself.

'Lewes,' I say, looking down at my feet. 'I'm staying in Lewes. In this place.'

I open my bag, take out the crumpled B & B brochure and hand it to her.

'Oh, okay,' she says, frowning. 'Now, why don't you get in the car and I'll drive you back. Sorry, I didn't catch your name.'

'It's Maggie Allan,' I say as I follow her to the car.

'I'm Julia,' she says, opening the passenger door for me. 'Julia Mathers.'

She gestures at me to get in the car. I step forward

but as I grab the door my heart lurches in my chest. I'm back at the riverbank, holding on to the car with all my might. I hear screams, desperate screams. It's Elspeth. She's trapped.

Mummy!

Elspeth. No!

'Maggie?'

I turn round and as I look at Julia's concerned face I remember something: a figure in red.

I close my eyes and try to will the memory back. The car rolling. Elspeth screaming. Turning to cry for help. A flash of red. A figure? Or just my mind playing tricks on me? I shake my head in frustration. The memory had seemed so clear just a moment ago and now it's gone.

'Maggie? Are you okay?'

I look up at Julia, another stranger taking pity on me.

'I'm fine,' I say as I get into the car.

But as we drive away all I can hear is the sound of Elspeth's screams.

'Is this the place?'

Julia has stopped the car outside the B & B. I look out of the window and see the stone lions standing guard outside the front door.

'Yes,' I say, my heart sinking at the thought of returning to that empty room.

I unclip my seat belt and open the door. I'm about

to turn and thank her for the lift when I see that she is getting out of the car.

'I'll see you in,' she says, shutting the door and locking it with her electronic fob. 'You were out cold back there. I want to check that you're okay before I leave you.'

'There's no need, honestly, I'm fine.'

'I'm sorry, Maggie, but I'm a doctor,' she says as we walk up the path. 'It's in my nature.'

I look at her. There is something in her face that draws me to her. She has kind eyes. I decide to trust her.

She looks up at the door then turns to me.

'Do we have to knock?'

'No, I've got a key,' I say, taking the bulky set from my pocket.

I unlock the door and we step into the dark hallway. Thankfully the reception desk is unattended. Mr and Mrs Hutchinson will be having their tea.

'It's this way.'

I gesture ahead, and Julia follows me down the narrow corridor to Room 2.

I open the door and step inside.

'Come in,' I say, turning to Julia.

She is standing in the doorway, a strange expression on her face.

'I'll make some tea,' I say, shuffling across to the kitchenette.

'No,' says Julia. 'You sit down. I'll do it.'

She has a doctor's voice, calm yet authoritative, and I do as she says. I watch as she boils the kettle and prepares the tea, grimacing at the pots of UHT milk.

'Here you go,' she says, coming over to where I am sitting on the wicker chair by the window and handing me a mug.

'Thank you,' I say, taking it and wrapping my hands round its warmth.

She sits down in the chair opposite me, watching as I sip my tea.

'Maggie, I want to apologize,' she says. 'For the way I spoke to you at the house. I had no idea that you'd been in an accident. I realize something like that can result in erratic behaviour and . . . well, if I'd known I'd have been more understanding.'

I put my mug down on the small coffee table between us then lean forward in my chair.

'I'm really sorry I walked in like that,' I say, clasping my hands together so tightly my knuckles go white. 'It was wrong of me. But I came to the house today for a reason.'

'Oh?' she says. 'What was the reason?'

I look down at my fingers, the raw flaky skin where my nails used to be.

'Maggie?'

'I wanted to remember,' I say, my eyes filling with tears.

And then it all comes out. Waking up to find that

Elspeth is dead. That my husband is missing. That the house she is now living in used to be ours. The whole sorry tale. When I finish I look up at Julia and see that the colour has drained from her face.

'Maggie,' she says, putting a hand to her mouth. 'I . . . I don't know what to say. I can't imagine what you must be going through.'

'I thought coming back to Larkfields today would help,' I say. 'Thought I might be able to make sense of it all, but it just raised more questions than it answered.'

'I didn't realize,' she says, shaking her head. 'I feel terrible; like I've made you homeless.'

'You weren't to know,' I say. 'And it's not your fault. Oh Christ, I don't care about the house. Nothing matters but Elspeth.'

I slam my fists on my lap. The room feels like it's closing in on me.

'I saw her,' I say, tears clouding my eyes. 'She was up on the hill by the stones. I know as a doctor you won't believe in all that stuff but I know my little girl and she was there. She asked me to find her. I've been having these strange dreams where she appears and begs me to help her and, you know, I can't shake the feeling that . . . oh, it doesn't matter.'

'No, do say.'

'Well, it's just I don't feel that she's dead. Not in here,' I say, pressing my fist against my stomach. 'As a mother you always know when your child needs you, when they're hurt or in danger, and by that reckoning I would feel it if she was dead, I would just know. You may think I'm crazy but, no matter what they've told me, I feel like she's somewhere out there.'

'That's understandable,' says Julia. 'You're processing your loss. It will take time, possibly even years, for you to come to terms with it.'

'No,' I say. 'It's more than that. Today when I went up to the meadow I saw her by the stones. She was there . . . right in front of me.'

'Grief can do that,' says Julia, her voice calm and steady. 'It's the brain creating what it wants to see.'

'It was Elspeth,' I cry. 'I don't care if you think I'm mad, I know what I saw.'

'I do understand, Maggie.'

'No you don't,' I snap. 'You could never understand what I'm going through. Have you ever lost a child?'

She shakes her head.

'Of course you haven't,' I say, my skin prickling with sudden anger. 'But that's all people keep telling me: they understand. The doctors and nurses, the social workers, now you, and I want to scream and yell, no you don't, you never will.'

I slump back in the chair, exhausted by my outburst. Julia looks at me for a moment then leans forward, her head to one side.

'You're right, Maggie, I've never lost a child,' she says. 'I've never been a mum. I've never been pregnant and given birth. I have no idea what it's like to produce another human being, to hold it and nurture it and form an unbreakable bond with it. But I do understand loss of a kind because my mother died when I was a baby.'

'Oh,' I say, wiping my eyes. 'I'm sorry to hear that.'

'People say to me that it isn't the same because I never knew her,' she says, picking at a piece of cotton on the hem of her jacket. 'That because I never had a relationship with her then I can't feel her absence as keenly as someone who lost their mum when they were older.'

I nod my head and imagine for a moment that Elspeth had survived and not me. The hurt she would carry for the rest of her life.

'But it's always there,' continues Julia. 'This mother-shaped hole, this absence. I've spent my life craving a mother. To have a relationship like the one Elspeth had with you; I wanted that. I needed that.'

'I'm sorry,' I whisper. And I mean it. It must have been hell to grow up without a mother.

'Anyway,' she says, sitting upright in the chair, regaining her composure. 'What I'm trying to say is that I'm not just spouting platitudes. I do understand a fraction of what you're going through and, if you'd let me, I'd like to help.'

'What do you mean?'

'Well, as I told you, I'm a GP,' she says. 'Newly qualified but don't let that put you off. My practice is here in Lewes, just off the high street. I don't know where you're registered at the moment but it would make me feel better – particularly as I've effectively made you homeless – if you sign up with me. I've had a lot of experience with depression and grief counselling and I think I could help, if you were up for that. But please feel free to say no, I won't be offended.'

'Oh, Julia,' I say, sighing. 'I know you mean well but no amount of talking or counselling is going to bring Elspeth back.'

'That's true,' says Julia. 'But like you said, there was a reason you came to Larkfields today. You wanted to trigger your memories of that night. You wanted to find answers.'

I nod my head, thinking again about that flash of red, the person standing on the riverbank.

'And your husband? Surely you want to find him?'

'Of course I do.'

'Well, to do that you need to get better,' she says. 'Not just physically but mentally too. Now, where are you registered at the moment?'

'Er . . . Newhaven.'

'Gosh, that's a long way to go to see a doctor,' she says, screwing her face up.

'We rented a place there when we first came to

Sussex. We were getting some structural work done on Larkfields,' I say, remembering those blissful few months in the little flat by the sea, me and Sean and Elspeth. 'And then we just stayed with the practice once we moved. It wasn't that far a drive.'

'Yes, but now things are different,' says Julia. 'And with your limited mobility you definitely need somewhere closer. Hang on, let me just check something.'

I watch as she takes her phone out of her bag and scrolls through.

'Yeah,' she says, looking up. 'I'm technically not scheduled to start until midday tomorrow but I can book you in as an emergency in the morning. I'll talk to the receptionist when I get in tomorrow. Shall we say ten thirty?'

I nod my head. This is all happening so fast but my life since I left the hospital has been one long round of appointments. One more can't hurt.

'I'll give you my card,' says Julia. 'This has the address on it.'

She hands me the card and I put it on the table.

'I must say, you're looking a lot better than you did earlier,' says Julia, standing up. 'Your colour's coming back.'

She smiles at me and I see that flash of red again. Elspeth screaming. Julia must sense my unease because her smile fades.

'Maggie? What is it?'

'Nothing,' I say, getting up from the chair. 'Just a twinge in my back, that's all. I'll see you out.'

'Okay,' says Julia. 'I can take a look at your back tomorrow when you come for the appointment.'

'Thanks,' I say as we walk to the door. 'And thank you again for driving me home. I do appreciate it though I know I've probably messed up your plans for the day.'

I take the latch off the door and pull it open, the smell of old cooking fat filling the air.

'I was glad to help,' says Julia, stepping out into the dank hallway. 'See you at the surgery tomorrow?'

'Yes,' I say, smiling politely.

Julia goes to say something but before she gets her words out Mr Hutchinson appears behind her.

'Mrs Allan,' he snaps, 'have you read the information pack?'

I look at him in bewilderment. I have no idea what he's talking about.

'Sorry, I . . .' I begin, but he raises his voice over mine.

'It's specifically stated in the information pack that all visitors must be signed in,' he says, gesticulating with his hands. 'If not, I don't know what kind of characters might be skulking about the place. Rules are rules. I told that social worker of yours that if you didn't comply you'd be out.'

'Sorry,' says Julia, turning to face him, her hands on her hips. 'Who are you?'

'I'm Frank Hutchinson,' he says, standing back. 'The proprietor of this establishment.'

'Right, well, my name is Dr Julia Mathers,' she says, her voice reverberating around the narrow hallway. 'I'm Mrs Allan's GP and I've been here on a scheduled home visit.'

She is a good five inches taller than him and he seems to cower under her gaze.

'Oh,' he says, looking at me suspiciously. 'Well, she should have told me. I don't feel happy having unauthorized people in here. But as you're a doctor I'm happy to let this one go.'

'Good,' says Julia. 'Mrs Allan has suffered an unimaginable tragedy and is in a physically fragile state. She is staying in your "establishment" for a few days until her new place is ready and you are being paid well for it. So maybe you'll offer a bit more empathy towards her for the duration of her stay.'

'Like I said, I had no idea you were her GP,' he says, holding his hands in the air. 'I meant no offence. Oh, and Mrs Allan, your carer said to call her on this number when you got back.'

He passes me a bit of paper then slinks back down the corridor. Julia keeps her gaze on his departing figure then turns to me.

'What an arsehole,' she says, shaking her head. 'He's clearly suffering from a serious condition.'

'What's that?' I say.

'Small man syndrome,' says Julia, giggling.

It's a funny comment and there was a time when I would have laughed along, but all I can manage now is a forced smile.

'Listen, I'd better go,' she says, her smile fading. 'You should get some rest. I'll see myself out.'

'Bye, Julia,' I say. 'Thanks again.'

As I watch her walk away I feel an odd sensation, a fleeting one but powerful none the less. She had listened to me; helped me. And she had done so without being condescending. It had felt like I was talking to a friend. Now that she's gone I feel so utterly alone it hurts.

I shut the door and go back inside. The bed is still unmade but I flop down into its folds regardless. Closing my eyes, I try to make sense of everything that has happened today. But try as I might, the figure in red is as much a mystery as it was earlier. As for my sighting of Elspeth: could Julia be right that my brain is seeing things it wants to see? I don't know the answer to any of it. All I know is that I need to press on with my search for Sean. When Sonia brings the new phone tomorrow I will call everyone on my list and if that doesn't bring up anything then I'll go back to the police. They can't just give up on him.

I turn over on my side and try to ignore my memories. But as I lie here my mind wanders back to last Christmas. Is this something to do with what happened then?

Sean had been working extra hours all through December. The firm had just secured a big contract and it was all hands on deck. He was crazy busy and would sometimes go days without seeing Elspeth or me. His behaviour started to change too. He became irritable and would lose his temper at the slightest thing. I would wake up in the night and find his side of the bed empty. In the morning he'd tell me that he'd got in late and gone to sleep in the spare room as he didn't want to wake me. I know I should have taken more notice of these things, should have talked to him, but I was busy with Elspeth. We had a packed timetable of school events: the Nativity play, the carol concert, Christmas parties to attend and Secret Santa gifts to buy. And I guess, if I'm honest with myself, I didn't want to acknowledge that there might be a problem. But then it all came to a head on Christmas Eve. Sean was meant to have finished work on the 23rd but he got a call late that evening from his boss asking if he could go in the next day. I begged him not to, reminded him that we were supposed to be going to the pantomime in Lewes on Christmas Eve, that Elspeth would be devastated if he didn't come with us. He assured me that he would only be going into the office for a couple of hours and that he would be home in time for the show. But by 3 p.m. the following day he still hadn't come home. I called his mobile but it rang out. I sent him text messages but got no reply. In the end I called his office. The receptionist answered and when I asked to speak to Sean she said that he hadn't been in that day, that his department was closed for Christmas and there was only a skeleton staff working. I didn't know what to think so I tried to put it out of my mind. I took Elspeth to the pantomime, then came home, put her to bed and started wrapping Christmas presents. Sean got home at midnight. When I confronted him he told me that he'd been working at his boss's house in Richmond and that the whole team had been there. 'Phone him if you don't believe me,' he'd yelled. I didn't think his boss would relish a phone call at midnight on Christmas Eve so I did what I always did and left it to fester inside me. The next day, Sean and I watched as Elspeth opened her presents, we ate turkey and Christmas pudding, drank champagne and watched the Queen's speech. That Christmas holiday Sean never left our sides. We went for long walks on the Downs, had lunch at the village pub, played board games. Sean and I even made love again for the first time in months. He told me he loved me and that he was sorry. So by the time he went back to work a week later, the whole Christmas Eve incident had been forgotten. Or rather, I chose to forget.

Until now.

23

Dear Mummy,

It was a weird day today. When I woke up I forgot where I was and for a moment I thought this had all been some horrible dream. But then I heard Zoe swearing at her phone and I realized I was still here. I lay on the bed thinking about my friends and my old school and that sadness lump in my chest got bigger and bigger until it felt like I couldn't breathe. I must have made a choking noise because the next thing I knew Zoe had jumped off her bunk and was leaning over me asking me if I was okay. I told her I felt poorly and didn't think I'd be able to go to school. She looked at me for a minute then did this weird laugh and said that if I wanted to survive here it would be best if I went along with what they want. But she said it in a nice way, like she was letting me in on a secret that was for my benefit. At breakfast she poured me a glass of orange juice and buttered some toast for me. 'If you're ill you need to eat,' she said. She was right, the food did make me feel a little bit better.

At school I kept my head down. Luckily we have maths every day and I just worked my way through the worksheet. The sums are easier than the ones we were doing at my old school but

I didn't say anything. I just kept quiet then went and sat in my usual spot at break and hoped nobody would notice me. But then that boy who had thrown the pebble at me the other day came over and started kicking soil at me. I asked him to stop but he just kept going. I got really upset and ran inside. The teacher found me sitting in the cloakroom. I was crying so much it made my voice all shaky. I told her that I wanted my mum and then she took me to see the school counsellor.

The school counsellor's name is Geoff. He's got a beard and he's quite fat. By the time I got to his office I'd calmed down a bit and didn't really feel like talking. But Geoff started asking me all these questions about how I was feeling and what was making me so sad. He was trying to get me to talk about you I think. But I didn't want to think about you or my sadness because then the stone would be back, sitting in the middle of my chest, and it would take me even longer to get rid of it. So I turned the tables and started asking him about himself. I asked him if he'd ever dissected a human brain and he said he hadn't. And I said that it was foolish of him to think that he could get inside people's brains if he'd never held one in his hands. He didn't know what to make of that so he just asked me a couple more questions, scribbled my answers in his notebook and then I left.

I've been reading the sections on the human brain in my science book. I've figured that if I learn everything there is to know about the brain then maybe I can figure out what was going on in yours when you sent me away. And if I can figure that out then maybe I can convince you to come back for me.

Anyway, at home time I was coming out of the main doors when pebble boy – Alex is his name – grabbed my bag from off my shoulder and went running off with it. He threw it to his friend and shouted, 'Catch the skank's bag.' They headed for the gate and I ran after them. I knew that Weasel Face would be furious if I lost my bag. When I caught up with them I asked them to give me it back. Alex laughed and said I had a funny voice. Then he threw it to his friend and said, 'Watch out for the fleas.' The friend flung it back at him and I jumped to try and catch it but I lost my footing and fell over. They burst out laughing and started chanting 'skank, skank' over and over again. Then I heard someone say my name. I looked up and saw Zoe. She was heading towards us, her face all angry. At first I thought she was angry with me but then she grabbed Alex by his neck and told him to give me the bag back. What she actually said was, 'Give her it back now or I'll kick your head in, you little fuck.' (Sorry for swearing.) Zoe was really scary. Alex dropped the bag immediately. Then he and his friend ran off. I said thank you to Zoe but she just shrugged her shoulders and we walked home in silence.

I wish you had been waiting for me at the gate, Mummy. I wish it with all my heart. I'm beginning to think that you have a really important reason for sending me away.

Anyway, when you are ready, please come and get me.

I love you.
Your lovely daughter xxx

24

Thursday 3 August

Sonia stays close beside me as we make our way along the high street towards Riverdale Surgery. Though I assured her when she arrived at the B & B this morning that yesterday's trip to Larkfields hadn't upset me, she could see by my swollen eyes that it had taken its toll.

'Are you absolutely sure you want to do this?' she says as we turn down a narrow side street and the sign for the surgery looms into view. 'It's just that I think the fact that the doctor is living in your old house could hamper your recovery process, Maggie. She'll be a constant reminder of everything.'

I pause as we reach the automatic glass doors, standing back to let a woman with a pushchair out.

'I know what you're saying, Sonia,' I say as we go through the doors and head into the large reception area. 'But I like Julia. She seems to understand what I'm going through. And I need to start getting myself back together. I need to be strong if I'm going to have any chance of finding out what happened.'

Sonia nods her head as we approach the reception desk.

'One moment,' mouths the receptionist, holding her hand up. She is busy taking a call.

I smile then turn to Sonia.

'Did you manage to get the phone?' I say.

'Oh, shit, I completely forgot,' says Sonia, grimacing. 'I'm so sorry. I was running late this morning, then my flatmate was hogging the bathroom. I tell you what, how about we pick one up on the way home?'

'That would be great.'

'Okay, ladies,' says the receptionist, putting the phone down. 'Sorry to keep you. How can I help?'

'I'm here to see Julia, er, Dr Mathers,' I say.

'And your name is?'

'Maggie Allan.'

I watch as she types my name into her computer, shaking her head as the phone starts ringing again.

'Here you are,' she says. 'Ten thirty emergency appointment with Dr Mathers. She booked you in herself. You're a new patient, is that correct?'

'Yes,' I reply. 'Dr Mathers said that it would be –'

'No problem,' interrupts the receptionist as another phone starts to ring. 'If I could just ask you to fill in these forms while you wait.'

She hands me a black clipboard with a purple and white form attached.

'Here's a pen if you need it,' she says, handing me

a black biro. 'Dr Mather's waiting area is just over there. If you take a seat she'll be with you shortly.'

'Thank you,' I say, but my words are swallowed up by the telephone ringing again.

Sonia leads me towards the seating area, which is on the left-hand side of the room. We sit down and I look at the people around me. There's an elderly woman with painfully swollen legs, a young man in his twenties with a bandaged arm, a mum reading a tatty cardboard-backed book to her pink-cheeked toddler who wriggles on her knee like a seal.

'He's teething,' I say to Sonia, who catches me looking at the child.

'How do you know?'

'Look,' I say, and we watch as he grabs the book and begins to gnaw it like a beaver.

'Elspeth got terrible teething pains,' I say. 'I remember I used to hold a pack of frozen peas on her face. It was the only thing that seemed to soothe it.'

My eyes fill with tears but I blink them back. Swallowing hard, I turn my attention to the registration form. I read the first line that asks for my status: Mr/Mrs/Miss/Ms. Taking the pen, I draw a circle round 'Mrs' but my hand shakes so badly I drop the pen on the floor.

'Here, I got it,' says Sonia, bending down to pick it up.

'I'm sorry,' I say. 'It's like my hands have forgotten how to use a pen.'

'Listen, how about you tell me the answers and I fill it in?' says Sonia, taking the clipboard from my lap. 'Now, let's see. Date of birth?'

'10/03/74,' I reply, glad to at least be able to remember that.

'Ah, a fellow Pisces,' says Sonia. 'I'm the 15th.'

She smiles then carries on with the form.

'Previous surname?'

'Carrington.'

'Home address?'

'Larkfields, Rodmell, Sussex, R—'

'I think it means current address,' says Sonia. 'Which would be the B & B. Don't worry. I can fill that bit in. I've got the address here on my phone.'

She takes her phone out but before she can get the address up someone calls my name.

I look up and see Julia standing in the doorway of the consulting room opposite us. She's wearing a pale-blue trouser suit with kitten-heel shoes.

'Maggie,' she says, her face beaming as I walk towards her. 'Do come through.'

I turn to Sonia, who has also stood up.

'I haven't finished filling in the form yet,' I say to Julia.

'Oh, don't worry. You can finish it after the consultation.'

'Do you want me to come in with you, Maggie?' asks Sonia.

'No, it's fine,' I say. 'It's probably best if I do this alone.'

'Okay,' says Sonia. 'But I'm right here if you need me.'

I smile then follow Julia into the consulting room.

'Do take a seat, Maggie.'

She points to a high-backed wooden chair that is wedged in front of her desk. As I sit down I look around. The room is sparse and white and there are what look like medical diagrams running the length of each wall like the stations of the cross.

'So how are you feeling this morning?' she asks brightly as she sits down at the desk.

'Okay,' I say. 'I've just taken my morning dose of codeine so the muscle pains have subsided . . . for now. And I had to stop a few times on the walk here to take my inhaler.'

She nods then types something into her computer.

'How about emotionally,' she says, leaning back in her chair and folding her hands together. 'When we spoke yesterday you seemed rather low.'

'I feel confused,' I say. 'My emotions go up and down throughout the day.'

'Okay,' says Julia gently. 'Well, that's normal.'

'Is it?' I say. 'Because, believe me, nothing about my state of mind feels normal. You know, when you left the B & B I went back into the room feeling determined to get strong, to find Sean, but this morning . . . it's just so hard.'

I start to cry then. Great big wet tears. Julia passes me a box of tissues and I pull out a big clump of them.

'Thank you,' I say in between sobs.

'That's okay,' she says. 'Take your time.'

I wipe my eyes and try to compose myself.

'Are you all right to continue?' says Julia.

I nod my head.

'Right,' she says. 'Well, your notes were sent over to me first thing this morning and I've just about managed to read them. You've got your first out-patient appointment at the hospital in two weeks, is that right?'

I nod my head.

'That's good,' she says. 'Though looking at the results of your recent CT scan, the recovery process is coming along extremely well. Your brain function was normal, though they did detect slight frontal-lobe bruising which will explain the short-term memory loss. Your last X-ray, taken before you were discharged, shows slight scarring on the lungs, though that is more likely to have been caused by the breathing tube. The scarring should heal within a couple of months.'

I instinctively put my hand to my chest.

'Are you in pain at the moment?' asks Julia, look-ing up from her computer screen.

'No more than usual,' I reply. 'Like I said, my lungs feel sore if I walk long distances or if I get agitated but the inhalers are helping. The muscle pain eases within about ten minutes of taking the codeine.'

'Okay,' says Julia. 'The muscle pain sounds normal for someone who has spent several weeks in the ICU. As for the lungs, we'll monitor the progress of their recovery closely You'll have another X-ray when you go for your out-patient appointment and that will pinpoint any anomalies. Otherwise, it appears that, physically, you're recovering well.'

I look down at my fingers. The skin is regrowing. It is pink and wrinkled, like a newborn baby. It makes me angry. The fact that my body, its skin and cells, are regenerating while my beautiful daughter is decaying in a grave.

'It's your psychological recovery that I'm more concerned about,' says Julia.

I look up. She is staring at her computer screen, her chin resting on her hand.

'Maggie,' she says, turning to me. 'If it's all right with you, I'd like to ask you some questions.'

'What sort of questions?'

'Don't look so worried,' she says, smiling. 'It's nothing scary, just part of the check-up.'

'I'm sorry,' I reply. 'Worry seems to be my default setting at the moment.'

Julia nods her head then pulls her computer key-pad towards her. I watch as she begins to type.

'I've noticed your hands are very shaky,' she says, without looking up.

'Yes,' I say, placing my hands palms down on the desk. 'They've been like that since I came round.'

'It's very common for that to happen after suffering hypoxia,' says Julia. 'Though your CT scan shows very little damage to the brain, your nerves will have been affected by the lack of oxygen when you were in the water. But in your case I think the tremors may be exacerbated by your emotions. So if we're going to treat it I think we come at it from a psychological rather than a physical angle.'

I look down at my hands. The shaking has stopped for a moment because I'm pressing my palms into the desk but I know that as soon as I lift them up it will start again. It's like they are shaking in tandem with my heart.

'Now you mentioned you're taking codeine,' continues Julia, turning from her computer to me. 'How are you getting on with that?'

'It's fine,' I say. 'But to be honest, I can deal with the physical pain.'

Julia raises her eyebrows.

'The not knowing is just . . . it's horrific,' I explain, choking back the tears. 'I just want to get my memory back.'

'I know you do,' says Julia gently.

'It's frustrating because I can remember snippets,'

I say, dabbing at my eyes with the sodden tissue. 'But that's all they are. I have no way of connecting them.'

'What do you mean?'

I look down at the stark white floor, remembering the flashback I had at Larkfields yesterday: Elspeth begging me not to put her in the car and then that flash of red, the person standing on the riverbank.

'Maggie?'

I lift my head. Julia is looking at me quizzically.

'I can't really remember anything, just fragments. It's like I'm being tormented by these flashbacks, like that's all I'm going to get.'

'Maggie, there is a good chance that your memory of that evening will return,' says Julia. 'But it's a long process and . . .' She pauses then looks down at her keypad as if trying to find the right words to say to me.

'What?' I say, looking up at her pleadingly. 'I will get there, won't I? I will remember what happened that night? I mean, I *have* to remember.'

'We can try our best,' she says, folding her hands together. 'But you have to be prepared for the worst too.'

'What do you mean?'

'Well,' she says. 'People assume that the brain retains every single memory we have and stores it away neatly but that's not the case. The brain is very much like a computer. It only saves the memories that are regularly recalled, the rest are just deleted.'

'What are you saying?' I gasp, my hands beginning to tremble again. 'That I might never remember what happened that night?'

'No,' says Julia. 'I'm just trying to make you aware of every eventuality. In cases like yours when the patient has experienced a traumatic event, the brain can actually wipe out a memory. It's like an act of self-preservation. That way the person doesn't have to relive the trauma.'

It feels like all the air has been sucked out of the room. My chest tightens and the panic attack that has been threatening all morning envelops me with a violent force. My heart pounds so fast it feels like I'm about to die.

'Maggie,' says Julia, getting out of her seat. 'Are you okay?'

She puts her hands on my shoulders. I stare into her eyes, desperately trying to control my breathing, but it's like I've got an elastic band tightening round my heart.

'I can't . . . catch my breath,' I gasp.

'Maggie, listen,' says Julia, speaking slowly and clearly. 'I want you to inhale very slowly through your nose, okay?'

I keep my gaze on her as I follow her instructions.

'Really deeply,' she says. 'Inhale as far as you can go then hold that breath until I tell you to let go.'

I do as she says.

'Now exhale.'

I breathe out.

'And again,' she says.

I inhale. Hold. Then on Julia's nod, I exhale, and the room stops spinning.

My heart rate slows down. It's over.

'Thank you,' I say, feeling embarrassed. 'I'm okay now.'

'Would you like some water?' says Julia.

'I have a bottle in my bag,' I reply, pointing to my crumpled rucksack. 'In the front pocket.'

She opens the pocket and takes out the half-drunk bottle of water.

'Here,' she says, handing it to me. 'Take small sips.'

I do as she says. The water is lukewarm but soothing.

'Thank you,' I say to Julia, cradling the bottle in my hands.

She looks at me and nods then returns to her chair.

'Do you get those often?' she says. 'The anxiety attacks?'

'If I let myself think about my reality for more than a few minutes, yes,' I say. 'It's just when you said I might never be able to remember what happened I . . .'

'I'm sorry, Maggie,' she says. 'I really didn't mean to upset you. I was just giving you the worst-case scenario. But in the light of that panic attack I'm thinking we should look at some options.'

'Such as what?'

'Well, there are certain forms of medication that might be suitable. I'm thinking anti-anxiety drugs in particular.'

'Oh,' I say, knowing where this is leading.

'Please don't worry,' says Julia, smiling.

'It's just . . .' I begin, my voice quivering. 'Well, I've been on that kind of medication before and it didn't agree with me.'

'Yes, I'm aware of your medical history. It was in your notes.'

She meets my eye and fear flutters through my body.

'It's okay,' says Julia, noticing my discomfort. 'The reason I'm raising this is it reinforces my feeling that we should look at some anti-anxiety medication in the short term. Now, according to your notes you have had some mental health issues in the past.'

I look down at my feet. Why does it always have to come back to this?

'Maggie, as your GP it would really help to know a bit more about this,' she says. 'You were admitted into a psychiatric unit, I believe, when you were a teenager?'

'Yes,' I say, staring at a black mark on the white floor. 'Almost fifteen.'

'Okay,' says Julia. 'And can you tell me why you were admitted?'

I don't answer. If I just stay silent then maybe she will stop.

'Maggie?'

'I don't want to talk about this.'

'I understand it's difficult,' says Julia. 'But in order to help I really do need to know a bit more about it.'

I look up at her. She is sitting forward in her chair, her hands clasped together.

'Maggie?'

'It was just a . . . something bad happened, with me and a boy I knew, that's all,' I say, trying not to meet her eye. 'It was a long time ago. It's not relevant any more.'

'It must have been pretty serious if you were admitted into psychiatric care,' says Julia, her voice hardening.

I take a deep breath.

'We got into some trouble,' I say, staring at the white tiled floor.

'What kind of trouble?'

'I told you, I don't want to talk about it.'

'Maggie, I just want to try to help you and to do that I —'

'I tried to kill myself,' I say, raising my voice. 'Okay? That's why they sent me to that place.'

It comes out in a rush. It's almost a relief to say it, after all this time.

Julia looks at me for a moment without speaking. Then she nods her head and turns to the computer.

160

'I'm sorry to have to pry,' she says as she begins to type. 'But any information you can give me at this stage really will help me come up with an appropriate care plan.'

She stops typing then looks up at me as if waiting for me to speak but I have no words. I feel like I've just been cut open and I'm sitting here, raw and exposed.

'You suffered from an eating disorder,' she says, her eyes fixed on me. 'For over ten years I believe.'

I nod my head. 'That's right,' I say shamefully. 'But that was a long time ago. I got better.'

'It was anorexia nervosa, yes?'

'Yes,' I say, willing her to stop. 'Look, I don't want to talk about that. It's in my past. I told you, I got better.'

'I know this is difficult, Maggie, but if I'm to help you then I do need to know as much as possible about your background.' She smiles and it puts me at ease. That feeling I had when she brought me home yesterday returns. This is a good person. I can trust her.

'The anorexia started before I went into the unit,' I tell her. 'When I tried to kill myself and it didn't work, well, I decided I'd starve instead. My mum couldn't cope with it so she –' A lump lodges itself in my throat. 'I'm sorry, this is just . . . it's really hard.'

'I understand,' says Julia softly. 'And you've done really well to tell me this much. Before we go on I'd just like to ask you a couple more questions, nothing too probing, I promise. Is that okay?'

I nod.

'We talked just then about the anorexia and where you think it stemmed from,' she says, leaning back slightly in her chair. 'Now in a lot of cases it can come about due to a traumatic event and I'm wondering . . .'

'If you're asking whether I've gone anorexic again, the answer's no,' I say, cutting her off. 'Sure, I don't feel like eating at the moment because my stomach is so twisted with sadness but . . . it's a different feeling.'

'What do you mean?'

'Well, when I was in the grip of anorexia food was all I could think about,' I say, remembering the room in the unit, the smell of boiled vegetables in the air, the weekly weigh-in. 'I was obsessed with it. I would dream about it. Now I don't give food a second thought. All I can think about is Elspeth and Sean and what happened that night at the river. That's the difference.'

'Okay,' says Julia. 'But I still think it's something we'll need to monitor.'

'I understand your concern,' I say. 'But I don't see why my background is important. What is important is getting my memory back.'

'Maggie, we can use your background to get you out of that B & B,' she says, looking up from the computer screen. 'Which I don't think is a suitable environment for someone in your current state. Your medical history just strengthens the case.'

She starts typing again. I sit and watch her, feeling utterly disconnected; a woman drowning on dry land.

'So, as your GP,' continues Julia, 'I'm going to call Lewes Social Services today and strongly suggest that as a mentally vulnerable patient you be moved into more stable accommodation as soon as possible. I'm also going to prescribe a course of antidepressants to deal with your anxiety.'

'Antidepressants,' I say, my breath growing shallow again. 'Are you sure? The last time I took them it wasn't a good experience.'

'The ones I'm recommending are much more advanced than what you were prescribed in your teens,' says Julia. 'Things have improved a lot since then.'

She looks at me and I feel like I'm being judged. She's seen my medical notes. God knows what she must think of me.

'What happened when I was a teenager . . . it was a very long time ago,' I say. 'I was so young . . . I didn't know what I was doing. But I would never do something like that again. I didn't harm Elspeth, you know that, don't you? I loved my daughter more than I've ever loved anyone in my life.'

Julia stares at me for a moment as though she's assessing whether I'm telling the truth. Then she takes a deep breath.

'Of course. Now,' she says, 'the reason I mentioned your medical history wasn't so I could haul you over the coals for your past behaviour. As I said, it simply adds weight to the case for getting you into more secure accommodation and tackling your anxiety issues. Both of which I consider to be urgent considerations and crucial to your recovery process.'

She stands up and retrieves a slip of paper from the printer.

'Here's your prescription,' she says. 'You can pop it into our on-site pharmacy. It's on the first floor.'

I take the prescription and ease myself out of the chair.

'And my memory,' I say as we walk to the door. 'You think it's gone for good, don't you?'

'The truth is, I don't know, Maggie,' she says. 'But what I'm trying to do here is help you get back on your feet, try to piece your life together. And who knows, with the medication I've prescribed and more stable accommodation, perhaps your memory will return. But you have to remember that it's not a race, your mind and body have a lot of healing to do.'

I nod my head meekly.

'Now let's see how that medication goes,' she says. 'Any problems, just come straight back and we'll reassess. And in the meantime I'll put in a call to the Social Services team. Does that all sound okay?'

'Yes,' I say, trying to be upbeat. 'It all sounds very sensible.'

'Good,' she says, opening the door. 'Now take care of yourself and remember that breathing exercise.'

'I'll try,' I say as I step out into the waiting room.

'Good,' says Julia. 'And, Maggie, one step at a time, okay?'

I turn to answer but she has closed the door and gone back into her room, the smell of her perfume trailing in her wake. I look down at the prescription in my hands. A year ago if someone had handed me antidepressants I'd have flushed them down the loo. Now, though, I realize that I need them. If I can get rid of this anxiety then I can start to think straight and once my head is clear then I can focus on what needs to be done. If Julia is right, and there is a possibility that my memory is gone for good, then I'll have to find other ways of getting to the bottom of what happened that night, and the only person who can help me with that is Sean.

As I make my way across the waiting room I make a vow to myself that, no matter what, I am going to find him. But I can't do it on my own.

25

Three hours later I am standing outside the police station. Sonia has gone home. After collecting my prescription we went into town together to buy a phone and managed to find a cheap model that has internet access. Though we still had to stop several times along the way so that I could take my inhaler, I feel a little of my strength returning. I'm determined to solve this now.

I look up at the glass doors and try to gather my thoughts. I'm holding a piece of paper with the name of the police officer who visited me in hospital. DS Grayling. The one whose voice reminded me of the girl I shared a room with in the psychiatric unit all those years ago. Hayley Redmond, that was her name. She had light-brown hair and freckles all over her face and chest. I remember she came from Leeds and was a self-harmer. Her arms and legs were covered in scabs and scars from where she had slashed herself. 'Poor girl,' my mother had commented on one of her rare visits. 'She'll never be able to wear a sundress.'

I try to wash all thoughts of the unit from my head. It's not helpful to be thinking about the past now. I have to focus, remember that I'm here to find Sean. I have to ignore the pains in my legs, where my under-used muscles are slowly coming back to life, ignore the panic that is fluttering through me and start behaving like a fully functioning adult.

But it's easier said than done and when I step through the glass doors and enter the busy entrance area I feel bewildered. I look around for someone to help me, then I see a glass unit on the left. There's a large bald police officer sitting behind it. I make my way over and stand for a moment waiting while he finishes typing something into his computer. Then he looks up and nods his head.

'Hello there. What can I do for you?'

His voice is loud, and I feel small and insignificant in his presence.

'Erm, I'm here to see DS Grayling,' I say nervously.

'You have an appointment.'

It's more a statement than a question.

'No,' I say.

'Right,' he says, sighing. 'Well, it's going to be difficult to see her if you haven't got an appointment. Can you tell me what this is about?'

I open my mouth to speak but I can't get the words out. I look at the man. He glares back impatiently.

'I was . . . involved . . . in an accident,' I say, the words slowly unlocking. 'DS Grayling has been investigating it.'

'What's your name?' he says, looking down at his computer.

'It's Maggie Allan. The accident happened in the river just outside the Plough Inn. My little girl drowned.'

The man makes an 'o' with his mouth and something resembling pity flashes across his hardened face.

'Let me see if I can contact DS Grayling for you,' he says, his voice softer now. 'Bear with me a moment.'

He lifts the phone receiver, presses a button then waits.

'Hi, Cathy, it's Des. Yeah, not too bad. Listen, I've got a Maggie Allan here at the desk. She'd like to speak to you if you're free. I don't know. I could ask . . . Are you sure? All right then, Cathy, see you in a sec.'

He puts the receiver down and the ghost of a smile flitters across his face.

'She'll be with you shortly,' he says. 'Why don't you go and sit over there?' He points behind my head. I turn and see a small waiting area. I thank him then make my way over to it.

When I sit down, tiny silver stars dance in front of my eyes. The anxiety is still as sharp as it was. I took the first of my anti-depressant pills an hour ago, but Julia told me it would be at least a couple of days before they start to take effect. I wipe my forehead. It is damp and clammy.

'Mrs Allan?'

I look up and see DS Grayling standing over me. She looks different to the last time I saw her. She's had honey-coloured lowlights put in her hair and she's wearing pale-pink lipstick. It makes her look softer.

'Hello,' she says, extending her hand. 'My colleague said you wanted to see me.'

'Yes. I hope you don't mind. I had some questions and you said at the hospital I could get in touch if I needed to . . .'

'That's fine. Listen, why don't we go somewhere a bit quieter?' she says, perhaps sensing that I'm starting to ramble. 'There's a free room along the corridor. It's just this way.'

I follow her past the glass reception desk and into the corridor. The walls are covered with posters proclaiming: 'See it. Say it. Sorted.' The words run through my head like a stuck record as DS Grayling ushers me into the room and closes the door behind us. See it. Say it. Sorted. If only life were that simple.

'Do take a seat,' she says, pointing to one of two plastic chairs that are tucked in facing each other on either side of the brown table. 'Can I get you a tea or coffee?'

'No thank you,' I say as I take my seat. 'I'm feeling a bit hot actually.'

'Water then,' says Grayling, and she walks over to

the large plastic water dispenser that sits by the window like some bloated sea creature. She pours me a drink and comes back to the table.

'Here you go,' she says, putting the plastic cup down in front of me.

'Thanks,' I say, taking a long sip. The water is icy cold and makes my teeth tingle.

'So when were you discharged?' she asks, folding her hands in front of her.

'Monday.'

'Okay,' she says, nodding her head. 'And how are you feeling?'

'Physically, I'm slowly getting there,' I say. 'Though I still can't remember anything about the accident.'

'That's frustrating,' she says, a frown line cutting into the middle of her forehead. 'For you, I mean, not for us. We know it wasn't your fault. You mustn't beat yourself up too much about getting your memory back.'

'Can you remind me,' I say, putting the empty cup down. 'You see, these last few days my head has got so fuzzy and I've been having such strange dreams I'm not sure if what I remember you told me is accurate or whether I've just bundled all the facts together and created a whole new version. The main thing that sticks in my head from what you told me is that I lost these gripping hold of the car.'

I hold up my fingers. Grayling doesn't flinch. She will have seen worse.

'That bit was accurate, yes,' she says. 'But I totally understand your confusion. There was so much information to take in that day and you'd just come out of a coma. What we pieced together from the fire officer's report is that it appears you parked your car behind the Plough, on the edge of the riverbank. You got out of the car, locking it with your key fob. Then the car began to roll. There's quite a hill there. The report found that the handbrake hadn't been engaged properly. The car gained speed and smashed through the car-park fence and rolled into the river. When you noticed we think you ran after it and tried to prise the door open. Traces of paint from the car were found on your fingers. At some point you got swept down by the current. Our conclusion and that of the coroner was that it was a tragic accident.'

I sit for a moment, unable to get the thought of Elspeth out of my head. What must she have gone through? I remember the metallic taste of river water in my mouth, the screams, the flash of red fluttering in front of me. There's a certainty strengthening in me with every moment. Something else was happening that day. Something the police don't know or aren't choosing to tell me.

'Was I wearing red?' I say.

'I don't know,' says Grayling, narrowing her eyes. 'Why?'

I think again about that memory: the flash of red

darting in front of me. And for a second I'm tempted to tell Grayling but then I stop myself.

'It's nothing,' I say.

'Was there anything else you wanted to ask?' says Grayling. 'Or anything you wanted to tell me?'

'Well, yes, actually,' I say, trying to keep my voice steady. 'I came here today because I need to find my husband and I wondered if you could help me.'

'I'm afraid when it comes to that there's not a lot we can do,' says Grayling.

'But he's missing,' I say. 'He left my bedside that evening and just disappeared. Surely your officers could put out a search for him?'

'Maggie, we looked into it,' she says, raising her eyebrows. 'And everything pointed to the fact that your husband left of his own accord.'

'But he was just going home to get changed,' I say. 'That's what he told the nurses. Why would he disappear? It doesn't make sense.'

'That's just it, Maggie,' says Grayling. 'He didn't disappear. He gave notice to your landlord, he tendered his resignation at work, withdrew money from his bank account. These are all considered actions. The horrible fact is that he left you when you were seriously ill and that is just unimaginable but it's not a crime. And as for searching for him, as he has done this of his own free will there's not much we can do. I'm really sorry.'

My chest is tightening as the anxiety I have been keeping at bay spreads through me like a virus. 'But you must be able to do something. Check the ports, the airlines. I have a list of people you could contact. I would be out there looking for him myself but my stupid body won't let me.'

'Maggie, we would only be able to do those things if your husband had committed a crime and we had a warrant for his arrest,' says Grayling, a hint of impatience threaded through her words. 'As it stands he is simply a man who has left his wife and we don't have the resources to undertake a manhunt for every person who walks out of their marriage.'

I look down at my hands. My wedding and engagement rings glint back at me. I've lost so much weight they're slipping off. I think back to the day Sean asked me to marry him. It was a Sunday afternoon and we'd gone for a walk in Battersea Park. He told me he felt tired and needed to sit down so we went into the little English Garden and sat by the pond. It was winter and the water had turned to ice. I was shivering with cold so Sean took his scarf off and wrapped it round my neck. He kissed my nose then told me he had something he wanted to ask me. I watched as he put his hand in his pocket and took out a green velvet box. Inside was a beautiful antique emerald ring. For a few moments time seemed to stand still; the whole park seemed to hold its breath, waiting for my answer. 'Yes,' I told him. 'A thousand times yes.' I was so happy that day. It felt like all the pain and anguish I'd suffered had led me to that moment; that I could stop punishing myself and just live. I look down at the ring now and feel utterly numb. Grayling asks me if I have any more questions but I'm unable to speak. All I can muster is a feeble shake of the head.

'I'll see you out then,' she says, pushing back her chair and walking to the door.

I get up and follow her out, down the dark corridor, past the posters.

See it. Say it. Sorted.

When we reach the reception area Grayling stops. 'I really am sorry for everything you've been through,' she says, placing a hand on my arm. 'And if we could do more to help we would but . . .'

'It's fine. I understand,' I say brusquely. I really want to get out of here now.

'Are you going to be all right walking home?' says Grayling. 'I can call you a taxi if you like.'

'It's okay,' I say, flinching as a siren squeals past the front door. 'I don't have far to go.'

'Well, if you're sure.'

'I am, thank you.'

I turn to go but then Grayling calls my name.

'Just one more thing,' she says, squinting into the afternoon sun. 'Your question about what you were wearing that day, whether you were wearing red. Is there anything I should know?'

'It's nothing,' I say, swallowing down my fear. I need to figure out what it is I'm remembering before I tell anyone. 'I'm still trying to piece things together, that's all.'

Grayling nods and I turn to go but as I make my way across the car park I can feel her eyes on me. Sweat gathers on my forehead. I go to wipe it away but as I do my rings catch my skin. Yanking them off my finger, I slip them into my pocket and with a sick feeling in my stomach make my way back to the B & B.

26

Dear Mummy,

The most amazing thing happened today. I had a visitor. Saturday is grocery day here and Weasel Face had taken me into town to go to the supermarket. When we got back Zoe came to the door and said there was someone here to see me. My first thought was that it was you, that you'd come to get me, but when I went into the living room I saw a woman with blonde hair sitting on the sofa. She jumped to her feet when she saw me and said I looked so much like my daddy. I just stood and stared at her for a moment. She was really beautiful. She was wearing a long pale-pink coat and a cream polo-neck jumper and her eyes, when she looked up at me, were the strangest colour – a mix of green and gold, like autumn leaves. She told me to sit down then she said that she had come to see if I was okay. She said she was a friend of Daddy's and that he had sent her with some presents for me. Then she reached down into her bag and handed me a parcel. The wrapping paper was covered in Disney characters. Inside there was a pack of coloured pencils, a Barbie doll and a bag of sweets. I said thank you and she smiled. Then I asked her why my daddy hadn't come and she said he wanted to but it was complicated and that he'd sent her instead. I asked if she knew you and she went all funny, like she'd caught a bad smell. I asked if you were coming to get me and she said she didn't know. When she said that I started crying and she put her hand on my shoulder and said she was sorry, she hadn't wanted to upset me. Then Zoe came in with cups of tea but the woman said she couldn't stay, that she had to get back. I asked her where she lived and she said it was a 'long long way away' and by the sea. When she stood up to go I told her to tell Daddy to come and get me. She said she would try her best. Then she told me to be a good girl and that she'd come back and see me again soon. As she went to leave I realized I hadn't asked her name. She looked a bit flustered, when I said that, like she couldn't remember it or something. But then she shook my hand and said, 'Just call me Freya.'

When she left I sat on the sofa and shared my sweets with Zoe. I told her about Freya and how she knew my daddy and that it meant he must be coming for me soon but Zoe just rolled her eyes and said that she's seen hundreds of visitors like her, that they're just do-gooders who get their kicks from bringing presents to kids like us, that she probably doesn't even know my dad. I got sad then and couldn't finish my sweets.

I hope she's wrong, Mummy.

I love you.
Your lovely daughter xxx

27

I sit on the wicker chair by the window staring at the spider's web that has appeared on the glass.

It's odd to see one in August. Perhaps the rain has made it visible. Yet, with the cool temperature and the brooding grey sky, you could be forgiven for thinking it was autumn out there.

Elspeth loved the autumn. She used to call it 'cobweb season'. Not only because the shops and houses in the village would be festooned with Halloween paraphernalia but because, unlike them, our windows at Larkfields would be adorned with the real thing. As I sit here looking at the web, the dew and moisture clinging to it like tiny diamonds, I think of Elspeth weaving her dream catcher. Why hadn't I helped her properly when she asked me to sit with her that night? Why did I always want to be somewhere else?

I look at the web again. Its centre is straining with the weight of the rainwater, but the spider that created this masterpiece is nowhere to be seen. The web is its only legacy.

I'm driven from the memory by a buzzing noise.

At first I think it's the smoke alarm but then I see my new phone on the floor, its screen illuminated. Fully charged.

Seeing as the police won't help me, this phone is the one tool I have to help me find Sean. My meeting with Grayling left me feeling uneasy and I've spent most of the afternoon staring at the wall. Now, as evening approaches, I feel a bit brighter. Maybe the pills are starting to work.

I put the phone down on the table then take the list I made the other day out of my bag. I start with Rob. After typing his name and the name of the company into the search engine I get his office land-line number. I type it in and wait. It rings five times then goes to voicemail. Clearing my throat, I start to leave a message, telling him that it's Sean's wife and could he please call me back on this number. What number? My brain stalls. I don't know the number of the new phone. I splutter my apologies to Rob Daniels' voicemail then quickly end the call, my palms sweating.

I stand up and try to locate the box that the phone came in then I remember Sonia saying something about taking it to put in the recycling when she left. I throw myself on to the bed, my head spinning with the pills and the stress of having to think like a nor-mal person. It's hopeless, I think to myself as the blown vinyl wallpaper on the ceiling swirls and loops in front of my eyes. I'm clutching at ridiculous straws. Sean was a bloody loner. There is no way he would have gone to any of those people for help. He never confided in people, not even me; if he had then I would have known that the house I thought we owned was a rental.

And then, through my cloudy head, a thought occurs. When Sean gave his notice to the landlords, he would have surely given reasons, perhaps even a forwarding address. I sit up and go back to the window, taking the phone and opening up the search engine.

What was the name of the company again? BH2 property, that's it. Strange how my memory of recent events is so much better than those from further in the past. The results dance in front of my eyes like confetti. There is a raft of property listings in Bournemouth with a BH2 postcode. By the third page I give up and search again, adding 'Rodmell, Sussex' to the name. This time I just get a list of properties for sale in Rodmell. One last try, I think to myself as I search 'BH2 Properties Rodmell Sussex Larkfields'. The results flash up. The first few are properties for sale. Then, halfway down the page, I see the name Larkfields and 'House to rent'. My heart feels loose in my chest as I click on the link but there is just a holding page stating that 'This property is no longer on the market'. I go to close the page then I see the name of the estate agent and a phone number printed at the bottom: Kingsland Farley Properties.

I stare at the number for a moment then at the clock. It's just coming up to 5.30. They might still be open. It's worth a try at least. My head is jumbled and I have no idea what I'm going to say but I type the number into the phone anyway and wait. After a couple of rings a young woman answers.

'Kingsland Farley Properties. How may I help you?'

'Oh . . . hello,' I say, my voice catching in my throat. 'Erm . . . my name is Maggie Allan. My house – I mean the house I was living in – was leased through your agency a few months ago and – well, I was in hospital, very ill, and – my husband –'

I'm not making any kind of sense. My head feels like a sponge and I'm finding it difficult to form the correct words.

'Sorry,' says the girl. 'I only caught a bit of that. You said you want to rent out your house while you go into hospital?'

'No,' I say impatiently. 'I said you had a house on the market – my house – a few weeks ago.'

'Okay,' she says, dragging the word out. 'So you're the vendor?'

'Yes. I mean, no, erm, my husband, he . . . we were renting.'

The girl sighs loudly down the phone.

'And how can I help you today?'

The question slurs through my foggy brain. How can she help me? What did I ring for?

'Er, yes,' I say, sitting up straight in the hope that the lost words will spring back into my head. 'Well, you see, my house, the house, was put up for rent by your agency a couple of months back.'

'What was the address?' she asks.

'Oh, the address . . . well, it's a name actually.'

'What was the name then?'

'Larkfields,' I say, reassured that I can at least remember that name.

'Oh, yeah,' says the girl. 'I know it. The Gothic lodge house on the outskirts of Rodmell.'

'Yes,' I say. 'That's the one.'

'We rented that out, ooh, about six weeks ago.'

'Yes, that's right,' I say. 'My husband, Sean Allan – well, we – were the previous tenants.'

'Yeah,' says the girl. 'So how can I help you?'

I take a deep breath. I have to get the story right.

'Well,' I say, keeping my voice bright and brisk. 'We need to get hold of our former landlords, BH2 Properties? Er, we have a friend who has a house that they'd like to sell and we thought BH2 might be interested in, er, buying it.'

There is silence on the other end of the phone.

'Hello?' I say. 'Are you still there?'

'Sorry about that,' says the girl. 'My colleague was

just asking me a question. You said you wanted to contact who?'

'BH2 Properties,' I say. 'The owners of Larkfields. I just wondered if you had their details.'

'I'm afraid I wouldn't be allowed to give that information out without consulting my boss and she's just gone home,' says the girl. 'If you leave me your number I can get her to call you back tomorrow.'

My number. The bloody number. I don't have it.

'Oh, gosh,' I say. 'It's completely slipped my mind. Erm . . .'

'Are you Mr Allan's partner?' asks the girl.

'Yes,' I reply. 'I'm his wife.'

'Well then, I think I've got your number here on our system.'

'Really?' I say. 'How?'

'Well, I've just brought up all the contact details for that property,' she says, her voice a drawl. 'And I have your husband's number as a first contact and then Freya Nielssen, which must be you.'

My whole body goes cold. Who? What is she talking about? I try to keep calm, try to stem the sickening dread that is rising through my stomach and up to my throat.

'Oh yes,' I say, laughing awkwardly. 'That's me. Which number have you got there? I'll just check it's the right one.'

The girl recites the mobile number and I scribble it

on to the cheap notepad, my hand trembling so badly I almost drop the pencil.

'Oh,' I say. 'That's my old one I'm afraid.'

'Right, well if you give me your new number I'll pass it on.'

'I'm sorry, I'm afraid I can't remember,' I say, trying to catch my breath. 'It's a new phone and . . .'

'It's okay,' says the girl. 'I can see it on the phone display.' She reads it out and I make a note of it.

'Thanks. I'm so sorry, my memory's very bad at the moment.'

'It's no problem, Miss Nielsson,' she says. 'I'll pass the number on to Sharon and she'll give you a call as soon as she can. Now is there anything else I can help you with today?'

'No,' I say, slumping down on to the bed. 'No thank you. Goodbye.'

I press 'end call' then sit for a moment, staring at the biscuit-coloured carpet.

Who the hell is Freya Nielssen?

28

It's dark outside now. I should close the curtains but I can't move from the bed. I try to remember the names of Sean's colleagues or associates. Was there a Freya Nielssen among them? I have no idea. The name means absolutely nothing to me but it meant something to Sean. Enough to name her as a contact for our family home.

I look down at the notepad. The phone number stares back at me like a challenge. All I have to do is phone this number and then I'll know. But I daren't.

The truth is, deep in my gut, I already know the answer and that is why I'm so reticent to make the call. All these weeks I've been racking my brain, trying to work out why Sean could leave me like this, and not once did I consider the obvious, that he'd been having an affair.

Whitstable. It was Sean's idea. He'd booked a cottage for a week in March as a birthday surprise for me. Elspeth was so excited. Whitstable was her favourite place. She spent the whole week before we were due to go packing her suitcase and planning precisely what she would do each day of the holiday. Things had been better since Christmas, and I'd decided it was just a blip. Then in February Sean and his team won a new contract that would require more late nights and occasional trips to Europe. In the run-up to the holiday he worked late and on the rare occasions he made it home for dinner would sit in silence, glued to his phone. When we got to the cottage Sean was distracted, his phone always to hand. And then on the second day he announced that he would have to head back to London, that he was needed at the office. 'I'm so sorry, Mags,' he said when I came back from the beach and found him packing. 'Work's just gone crazy.' I told him that this was a holiday, my birthday present, that surely he could delegate whatever problem had arisen to one of the team, but he said there was some legal issue that could turn nasty and he was the only one who could sort it out. Elspeth and I had tried to enjoy the rest of the break but Sean's leaving cast a shadow over it. When it started raining on the fourth day we decided to give up and go home. We were halfway back when I got the text from Sean. He said that he was flying to Stockholm, where the sports company was based, for an urgent meeting. 'I'll make it up to you, Mags,' he said at the end of the text. 'And tell Elspeth I'll get her something special from Sweden.'

Sweden. I look down at the name written on the piece of paper in front of me and a chill courses through my body. Freya Nielssen. What if he met her on that trip to Stockholm? Did she work for the sports company? I need to know, I tell myself, as I carefully enter her number into the phone, otherwise I'll be trapped in this limbo for ever. I close my eyes, press the 'call' button then hold the phone to my ear.

There's a pause and then I hear a robotic voice.

'The person you are calling is unavailable. Please leave a message after the tone.'

I don't leave a message. Instead I press 'end call' then sit with the phone in my hands as it slowly sinks in.

Sean has left me for another woman.

29

Friday 4 August

I stand in the shower and look down at my broken body. What is the point of being clean? What is the point of getting through another day when I've lost everything?

I turn off the water and take a towel from the rail. As I dry myself I catch sight of my face in the small round mirror above the sink. My long hair is straggly and dry, the red now threaded with grey. My eyes are swollen from crying; my lips are dry and cracked. I have become an old woman in the space of a few weeks. And then I think of Freya Nielssen. I imagine a perfect blonde with flawless skin and a young lithe body. A woman unencumbered by mental illness, a happy extrovert who likely sidled up to Sean after their meeting and suggested they go for a drink. Or was it the other way round? Did he initiate it? I think back to the day we met, his insistence we go for a drink. Did he do the same with Freya? And then to torture myself I think about them together. Her perfect naked body draped across his, my husband doing things to her that he did to me, things that were unique to us. I imagine him cupping her face in his hands, telling her he loves her.

Stop it, I will myself, nausea creeping up my throat. Just stop it. I come out of the bathroom and put on yesterday's clothes. I'm in a daze. It's like my brain has finally said 'no more' and is shutting down.

Then there is a knock at the door and I hear Sonia's voice.

'It's just me, Maggie. Are you decent?'

I walk towards her voice, trying to compose myself.

'Hiya,' she says, smiling broadly as I open the door. 'How are – oh, what's the matter?'

It's the sight of Sonia, so warm and reassuring, that makes me crumple. And once I start crying I can't stop. I stagger to the window and slump down on the wicker chair.

'Maggie, what is it?' she says, closing the door and coming over to me. 'What's happened?'

'It's Sean . . .' I say, my chest heaving with sobs. 'He was having an affair.'

'What? How do you know?'

'I called the estate agency that dealt with the rental of Larkfields and on their records they had Sean listed alongside his partner, a woman called Freya Nielssen.'

Sonia's eyes widen and she shakes her head.

'I suppose it could be a business partner,' she says optimistically.

'It was quite clear what kind of partner it meant,' I say, rubbing my forehead with the palm of my hand. 'I think it's someone he met at work.'

And then I tell her about the disastrous Whitstable holiday and Sean's urgent trip to Stockholm; his disappearance on Christmas Eve and his strange behaviour in the months that followed.

'Oh, Maggie,' says Sonia, squeezing my hand. 'I don't know what to –'

A knock at the door interrupts her sentence. I sit up on the chair, rigid.

'Oh God, it'll be Mr Hutchinson,' I say. 'He comes in to empty the bins at this time. Can you get rid of him?'

'Of course I will,' says Sonia.

She stands up and goes to the door.

'Who is it?' she calls.

'It's only Amanda. Can I come in?'

I quickly wipe my eyes and try to compose myself while Sonia opens the door.

'Sorry about that,' she says as Amanda strides in on a wave of vanilla oil. 'We thought it might be the creepy landlord.'

'Well, we won't have to worry about him any more,' says Amanda. 'Did Sonia tell you the good news?' She doesn't seem to notice my dishevelled appearance.

'I haven't had a chance yet,' says Sonia.

'What is it?' I say.

'Well,' says Amanda, coming to sit on the chair next to me. 'We've managed to find you secure accommodation.'

My heart sinks. In my light-headed state I'd thought for one precious moment that Amanda was going to open the door and bring Elspeth in, tell me that this had all been some dreadful mistake.

'It's a nice little flat off the Western Road,' she continues. 'I've just been to see it and I think you'll love it. There's a nice bedroom, a big spacious living area and a kitchen with white goods. Everything you need.'

'Western Road?' I say, trying to keep up.

'Yes,' says Amanda. 'Really accessible for town and all the amenities. Now, dear, I've got the car outside. Why don't we get packing and we can be in the new place by this afternoon.'

'That quick?' I say, feeling overwhelmed by it all. 'Are you sure?'

'I don't think we should hang around here any longer than we need to,' says Amanda, taking a jumper from the back of the chair and folding it over her arm. 'Sonia, you grab Maggie's rucksack and pop these clothes in. I'll go and get the toiletries from the bathroom.'

I stand impotently in the middle of the room, watching as the two women collect my meagre belongings.

'Right, we're all set,' says Amanda, gesturing to the rucksack and two carrier bags that constitute my worldly goods. 'Shall we go?'

I take my coat from the bed and as I'm putting it on I notice the ICU diary lying on the bed, among the crumpled sheets. I grab it and put it into my coat pocket.

'Right,' says Sonia, guiding me out of the door. 'Let's go find your new home.'

30

Dear Mummy,

I've written you a poem. This is it:

When I think of home I think of you and me.
A warm cosy place, a place where I feel free.
I think of all the good times
That we would have in there.
A big lovely house, pretty and fair.
When I think of home, there's water all around.
Running down the windows.
Rising up through the ground.
The river's always flowing
Down towards the sea.
It's carrying a secret.
That belongs to you and me.
I love you Mummy.

Xxx

31

I sit on the lumpy sofa in my new home, cradling the phone in my hands. I've spent the last few minutes searching the name 'Freya Nielssen' on Google but by the third page the only people coming up are an elderly Canadian vet and a Hollywood personal trainer, neither of which I could see Sean running away with.

It's 8 p.m. Sonia and Amanda left an hour ago after spending the afternoon getting me settled. It's a ground-floor flat in a quiet street, and though I suppose I should feel grateful, it isn't my home.

There are two armchairs as well as the sofa and a large flat-screen television hangs on the wall above the fireplace, its bulk dominating the entire room. From where I am sitting on the sofa I can see my reflection in it. I look crooked and small.

There are some built-in shelves next to the television that Sonia said would make wonderful bookshelves. I told her that I don't have any books; that all of mine had been in Larkfields and who knows where they are now. She'd suggested we go to Oxfam to buy some more but the last thing I want to do right now is read.

Once, books were my lifeline, my sanity; now it feels like that part of my brain has been closed for good.

I get up from the sofa and walk through into the narrow galley kitchen. Sonia drove me to Aldi to get some shopping before she left. My money is depleting fast. I had never been to Aldi before, though Sonia assured me it was the best of the supermarkets in terms of value for money. She has set my weekly food budget at £20 and recommended that I buy basic items and cook meals that can last a few days – like casseroles and soups.

She means well but if I'm honest food is the last thing on my mind. When I was sent away as a teenager I stopped eating. After the bad thing happened I wanted to punish my body and I did a very good job of it. When I came out my mother gasped because I was so thin. She tried feeding me up but I couldn't eat more than a few morsels without feeling sick. I was still suffering when I met Sean. He knew I had issues with food but he never pushed it or made me feel uncomfortable. In the end it was getting pregnant with Elspeth that made me better. The fact that my body had been given a second chance, that I had another life inside me, made me want to nurture it. When she was born and they placed her in my arms I made a promise to her that I would stay strong for her, that I would never get ill again.

But I didn't keep my promise. I let her down. I look at the small round dining table standing in the middle of the kitchen and I feel sick. How could I even begin to think about cooking a meal? The very act of setting a table just for me, without Sean and Elspeth, is too painful to contemplate. I can hear the old voice rising up again, the one I used to hear when I was sent away, the one that told me it was my fault, that I should punish myself. My stomach rumbles with hunger but I ignore it. The voice is right. I deserve to be punished.

I rinse my coffee cup and put it on the draining board. But as I turn to walk out of the kitchen I hear something. A voice. I look up at the ceiling. According to Amanda, the tenant in the upstairs flat is a bedridden elderly woman. 'No loud parties, then,' Sonia had remarked. But the noise is not coming from above, it's coming from next door, from my bedroom.

'Hello,' I call as I tiptoe out of the kitchen, my skin prickling with fear. 'Who's there?'

This is a ground-floor flat. A prime target for burglars. I should call the police but my phone is on the sofa in the living room and I am here, standing in the dark hallway that connects the kitchen to the bedroom and bathroom, frozen with fear.

And then I hear something that makes every hair on my head stand on end. Someone is singing. As I edge along the corridor it gets louder and that's when I recognize the voice and the song.

'The moon is shining bright tonight.'

'Elspeth?' I whisper as I approach the bedroom door. 'We're all warm and cosy tight.'

'Elspeth, baby, where are you?'

I push the door open, every fibre of me expecting to see my little girl lying in the bed singing the song my dad had sung to me at bedtime and that I had passed on to her. But the room is empty.

'It's the pills,' I think to myself as I stagger inside and sit down on the single bed. They're playing tricks with my head.

I lie on the bed, tucking my knees to my chest. I want someone to hold me and let me cry and cry until I have no tears left in my body. This loneliness is unbearable.

I turn on my side and see the ICU diary sitting on top of the chest of drawers. I need to distract myself, need to fill this unbearable silence. So I sit up in the bed and grab the diary. I read the next of Claire's entries where she notes that I was 'twitching my hands a lot this morning' and that my 'eyes flickered when we turned the radio on'. I turn the page and what I see makes my stomach flip. Sean's handwriting. He has written in this diary. How could I have missed it? I turn the pages. There are several entries, all in his distinctive jagged handwriting. I'm light-headed with shock. Turning back to his first entry, I begin to read.

32

14th May 2017

Hi Mags

They've told me that writing in this diary might help, whatever that means. Will it help bring Elspeth back? Will it help you wake up? Christ, these last few hours I've been sitting in this chair like a zombie, unable to even fathom what has just happened let alone write it down. But the images of yesterday are hammering against my head, begging to be let out. I can either scream and rage and bang my fists on the walls or I can write it down here.

I've been to see her, Mags. The doctors came in and said she was ready and for a split second I was sure they were telling me that it had all been a big mistake, that Elspeth was waiting in one of the cubicles, ready to come home, that it was some other poor soul's child that died. Not ours. Not our Elspeth.

So I went with them, the doctors, down this long sterile corridor, the road to hell. There was a policewoman there too, the same one who came to our front door. She didn't say anything as we walked along, just smiled this sickly smile. I wanted to rip it off her face. I mean, who smiles when you're about to see a dead child?

And then we got to the door. They opened it and, Christ, Maggie, it was the most horrific thing I've ever had to do. It was so cold in there, freezing, and there was this weird smell. I started to shake then and I couldn't stop. Even my teeth started chattering. The policewoman grabbed my arm. It wasn't real. It couldn't be. Think of the worst nightmare you've ever had then multiply it a million times.

Someone said my name and I saw a woman coming towards me, dressed in green scrubs. The pathologist.

She started talking but I couldn't really take in what she was saying because she was there. Elspeth.

I heard the woman say something. She was asking if this was my daughter. And every part of me wanted to say, 'No, that's not my daughter. My daughter's at home, safe and well.' But when I looked down there was no question who it was. Her little face was so white and she had a big purple bruise underneath her right eye. I just wanted to lift her off that block and carry her out of there, take her home. I wanted to shake her until she woke up.

God, Elspeth.

I can't really remember much after that. Everything just blurred. The police officer led me out of there and the doctor asked if I was okay. I told him that I would never be okay again, not after what I had just seen.

But as they walked me back to your bedside all I could think was that this was my fault. That you'd found out what I'd done.

15th May

Dear Mags,

I'm sitting by your bed and all sorts of feelings are battling inside me: fear, guilt, anger, confusion.

Yesterday I blamed myself. You'd found out, I was sure of it. You'd found out what I'd been up to and you were driving towards the station to confront me. But there are so many things that don't make sense. Why would you stop at the pub car park? You can't have been going in there. We hated that pub. Why would you get out of the car and lock Elspeth inside it? Jesus, Mags, you left the bloody handbrake off. Our little girl was in the car and you didn't secure it properly.

Anyway, I'll only get the answers to those questions when you wake up. If you wake up.

It's really quiet in here now and I'm glad of the peace. During the day there's a steady stream of doctors and nurses coming in to prod and poke you but they never have anything new to say. The way they look at you then scribble down their notes just makes me anxious. There's a lot of talk online about positive thinking, positive communication and the strength of the human spirit and I'm trying, Mags, I really am, but to be honest I don't even know if I want you to make it.

16th May

Dear Mags,

Christ, I miss her. I keep seeing her, in the corridor, in the car park. I can hear her voice, clear as a bell. How can she be gone, Mags? I just can't get my head around it.

Do you remember the day she was born? It was in a room just like this. The Griffin Room in Chelsea and Westminster Hospital. We called it our 'private suite' though we'd only been put there because you'd had a caesarean.

I remember I sneaked out one morning to get some food and when I came back you and Elspeth were gone. I charged out of that room like a madman, grabbed some poor nurse and demanded to know what had happened to my wife and daughter. Turns out you'd taken her to the bathroom with you. When I came back to the room there you both were, all safe and sound and cuddled up. But I'll never forget that feeling, that panic, because it was my first experience of the terror that comes with being a parent, the raw fear that the two people you love more than anything in this world could be taken away from you.

I loved you back then, I really did, Mags. I knew what you'd been through and how fragile you were, but you were also strong. The strongest person I've ever known. But the pressure of these last few years just got too much. All I ever wanted was to make you happy but you pushed me away. You only smiled when you were in your study typing away on the computer or if you and Elspeth were playing together. I saw the way your face would cloud over when I walked into a room. You pushed me so far away that I couldn't get back to you.

I miss you. I miss Elspeth. I miss us.

Please make it. I need you.

17th May

Hello Mags,

I'm sitting here because I don't want to go home. If I go home then all this is real. While I'm here in this hospital I can fool myself that this is a dream or that Elspeth has gone off on a school trip somewhere and will be back any day now full of stories and excitement.

Another reason why I don't want to go home is that I know I'll have to start planning the funeral.

Once the coroner's report comes back then her body will be released and I will have to think of . . .

You know last night I was trying to work out what she would like to have at her funeral and all I could think of was bowling. Bloody bowling. Do you remember for her last birthday she was adamant that she wanted a bowling party but we'd left it too late and they were all booked up. We ended up taking her friends to that pottery place in Lewes where they could decorate their own mugs. I'm talking gibberish, Mags, I know I am, but Christ I would give anything to just take her bowling now. To take the day off work for one lousy afternoon and see my daughter having fun in a bloody neon-lit bowling alley.

So here I am, Mags, trying to plan her funeral like we planned her birthdays. We used to say to each other, didn't we, in the weeks before her birthday, what would Elspeth want? And you would always know better than me. You knew that she preferred chocolate cake to vanilla; knew that she wouldn't want to invite that spiteful kid from the village even though she'd invited Elspeth to her party. You knew which of the kids had a dairy intolerance and who was veggie. You knew that the cherry tomatoes always got left at the end and that you couldn't go wrong with a few extra bowls of Hula Hoops. I'm trying to think like you, Mags, but inside I'm screaming, 'I can't do this.'

You knew her better than I did. I was always on the outside looking in. You and Elspeth were this invincible team and I had no chance of joining. I look back at the last few years and the chasm between us just got bigger and bigger.

I should have told you. I should have come clean and then none of this would have happened.

I'm sorry, Mags. I'm so sorry.

2nd June

Mags.

Today was Elspeth's funeral. My heart is ripped to shreds. I've never known pain like this, Maggie. I can barely breathe. How is it possible to be burying your own child?

Sophie Bailey brought her CD player and played their favourite Taylor Swift song, the one Elspeth used to sing over and over. I'll never be able to hear that song again. I asked she be put in her purple dress, her favourite. Do you remember she used to say that the colour purple had magical powers, that it could protect you from harm? And as I was standing in that church, listening to the vicar talk about the purity of childhood and how Elspeth is safe with the angels, I asked myself why she wasn't wearing purple that night, why both of you weren't wearing sodding purple to protect you from harm.

3rd June

Writing it down will make it better, they said. Writing it down will help make sense of it all. So I'm sitting at our kitchen table with this bloody diary in front of me, trying to find the words that will make sense of the last twenty-four hours but I don't think that is possible.

So I'll just be brief, Mags, and tell you what I know.

They gave me your phone.

It's all on there, everything you tried to hide from me. Your secret.

And when I read it I felt sick.

How could you do this?

It was your fault, Maggie, all of it.

You killed our daughter.

PART TWO

33

I'm with Ben. We're down by the river. It's hot, stiflingly hot. He kisses me. I tell him to stop. We shouldn't be doing this. 'Come on, Maggie, for old time's sake,' he whispers. And I relent. Like I always do.

I open my eyes and the dream dissolves.

Then slowly, like a rash creeping across my body, the revelations of the previous night come back to me. Sean. The diary.

I turn on my side, trying to stem the images that are multiplying in my head. Elspeth lying in the morgue, her face battered and bruised. Dr Elms said she wouldn't have felt a thing, but how does he know? It kills me to think that she could have been in pain before she died and that I couldn't get to her. Her fear. Her panic.

Is Sean right? Was I responsible?

I lean across the bed, my head thick with sleep, and take the diary from the bedside table. I read the last page over and over, the venom of Sean's words penetrating my skin. *They gave me your phone.*

And in that moment, I remember something. Ben.

He had been back in touch. I'd spoken to him on the phone, the day before the accident.

I sit up straight, my heart thudding against my chest as bit by bit it comes back to me.

The conversation was brief, and I was defensive and wary. He said he was sorry, that he felt guilty. What we did was bad, he said, but it's time we forgive ourselves. When the call ended I felt strange, like I'd just been winded.

I put the diary back on the table, my hands shaking. What was on that phone? Had Ben sent messages too? What exactly did Sean find out?

Then my phone starts to ring. I stare at it for a moment, too scared to answer. But it could be important. I reach over and pick it up.

'Hello.'

'Oh hello, is that Miss Nielssen?'

'Sorry?' I say, my skin prickling. 'Who is this?'

'It's Sharon Jarvis from Kingsland Farley. My colleague asked me to give you a call. You were enquiring about one of our properties?'

'Oh,' I say, remembering the estate agent. 'Yes, thank you for calling but actually my name is not Nielssen. It's Maggie Allan. Sean Allan's wife.'

'Oh, I'm sorry, my colleague said your name was Freya Nielssen. She must have got mixed up.'

'It's okay,' I say.

'It's about Larkfields, is that right?'

'Yes,' I say, pulling the covers up.

'Well, I'm glad you called,' says Sharon. 'Because we have a key fob here with your name on it but we had no number to call you on.'

'My name?'

'Yes, Maggie Allan?'

'On a key fob?'

'That's right,' says Sharon. 'We received instructions to hold on to the fob and to pass it on to you. This was done through a previous letting assistant who's now left the company. She was a bit of an airhead, to be honest, forgot to take people's numbers if they called with an enquiry, double-booked viewings. It seems she'd done it again with the Larkfields notes.'

'You say you were given instructions,' I say. 'Was it Sean?'

'I actually don't know, Mrs Allan,' she says, her voice flat. 'As I said, it was my previous colleague who dealt with it all but reading between the lines it looks as though the house was emptied by a third party after the tenancy ended and the contents placed in a storage unit. We were entrusted with the key to that unit and on the notes here it says that we were to hand the key over to you if you made a recovery; if not then we were to donate the contents to charity. Does that make any sense to you, Mrs Allan? Have you been ill?'

I put my head back on the pillow. None of this makes sense.

'Mrs Allan?'

'Sorry, yes, I'm still here,' I say. 'I'm just trying to take it all in. I have no idea why my husband has acted in this way. We were very happily married, everything was fine and then I had a car accident, my little girl was killed and he . . . he did this.'

My voice catches and I try my best to suppress the tears that are building up.

'Oh gosh, I had no idea,' says Sharon. 'I'm so sorry.'

'You say you have this key fob at the office,' I say, edging my way through her sympathetic noises.

'Yes,' she says, her voice lifting. 'You're welcome to come and collect it whenever you like.'

'I can come this morning,' I say, looking at my watch. It's just after 9.30.

'Fine,' says Sharon. 'I'm here all day. We're just opposite the war memorial. You can't miss our sign.'

'Okay,' I say, getting up from the bed. 'I'll be there in ten minutes.'

'Mrs Allan?'

A woman with a toothy smile greets me at the door as I walk into the estate agents.

'Yes,' I say. 'You must be Sharon.'

'That's right,' she says.

She's a large woman – big-boned, as my mother would

have said – with blonde hair cut in rather dated layers. Her face is overly made-up and she smells of talcum powder. She reminds me of the women who worked behind the make-up counters in the department store my mother used to drag me through when I was a child.

'Do come through,' she says. 'I just have to retrieve the fob from our safe downstairs. Can I get you a tea or coffee while you wait?'

'No thanks, I'm fine,' I say, still reeling from the shock of reading the diary and remembering Ben's call. Caffeine would be a bad idea right now.

'Okay,' she says, smiling politely. 'Do take a seat and I won't be a moment.'

As Sharon disappears down the stairs I sit down at her desk. As I wait I try to compose myself. I look around. There are four other desks dotted about the room, each with a person sitting behind it, either typing on computers or talking on the phone. None of them look up at me. The walls are covered with properties for sale. I read the details of the one just in front of me. A five-bedroom detached house in Ifield, on the market for £860,000. 'A perfect family home,' is how it is described on the front. As I look at it I think of how we stretched ourselves to get Larkfields even though we offered the lowest possible price, which was miraculously accepted. It seemed the Gothic facade and potential flood risk had put other buyers off. Still, Sean assured me that it was all fine, that work was going well and he would be in line for higher bonuses as he worked his way up the ladder. 'It's your childhood home, Mags,' he'd said to me as I sat there, six months pregnant and weeping at the thought of someone outbidding us. 'There is no way we're going to lose it.' And I was such a ball of hormones and baby head that I trusted him to deal with the intricacies of the sale. He signed all the papers and dealt with the bank and the estate agent and I believed him when he came home and said the house was ours. And it was. Until he sold it to some property firm. If only I knew why he had done that. And why he kept it from me all these years.

'Sorry to keep you waiting.'

I look up and see Sharon coming back to the desk. She is holding an orange file in her arms.

'I just need you to sign a couple of forms,' she says. 'And then I can hand you the key.'

She opens the file and takes out a sheet of paper.

'If you could sign and date this one, just at the bottom there,' she says, pointing her pen at the relevant place.

I scan the form. It's a solicitor's note. They are working on behalf of BH2 Properties who are registered to an address in the Channel Islands. The official language makes my head hurt but then as I get to the bottom I freeze. 'Designated key holders for storage facility: Margaret Allan and Freya Nielssen.'

That name again. Not just stated as Sean's partner

on some estate agency contact sheet but named as a 'designated key holder' on an official document for a storage unit that contains my belongings.

'I'm sorry,' I say to Sharon, handing the form back. 'Here's this name again. Freya Nielssen. Why is she on here?'

'I don't know,' she says, shaking her head. 'As I said on the phone, the tenancy termination for this property was dealt with by my colleague. I was on holiday at the time.'

'And the colleague,' I say, trying to collect my thoughts. 'You said that she's now left the agency.'

'That's right.'

'Well, is there any way of contacting her?' I say. 'To ask her about this woman and why she's been named both as my husband's partner and on here.'

'Contact Maxine?' says Sharon, her eyes bulging as if I've just asked her to commit murder. 'I'm afraid I wouldn't be able to help you there. Last I heard she'd gone travelling with her boyfriend: South East Asia then on to Australia. She only took this job to fund the trip and, if I'm honest with you, it showed. She had zero commitment, zero work ethic, last one to arrive on a morning and first one out the door at five thirty. I mean, no wonder there were mistakes and inaccuracies on her tenancy records, she spent most of her time on the internet looking at travel forums, but that's millennials for you.'

I look down at the form again, feeling even more confused. If this Freya Nielssen is the woman Sean is having an affair with then why would he want her to have access to our belongings? Surely they would be together. It just doesn't make sense.

'I'm sorry I can't be of any more help,' says Sharon. 'But at least your name's on there, eh? You can access your things now.'

I nod my head as she passes the duplicate slip. I scribble my name then she hands me a blue plastic fob with a large yellow key ring attached.

'Here you go,' she says. 'Now I'll write down the address of the storage unit. It's not far from here, just off the Piddinghoe Road. It'll only take a few minutes in the car.'

'It'll have to be the bus,' I say. 'I don't have a car.'

'Oh gosh,' says Sharon. 'That was so insensitive of me. Of course you wouldn't be driving after what happened. I'm very sorry about your little girl by the way. I do remember it now. It was in the papers.'

'Yes, I believe it was,' I say, getting up from the chair to stop her saying anything else. 'Anyway, thank you very much. You've been very helpful.'

34

The industrial estate, where the storage facility is housed, makes me think of a nuclear fallout zone. Large corrugated-iron buildings loom ominously in front of me as I try to decipher the labyrinthine map on the entrance gate. According to the map the storage units are in the yellow quadrant towards the centre of the estate. As I make my way across I take out my inhaler. I'm utterly exhausted and I haven't even got there yet.

Eventually I see the name of the unit and a set of automatic glass doors with RECEPTION written above in big yellow letters. When I step inside I see a young woman in a navy-blue uniform sitting behind a desk. As I approach, my eyes are drawn to the badge on her lapel which says: 'My name's Kelly and I'm here to help.'

'Hi,' I say. 'Could you tell me where . . .' I pause to consult the piece of paper Sharon gave me. 'Where Unit 428 is, please?'

'Sure,' she says, taking a leaflet from the front of the desk and opening it out. 'This is a map of the Yellow Bay. The four hundreds are situated on the fourth floor.'

She takes a red pen and circles the relevant place on the map.

'Your best bet is to take the lift, which is just over there,' she says. 'Then once you get to the fourth floor you need to turn right and you'll find the even-numbered units.'

'Thank you,' I say, taking the map. 'You've been really helpful.'

I go to the lift and press the button. As I wait for it to arrive I feel an odd sensation in the pit of my stomach. I have no idea what is waiting for me up there.

Then the lift doors open with a jolt and I step inside. I press the button for the fourth floor and close my eyes. I have never felt so strange. The anxiety, which had felt like sharp needles stabbing my skin, has been replaced with an odd sense of remove, like I am watching myself from above.

Everything that I have learned these last couple of days – Freya Nielssen, Sean's accusations, the phone call from Ben – it all feels like it's happened to someone else. I should be feeling horrified or upset. Instead I just feel numb.

After a couple of moments the doors open and I step out into a narrow corridor. The walls are painted an acidic yellow and the carpet is bright blue. The clashing colours make me feel disorientated. I turn right and count down the numbers on the metal doors.

420, 422, 424, 426 . . .

428.

I stop outside the door. There's a small square pad in the centre of it. I take the fob out of my pocket and hold it against the pad. A green light flashes. I push the door open and step inside.

A neon strip light splutters into life as I enter, flooding the room in a sickly artificial glow. It's a small space, about the size of an average garden shed, and it is stacked from floor to ceiling with white cardboard packing boxes. As I step closer I see that each box has been labelled in black marker pen, but I don't recognize the handwriting. It is definitely not Sean's.

The first box is marked *Elspeth: Bedroom*. I put my hands on the lid. It has been sealed with thick masking tape. I go to pull the tape away then stop. I'm not ready to see what is inside. Not just yet.

I step further into the room. There must be around a hundred boxes of various sizes all piled up. I see *Elspeth: Playroom, Elspeth: Bathroom*. My heart hurts when I see a box labelled *Elspeth: Miscellaneous* as I know exactly what that will contain; all of her oddities and precious things, her latest obsessions. 'Miscellaneous' is a good word to describe those things, I think to myself, though it is a word Sean would never have used. He was so respectful of Elspeth's obsessions, much more than I was. Spending every day with Elspeth meant that I grew impatient quickly. After the sixth day in a row of hearing Native American facts I would get frustrated and shout at her. Yet Sean, because he was out at work all day, would come home and give her his undivided attention. Whatever new thing had piqued her interest that particular week he would give as much reverence and attention to as the previous one. He was a better parent than I could ever be.

I step across to the other side of the room where more boxes have been piled up. But when I read the labels I go cold. In the same neat handwriting as the ones on Elspeth's boxes someone has written:

The Bitch: Bedroom
The Bitch: Kitchen
The Bitch: Bathroom
The Bitch: Office

The words drip with venom and hatred. This can't be Sean. He has never called me a bitch in his life. And, besides, this isn't his handwriting. Who could have written this? Who could hate me so much?

I slump down on the floor. I have no idea why someone would have so much hatred for me that they would dismiss me as 'The Bitch'. Surely it can't be Sean. But then I think of his last entry in the diary: *You killed our daughter.* And Freya Nielssen. Could it be her handwriting? After all, hers is the only name, apart from mine, that is linked to this place. Is she behind this? Did she make Sean believe I killed Elspeth so that he would hate me and they could be together? My head hurts from trying to make sense of it all.

I count the boxes. There are forty-three. Eleven years of marriage and one longed-for child and all I have left are forty-three cardboard boxes. How can this be my life?

I feel my chest tighten and I start to wheeze. I take my inhaler out of my bag and put it to my mouth. I inhale twice but my chest seems to get tighter. It must be the dust. I need to get out of here.

I stand up and make my way to the door but as I do I see something on the floor, just next to the first row of boxes. It's an envelope. I pick it up. It has my name written on it in capital letters. I slice it open and pull out a piece of paper. It is Elspeth's handwriting.

I rest my hand on the wall and begin to read:

Dear Mummy,

I've written you a poem. This is it:

When I think of home I think of you and me.
A warm cosy place, a place where I feel free.
I think of all the good times
That we would have in there.
A big lovely house, pretty and fair.
When I think of home, there's water all around.
Running down the windows.
Rising up through the ground.

The river's always flowing
Down towards the sea.
It's carrying a secret.
That belongs to you and me.
I love you Mummy.

Xxx

I clutch the letter to my chest, the words searing into my heart. My beautiful little girl. I imagine her sitting at home, a notepad in front of her, writing a poem that I never got to read. I look at the envelope again. No postmark. She must have written this for me, but when? It looks like her handwriting from a couple of years ago. I think back to all those times I shooed her away when I was working in my study. I can hear her little voice now: 'Mummy, can I just show you something?' And I was so absorbed in my imaginary world I wouldn't even turn round, wouldn't look at her. 'Mummy?' 'Not now, Elspeth, I'm busy.' What if she'd tried to show me this poem, a beautiful poem about home and what it meant to her, and I'd sent her away? How did I become so detached? From the moment Elspeth was born I had wanted to shower her with love, create the warmest of homes for her, protect her from the monsters that had plagued me. And then somewhere along the line it all got too much and I retreated; from Elspeth, from Sean, from the world.

The air is growing thinner inside the room. I really do need to get out now. I take the letter, grab my bag and the key fob and pull the heavy door open.

As I run down the hideous yellow corridor, tears stream down my face. My lungs are so tight now I can barely breathe. When I get to the lift I stab my fist at the button.

'Come on,' I cry as I watch the neon numbers slowly rise from one through to three. Finally, after what seems like hours, it strikes four and when the doors open I half fall inside. When the lift doors open on the ground floor I stagger out. Past the reception desk where 'I'm here to help' Kelly sits glued to her smartphone, through the automatic doors and out into the deserted car park.

Crouching on the tarmac by some bins, I look at the vast industrial wilderness around me and I know that this can't be it. I can't live in this limbo, this confusion.

I need to go back. Back to the river.

35

Dear Mummy,

Freya came to see me again today. She was sitting in the kitchen drinking tea with Weasel Face when Zoe and I came home from school. She said that Daddy was so glad I was well and that I just had to be a brave girl and stick it out and then everything would be fine. Then she asked if she could see my bedroom. I took her up there and when she walked in she gasped and said it was very bare and that next time she comes she'll bring me some cushions and pictures to 'cheer the place up'. Zoe was lying on her bunk and she made a snorting noise when Freya said that. I don't think she likes Freya. But then Zoe doesn't really like anybody.

When Zoe left the room I asked Freya about you again. She said you and Daddy weren't together any more but it was for the best. I told her that I'd been writing letters to you. She asked if she could see so I showed her my notebook. She read the letters and said that I was a very good speller. Then she said that you would love to read them and that perhaps she could pass them on to you. I nearly fell off the bed when she said that. I asked if she knew where you were but she said you weren't very well so you were in a special place where you could rest. Then she picked up my red ink pen and wrote her address on the back page of my notebook and said that I could send the letters to her. She told me to put them all in a big envelope and she'd make sure you got them.

When she left I sat at my desk and carefully ripped out each of the letters I've written so far so I can put them all together. Zoe says I'm deluded and that Freya is 'shifty' but I don't think she is. I think she must be a friend of yours and Daddy's and she's helping you.

Anyway, the next time I write you a letter it will have my address on the front in big letters so that when you receive it you'll know just where to find me.

I can't wait to see you Mummy.

I hope you're getting better.

I love you.
Your lovely daughter xxx

36

A light rain begins to fall as I walk along the bridle path. The air smells of smoke and silt. I hear a dog bark in the distance and a rustle of leaves. Birds? Or something – someone – else? Keep focused, I tell myself, keep walking and don't look back. But as I walk it is impossible not to look back, not to think about the events that have brought me here.

I'd walked this same route towards Ketton House Farm with my parents all those years ago. The night of Barbara's fortieth birthday party.

'Come on, Margaret. We're going to be late!'

My mother's voice returns to me from that golden summer.

I had spent hours getting ready. Ben was home from university and was going to be at the party. I had to look perfect. In the end I had opted for a black velvet dress that clung to my body like a second skin. My hair was scooped back in a sophisticated chignon and I'd painstakingly lined my eyes with smoky black kohl.

But Mum didn't like seeing me dressed up and had wanted me to change.

'Leave her be, Marion,' my dad had said, shaking his head at my mother. 'She looks lovely. A proper Audrey Hepburn.'

I shiver as I think of what followed. *Unhinged*; that's what Barbara had yelled as they took me away.

When I reach the river path the air grows cooler. I zip up my thin jacket and head towards the spot: the small patch of riverbank where the two alder trees meet.

When I get there I'm overcome with the scent of meadowsweet. It smells just like marzipan, intensified by the dampness in the air. The scent takes me back to the beautiful spring morning when Elspeth and her classmates took part in the annual May procession. She had spent weeks perfecting the flower garland that she would wear on her head. She wanted to have meadowsweet in it because she liked the fuzzy, cloud-like petals; thought they looked like angel hair. Like everything Elspeth made, it had to be just so. I can hear her little voice singing the hymn to the May Queen as I walk.

'Bring flowers of the rarest, bring blossoms the fairest . . .'

I was so proud of her that day. She had been chosen to lead the procession. In the past this would have resulted in a meltdown of epic proportions, but something had changed in Elspeth in her final few months, she had become more confident. I'd taken lots of photos on my phone and messaged them to

Sean who couldn't be there, even though it was a Saturday. He hadn't replied to those messages and at the time I thought nothing of it. Now as I stand here in the shadow of the two alder trees I wonder if he was with Freya Nielssen that day, if he was planning his escape. I see my beautiful girl in her shimmering white dress, her auburn hair threaded with blossoms, and a chill courses through me. Less than two weeks later she was dead.

I stand for a moment and look at the water. A thick green film of algae coats the surface. I think of Ben, his persuasive voice, urging me on: 'Come on, Maggie, don't be such a bore.' Why hadn't I just walked away? How different my life could have been.

But then, after all the hurt, I got a second chance at happiness; a chance to prove that I was a good person. And it came in the form of Elspeth, a child with piercing green eyes and an old, knowing soul.

I can't live like this, I think to myself, as I step towards the river's edge, clutching Elspeth's letter in my hands.

I look down into the water. Its brown murky depths seem to be taunting me. *I will go on after you're gone*, it whispers. *I am all that matters. Do it. Jump. Jump.*

Raindrops bounce on the glassy surface, sending little droplets of water spluttering into the air. I can feel the rain on my head, my hair, my body, but I don't move. Instead I stand, transfixed by the river.

It would be easy. Just a little struggle, then thick, black oblivion. I have nothing left. This is the only way.

And then I see her; a little face rising above the surface. She's about three metres away, in the centre of the river. Her arms are flailing as she battles the current.

'Elspeth!' I cry. 'Elspeth! It's okay. Mummy's coming.'

The rain is falling more heavily now, obscuring her from my view.

'Elspeth!'

I take a step forward, feel the thick, slippy mud under my feet, but as I go to enter the river I hear a voice.

'This rain looks like it's setting in.'

I turn my head then take a few steps back on to the bank to steady myself. There's a man standing there. As he comes towards me I recognize him. It's the man from the bus station. There's a dog with him, a slender greyhound with a brindle coat.

'Lenny can't stand the rain,' he says, gesturing to the dog. 'Makes him shiver. I was just making my way back to the village. You want to get yourself back, too. It's forecast storms.'

'I'm fine here for now, thank you,' I say. I turn back towards the river and hope that he will go.

'You're the lady who was looking for Rodmell,' he says. 'The Virginia Woolf admirer. Listen, you don't want to stand that close to the edge or you'll end up like her.'

'I was just clearing my head,' I say. 'I know this spot. I used to live here.'

'I see,' he says. 'I'm Tom by the way. What's your name?'

I don't answer. Maybe if I ignore him long enough he will just go away.

'Listen, why don't you step away from the edge a bit?' he says. 'It's not safe. I wouldn't forgive myself if I left you here and you slipped. Come on, dear.'

The wind lashes my face and my eyes start to stream, a mix of rain and tears. I wipe them with the back of my hand then look out across the river. There is no sign of Elspeth. It must have been my mind playing tricks on me again.

'So are you going to tell me your name?'

I turn round and stand facing him, my arms hanging limply by my side.

'It's Maggie.'

'Maggie,' he says brightly. 'That was the name of my elder sister. It's a good name.'

'I don't know about that,' I say, shivering with the cold. 'There's nothing good about me.'

'Why do you say that?'

I shrug my shoulders.

'Come on, Maggie, there must be something good about you. Everyone has good in them.'

'My daughter was good,' I say. 'She was perfect and beautiful and eccentric. But most of all she was good.'

He nods his head and smiles.

'And you were her mum,' he says. 'So you contributed to her goodness.'

'I snuffed it out,' I say. 'I didn't protect her.'

'What happened to your daughter, dear?'

'She drowned,' I say. 'And I don't know why.'

'That's terrible,' he says, putting his hand to his mouth. 'Just terrible. Oh, I am sorry.'

'Do you know how many times I have heard those words these last few weeks?' I cry. 'And do you know how futile they are? Why are you sorry? You don't know me. You didn't know my daughter.'

He looks at me sadly for a moment. 'It's just natural, isn't it? People are always sorry to hear of someone's death,' he says. 'Particularly a child. But I'm also sorry for you, for the pain you must be feeling.'

'I was driving the car,' I say. 'It went into the river, and I have no memory of it. Nothing. I would say that it was my fault but I don't even know what I was doing out that night.'

'Did it happen here?'

I shake my head.

'It happened up by the Plough Inn,' I tell him. 'I came here because . . . God, I don't know why I came here. I –' My voice breaks. 'I just don't think I can get through this. I'm not strong enough.'

There's a crack of thunder. The dog pulls at its lead.

'Look, you go,' I say to Tom, raising my voice above the pounding rain. 'You're going to get soaked. I'm fine here, honestly.'

'Not unless you come too,' he says, grimacing as the rain beats down. 'I'm not leaving a young lass like you out here in this weather. And you don't want to be responsible for me getting hypothermia, do you?'

'I just wanted to be able to remember,' I say, putting my hands to my head. 'That's all.'

'And you will,' he says, raising his voice to be heard above the rain. 'But sometimes memories come back when you least expect them.'

I turn and look at the water. Maybe he's right.

'Is there someone I can call?' says Tom. 'Someone who can come and fetch you?'

'There's Sonia,' I say.

'Who's Sonia?'

'She's my . . . my friend.'

'All right,' says Tom. 'Why don't we go and get to the main road and then we'll call Sonia? Come on, love.'

He holds his hand out and I stumble towards him.

'That's a good lass,' he says, guiding me away from the river. 'We'll call Sonia and it'll all be fine.'

I nod my head and walk next to him in a daze. As we make our way back to the path I look down and notice that I'm still holding Elspeth's poem in my hands. It is sodden from the rain but I hold it to my face and kiss it, one, two, three times.

37

Dear Mummy,

Here it is, the first 'official' letter that you will actually receive in the post. (Though I'm going to put all the ones I've written so far in the envelope too so you'll have loads to read!)

Anyway, because this is your first proper letter I wanted it to be a good one. The others that I've already written are all a bit sad and I'm crying in most of them but this one is going to be happy because yesterday I had a really happy day. Let me tell you about it.

Well, we went on a school trip to a museum in London, but it wasn't an ordinary museum full of stuffy old furniture and oil paintings, no, this museum was filled with blood and bodies.

I've found that if I concentrate on things that really interest me then it doesn't hurt as much – by 'it' I mean not being with you and Daddy – and the thing that interests me at the moment is blood. Not like gruesome, horror-film blood, but real blood. I bet you're wondering why I'm so interested in it, well I'll tell you. A couple of weeks ago I had the worst nosebleed ever. I woke up in the night and my pillow was all wet so I jumped out of bed, turned the light on and looked in the mirror. At first I was scared because it looked like I'd been in an accident or something but then I ran the water in the sink and started to wash my face and as the blood mixed with the water it made the most beautiful pattern. It made me think about the colours inside our bodies and how they are much more interesting than our boring skin colours. Anyway, ever since that night I have wanted to find out more about blood, and in this amazing museum it was everywhere.

A man called Charles showed us around. He was the head curator and had studied at Cambridge, which is this amazing university. The others were bored and kept tutting and rolling their eyes at him. They just wanted to go and buy rubbish in the souvenir shop and eat chips in the cafe but I stuck with Charles. He was really friendly and answered all my questions. I found out that in scientific language dead bodies are known as cadavers. I even saw one. It was preserved in a liquid called formaldehyde (I copied that word in my notebook so I would remember how to spell it) and all the blood had been drained from it. I don't know whether you are aware of it, Mummy, but a body without blood is very drab and boring, it just looks like a piece of old cardboard. Blood is what makes us beautiful, Charles said, and I agree with him. He also said that science was all about moving from darkness into the light and as I walked around the museum, looking at all the amazing displays, that is exactly how I felt.

Next he showed me a shelf that was filled with tiny vials of blood, all a different shade. One was almost black. It was so wonderful. I just stood there staring at them. I really wanted to pick one of them up – the scarlet one – and dip my finger into it, but Charles was standing next to me the whole time. Anyway, these things were rare artefacts. I could have been thrown out if I'd tampered with them, or worse, I could have been sent to prison!

Anyway, the best bit for me, after the blood, was this amazing book by a man called William Hunter. I wrote down the name of the book carefully as I wanted to remember it for ever. It was called 'The Anatomy of the Human Gravid Uterus' and it was made in 1774. 'Even before I was born,' said Charles. He was very funny. Anyway, this book had lots of drawings, hundreds of them, showing the inside of a woman's body when a baby's inside it. And oh my goodness Mummy it was gruesome and lovely all at the same time. The baby was squeezed into this tiny space, its head facing downwards and its bottom in the air and there was no room to move. But the weirdest thing about this drawing for me was that the artist, Mr Hunter, had chopped off the woman's legs so they looked like two bits of meat, like the disgusting lamb chops they serve us for dinner here.

And then I felt sorry for the upside down baby because it was just like me, all alone. I asked Charles if I could see another page but the book was kept under glass and nobody was allowed to touch it in case it fell apart. So I just stayed *there for the rest of the afternoon looking at that baby and wondering why Mr Hunter had made its mother dead.*

Please write back.

Or just copy down the address at the top of this letter and come and find me.

I love you.
Your lovely daughter xxx

38

Sunday 6 August

I can hear the faint noise of the radio trickling along the hallway. Sonia is here. She's spent the whole morning in the kitchen making various soups and stews to put in the freezer. The smell of garlic and frying onions wafts through the air. It's a comforting, homely smell, but it only serves to make me feel more alone as I lie here in this borrowed bed. All I can think about is Elspeth's poem, its heartbreaking description of home and the glaring truth that she had written it as a way to get my attention. If I could go back in time I would rip up every book I ever bought, destroy every note, every document, because it was my reliance on them and my need to be validated as an intelligent person rather than someone who flunked their exams and worked in dead-end jobs for years that destroyed the greatest gift of all: being a mother to Elspeth. That little girl had drifted in and out of my life like a feather on the breeze and I should have scooped her in my arms, brought her down to earth, taken notice of her instead of locking myself away.

And now it's too late.

I turn over and look at the rust-coloured curtains that hang either side of the bedroom window. There's a brown stain on the bottom corner. 'Never let your iron overheat or you'll burn right through the fabric.' My mother's voice drifts down the decades, though I never ironed curtains – I never ironed anything, I was much too busy. Or at least that's what I told myself. Outside I hear a car door slam then footsteps making their way up the path. The doorbell rings and I sit up in the bed.

'Just coming,' calls Sonia, clattering a pot down on the kitchen counter.

She opens the front door and I hear Julia's voice, asking how I am.

I run my hand through my hair in a half-hearted attempt to tidy myself up then give up. Julia is a doctor. She regularly sees people at their very worst. Why should I be any different?

'She's just down here.'

Sonia's voice echoes along the corridor. My bedroom door opens and she peeks in and smiles.

'Oh, good, you're awake,' she says gently. 'Dr Mathers is here. Shall I send her in?'

I nod my head then pull the covers up to my chest. I hear Sonia whispering outside, then after a few moments Julia comes into the room.

She is dressed in her usual elegant trouser suit and kitten heels combination. Today the suit is a deep emerald colour that brings out the green in her eyes. I look down at my thin polyester nightdress and feel ashamed. Then I think about Sean and wonder what kind of clothes Freya Nielssen wears. I imagine her as a glacial Nordic blonde, glamorous and elegant, everything I'm not. I imagine him lying in bed with her, nuzzling her.

'I'm sorry I couldn't get here any sooner,' says Julia, interrupting my thoughts. 'I had some paperwork to catch up on this morning.'

She sits down on the end of the bed and clasps her hands on her lap. It's then that I see her appearance is not as immaculate as I first thought. Her hair is scraped back in a messy bun and there are dark circles under her eyes. I feel a stab of guilt. Her job must be busy enough without me causing her trouble.

'It's very good of you to come,' I say. 'I do appreciate it.'

She nods her head.

'So, Maggie, do you want to tell me what happened?' she says, cutting though unnecessary pleasantries. 'When Sonia called me last night she said that you'd got caught in the rain and were in a pretty bad state.'

'Yes,' I say, wishing I could disappear into the folds of the bedclothes. 'I went down to the river by Ketton House Farm.'

'Why did you go there?'

'It was ... it was a place where something bad

happened,' I say, not meeting her eye. 'Something that I have a strange feeling might be connected to the accident.'

'I see,' says Julia, frowning slightly. 'And do you want to talk about this bad thing?'

'No,' I say firmly. 'It's, well, it's rather personal. Besides, I'm fine now. The shivers have gone. Sonia made sure I had a hot bath last night.'

Julia narrows her eyes. She doesn't believe me for a second.

'Sonia also told me that you thought the pills were making you feel dizzy,' she says, tucking a stray piece of hair behind her ear.

'I was in a bad state when I said that but . . . well, it's true, since I've been taking the pills I've been feeling strange.'

'What do you mean by strange?'

'I've just been feeling numb, like all my responses have slowed right down.'

'That could be the neurological effects of the accident rather than the medication,' says Julia, her face serious.

'That's what I thought at first,' I say. 'But this felt different to the memory loss and actually that side of things was starting to get better, I was beginning to remember things, but then I heard Elspeth singing and –'

'Hold on,' says Julia, looking utterly confused. 'You heard Elspeth singing?'

'Yes,' I say, and then, taking a deep breath, I tell her about the night I heard Elspeth singing. I tell her about Sean's diary and his accusations. I explain the phone call from Sharon and the woman's name on the estate agents' notes; the storage unit and all my things packed away in boxes marked 'The Bitch'.

'Okay, Maggie,' she says, her voice a steady contrast to my agitated one. 'Let's slow down a bit. What I'm most concerned about here is what you've just told me about hearing voices.'

'You think I'm going mad, don't you?' I say, sitting up straight. 'But I'm not – I –'

'No, I don't think you're going mad but I do think, taking into account your medical history, we have to act fast on this.'

I feel exposed. She is seeing my past, all the horrors I've hidden for so long. She knows what I'm capable of.

'And for that reason I'm going to prescribe a different form of anti-anxiety medication,' she says. 'I'll print off the prescription first thing tomorrow morning then either you or Sonia can come and collect it.'

'More pills?' I say.

Julia nods her head.

'I think you'll find these a lot gentler but no less effective,' she says.

She stands up from the bed and straightens her jacket.

'I'll let Sonia know,' she says. 'In the meantime, do try to get plenty of rest, eat well and let's organize an appointment at the surgery in a week's time to see how the medication is going.'

I nod my head then watch as she opens the door and steps out into the hallway. I hear her talking to Sonia about the prescription and then all is quiet. A couple of minutes later the door opens and Sonia comes in.

'I brought you a cup of tea,' she says, putting a bulky blue mug down on the table beside me. 'How are you feeling?'

I can't think how to answer truthfully, so I close my eyes and lay my head back on the pillow.

'I know this is hard, Maggie,' she says, sitting down beside me. 'And if I'm honest I've never had to deal with someone who's gone through what you have. My last job was an old woman with mobility problems and the one before that was a middle-aged fella who'd broken his leg. He was a stubborn old sod that one. Anyway, what I'm saying is that in my eyes you're doing amazingly considering what you've been through.'

'Thank you, Sonia,' I say.

'Hey, it's what I'm here for,' she says. 'Listen, I've been thinking. How about we try to get your stuff back from that storage unit? It will be good for you to have your familiar things around. Perhaps having some of Elspeth's stuff will help too.'

'I don't know if I could afford to,' I say, taking a sip of tea. 'I'd have to hire a van and that would be expensive. I've got just about enough in the bank to last until my benefits come in.'

'Now that's where I can help,' says Sonia, smiling. 'I've got this mate, Sid. He's got a big old transit van and he owes me a favour. I spoke to him this morning while you were sleeping and he said he'd come with me to empty the unit. We could have it all done by tomorrow. What do you think?'

'If it's not too much trouble for your friend then that would be wonderful,' I say, my eyes filling up. 'Thank you, Sonia. I mean that, thank you, I don't deserve . . .'

And then all the pain and anguish of the last few months comes spilling out and I begin to sob.

'Oh, Maggie, love, don't cry,' says Sonia.

She takes the mug of tea from my shaking hands and puts it on the bedside table. Then she takes my hand and strokes it gently.

'Hey, it's going to be okay, I promise you,' she says, and though I know she's wrong, it will never be okay, I allow myself to close my eyes and for one moment let her hold me.

39

Dear Mummy,

You didn't reply to my letter. I hope you are okay.

Things aren't very good here.

Zoe has been acting really strangely. Weasel Face took her to the hospital yesterday and when she came home she just laid on her bunk making strange noises, like she was in pain or crying or both. That is odd because Zoe is one of the strongest people I know and she never cries.

When I was getting ready for bed she asked if I'd heard back from you and when I said no she said that it was no surprise. She said parents always let their kids down; that it's part of life. She said that if she was me she would stop writing and just get on with things, stop deluding myself.

But I think she was saying those things because she's poorly, because of whatever happened at the hospital and because of the pain.

I know you wouldn't leave me here Mummy. I just know.

Anyway I'm going to put a stamp on this letter and send it to Freya first thing in the morning.

I've written my address on the top again. You can't miss it.

I love you.
Your lovely daughter xxx

40

Tuesday 8 August

'Jesus, Maggie, where are we going to put all this stuff?'

Sonia is sitting in the middle of the living-room floor surrounded by piles of books and papers, the bulk of the contents of my 'office' boxes.

'It must have taken you years to build up this collection,' says Sonia, opening up a crisp hardback edition of *To The Lighthouse*.

'Yes, it did,' I say. 'But then I've always loved books, always needed to have them around me. When I was little my family would buy me them for Christmas and birthdays and then . . . well, I made a great hash of my life when I was fifteen and I ended up flunking all my exams.'

'Is that when you were admitted to the psychiatric unit?' says Sonia.

'How do you know about that?'

'When I collected you from the riverbank the other night you were quite delirious,' she says, her face flushing. 'You were begging me not to take you back there. To the unit. Look, I'm sorry if I've over-stepped the mark.'

'It's okay,' I say. 'It's actually quite a relief to not have to hide it. I've become very good at hiding things.'

'It's nothing to be ashamed of,' says Sonia. 'Most people will suffer with some kind of mental health issue in their lifetime.'

'Yes,' I say, looking down at the books. 'But most people don't then go on to lose their daughter too.'

'No,' says Sonia quietly.

I feel bad then. She's just a young girl. How can I expect her to understand?

'Anyway,' I say. 'Where was I? Oh, yes, my exams. I should have done resits but I was in no fit state. But books, reading, writing, those things were always a huge part of my life, particularly Virginia Woolf's books. They got me through so much. When I read her books real life fell away and I could block out all the bad stuff. Sean used to tell this story of how we first met. I was temping as a receptionist at an asset management company. I had to sit behind this vast wooden desk and smile politely at all the suits as they arrived each morning. This one morning Sean came in for a job interview and I completely blanked him because I was so engrossed in my book.'

My voice catches then and I stop, lost in the memory of Sean, his beautiful smile, the way he just seemed to understand.

'That's a great story,' says Sonia gently. 'What a way to meet your future husband.'

'Yeah, well,' I say, trying not to think about that day and all its promise. 'It didn't turn out so great, did it?'

I stand up and look at the rest of the room. My newly discovered laptop is charging next to the socket, and there's a pile of unopened boxes stacked up against the far wall. Those ones are Elspeth's and though Sonia has offered to help go through them I know that I need to be alone to do that.

'Shall I start putting these on to the shelves?' says Sonia, gesturing to the books.

'No, there's no need,' I say. 'I can do that later. Why don't you head home now? You've been such a help.'

'If you're sure,' says Sonia, standing up. 'I'd planned to meet my mate Tina for a drink later.'

'That sounds nice,' I say as I walk her to the door. 'Where are you going?'

'Just into town,' she says. 'There's a new bar just opened that Tina likes the look of. It'll be full of hipsters but it should be a laugh.'

'Well, enjoy yourself,' I say, suddenly feeling very old.

'I'll try to,' she says, opening the door. 'Though we'll probably just end up talking about our dissertations. We're such a pair of bores. Anyway, have a good night too, Maggie. And if you need me for anything I'll have my phone right next to me all night.' She looks at me warily.

'I'll be fine,' I say brightly. 'You go and enjoy your evening.'

'Okay,' she says, smiling. 'I'll see you tomorrow.'

'See you tomorrow, Sonia, and thanks again,' I say, closing the door behind her.

I go into the kitchen and open the cupboard. There's a bottle of red wine in there. Sonia bought it for me when I moved in last week, a sweet house-warming gift. I shouldn't really be drinking while I'm taking the antidepressants but one won't harm. I don't have any wine glasses so I take a mug from the draining board and pour a good measure into it. Then I take it into the living room and go over to the pile of boxes. I pull one of them towards me – it's marked 'The Bitch: Office' – and slowly pull the masking tape off the seal. When I open it up I get a whiff of Pomegranate Noir. The two scented candles that used to sit on the bookshelves in my study have been placed on the top. I take them out and put them on the floor beside me; relics from another life. Then I dig deeper into the box and lift out notepad after notepad. I flick through them. They are filled with ideas for new books, for short stories, even a screen-play. One of the pages is filled with messy handwriting. I look closer and see that it's an early outline of my novel. It was initially called *Afternoons with Virginia*, then, when it started to evolve, I'd changed the title to *Drowned Words*. It seemed to fit with how I was feeling. The premise was the same though: a lonely young mother conducting imaginary conversations with a dead writer. I'd thought it up when I was sitting by the stones with Elspeth a couple of years ago. She used to love to count the stones; it was a form of meditation for her. That day she had been so lost in her counting she wouldn't answer me when I tried to engage her in conversation. So I began to talk to Virginia Woolf in my head, remembering how her words had made me feel centred when I read them at the unit. Elspeth had stopped counting then and asked what I was doing – I must have been moving my lips. When I told her, she shrugged her shoulders and said, 'Well, don't expect her to answer you back. I've tried and she never does.'

My funny, eccentric girl. God, I miss her. I put the notebook back in the box then turn to one of the boxes marked Elspeth.

I run my finger round the letters of her name, remembering the day I chose it. Sean and I were sitting having brunch at a little place on Battersea Rise. I was two weeks shy of the due date, the morning sickness that had dogged me in the early days had dissipated and I felt wonderful, like a newly ripened peach. 'She's kicking,' I said, grabbing Sean's hand and placing it to my tummy. 'Can you feel it?' Sean's eyes were gleaming with happiness. He drew closer and whispered to the bump: 'Hey there, missy. What are you up to in there? You ready to come out yet?' Then he'd looked up at me and said, 'We should think of a name, now that we know it's a girl.' And without thinking, I said, 'What about Elspeth?' Sean had repeated the name under his breath then nodded and said, 'I like it, where did it come from?' I told him it was the first name that came to mind. And it was true. It was like the name had been buried in my sub-conscious all these years, waiting for my baby to come along and claim it.

Taking a long sip of wine, I slowly peel the masking tape from the seal. The box falls open and I see the unmistakable floppy shape of Momo, Elspeth's favour-ite toy rabbit. I take it out carefully and hold it to my face. It still smells of Elspeth, a mix of talcum powder and sugared almonds. 'Oh, Momo,' I whisper.

But as I place the toy on to the sofa, a sick feeling courses through me. This means Momo hadn't been in the car with us that night. Elspeth always had to have him with her whenever we went out in the car. It all stemmed from the fright she'd got when Sean locked her in the car outside the dry-cleaner's. For months afterwards she would scream and cry when-ever we tried to get her into the car. Then Sean had an idea. He remembered Momo. The little toy had been Elspeth's comforter when she was a baby. As she got older she had consigned Momo to the toy cupboard with the rest of her baby things but now he was needed again. I'll never forget the look on her face when Sean came out of the house holding Momo. She was reticent at first but then Sean told her that Momo was her lucky mascot and that if she held on to him the fear would go away. After that we took Momo on every car journey. Elspeth insisted on it. So how the hell did I get her in that car without him?

I flop down on to the sofa and take the toy in my hands. Closing my eyes, I see that image, the one that has flashed in front of me so many times since I woke up. I'm strapping Elspeth into the back of the car. She looks up at me with indignant eyes. 'I'm not going, Mummy, and you can't make me.'

Momo wasn't with us. If that was the case then we must have left in a dreadful rush. Why was I in such a hurry to go out at that time of night? Any other evening Elspeth would be in bed by then and I would be happily ensconced at my desk, plunging into the next chapter of my novel. The thought of driving off into the night just doesn't make any sort of sense.

I place Momo back on to the cushion beside me. I sit for a moment trying to summon the courage to empty the rest of the boxes but I feel prickly with nerves. I take another sip of wine and close my eyes.

'Think, Maggie, think,' I mutter to myself. 'Where the hell were you going?'

Then I glance across at my laptop. It must be charged by now. I get up from the sofa, taking my wine with me. I sit down on the floor and take the computer on to my lap. Opening the lid, I hold my breath and wait for the dark screen to come to life. After a couple of moments it does and my heart does a little somersault in my chest as the screensaver appears. It's a photo of me, Sean and Elspeth, taken on holiday in Whitstable a couple of years ago. We're sitting on the shingle beach, all huddled together. Elspeth is in the middle and Sean and I have our arms wrapped round her, like a precious gift. Her hair is in bunches and she is wearing a purple T-shirt with 'Whitstable Oyster Festival 2014' emblazoned across the front.

Oh, how she loved that holiday. The best thing about Whitstable for Elspeth was that the beach was made of shingle instead of sand. She'd spend the day counting stones and putting them into piles of even numbers while Sean and I sat back on our deckchairs and read our books. The other children would be running around, splashing in the sea and playing Frisbee, but Elspeth was perfectly content to just sit amongst her stones.

I put my hand towards the screen and touch her face. My beautiful girl. Then I think back to that last trip to Whitstable, the one cut short because of Sean's work commitments, and a cold sensation ripples through me. There will be no more holidays now, no more smiles.

The computer starts to load and Elspeth's face is soon obscured with tiny blue folders. Wiping away a tear, I read the names of the folders and remember the life I once had, the person I once was.

- Household
- Elspeth School
- Photos
- Afternoons with Virginia Notes
- Rodmell History
- Lewes Loves Libraries Blog
- Short stories
- Ideas
- Motivational Quotes
- Reading List: Drowned Words
- Novel: Draft 1
- Novel: Draft 2
- Novel: Draft 3

Then Word starts to load up. All the documents I had left open that day appear on the screen, one after the other. The first is the chapter breakdown of my novel. I always kept that open as I worked so I could refer to it. The next is the latest draft of the manuscript. I scroll through to see where I ended up that day. The word count sits at 67,529. The very last sentence I had written was: 'She mulled the idea over and over in her head. The temptation to jump was a momentary one, a flutter of wings across her consciousness but . . .'

And there I had stopped, left the sentence hanging, the cursor flashing on and off like a siren. I think back to the flashback I'd had in the job centre, my phone buzzing on the desk. Was that why I'd left the sentence unfinished?

I minimize the manuscript and see that another document has opened up. It's a consent form sent by the school secretary. Elspeth was due to go on a class trip to the Jurassic coast in Dorset. As usual, I was to go along as a helper. Elspeth insisted I did. She wouldn't settle otherwise. I imagine how much fun her classmates had on that trip, the midnight feasts, the fossil hunting. And my Elspeth . . . I quickly close the document, unable to read any further.

I scroll down to the bar at the bottom of the page and click to open my emails. I have to try my very best to keep a cool, calm head. The fact that I left my sentence unfinished like that means that either there was an emergency with Elspeth or I got an urgent text – possibly from Sean? With no phone to check, my inbox may provide an answer.

The page opens up and I gasp as I see I have 3,064 unopened emails. I feel dizzy as I scroll. Most of them are junk. I skim through them, working my way from the first email, advertising 2 for 1 on skin care at Boots, sent yesterday, all the way back through

August, July, June and May. There are tons of condolence messages from the parents of Elspeth's school friends. I can't read those. Not now.

When I get to 12th May I slow down. Surely the answer will be here, there will be an email to explain it all. But there is nothing. Three emails. One sent in the morning from the school with the consent form attached, one from Amazon suggesting books I might like and one notification that I have a new follower on the Twitter page I set up years ago but have rarely used. I click on the name of the follower. It's a man called Tony Martinez, a fantasy writer from Idaho who has 1.3m followers. A spam bot.

I shake my head, take a sip of wine and then click on 'sent messages'. The only message I sent that day was a reply to the school secretary saying that I would sign the consent form and get it back to her ASAP and also confirming that I would be coming along as a parent helper. Nothing in my emails points towards some urgent situation where I had to leave my desk, bundle Elspeth into the car and go speeding off into the night.

I click back on to my inbox and scroll through again. And then I see a name, clustered amongst the emails from sympathetic parents, that makes me go cold. On 26th June I received an email from B. Cosgrove.

Ben.

I sit for a moment, my shaking hands hovering over the mouse pad. Then I close my eyes and click it open. But the name at the bottom of the email is not Ben's; it's his mother, Barbara. I enlarge the message and start to read.

Maggie,

Well Larkfields now has a new occupant and I hope that it heralds the end of you and your family's link to this area for good. Now Harry has died I no longer have to keep up the pretence. You don't fool me Maggie, unlike the rest of them, Harry included, who were sucked in by your lies. I know exactly what you were planning on doing that night by the river and though I am glad that your plan was thwarted I am sickened that your little girl had to lose her life because of her mother's idiocy. I have spoken to the hospital and they don't seem too hopeful that you will come through this. Maybe that is a blessing. Maybe then we can all get on with our lives, your husband will be able to grieve his child and I will be able to protect my son.

It's taken me almost thirty years to say how I really feel, Maggie. Perhaps now I can sleep soundly at night.

Barbara

I slam the lid of the laptop shut, and take my cup into the kitchen. Barbara's words twist through my head. I'm sad to hear that Harry, Ben's father, who was so kind to me when the bad thing happened, is dead, but I can't really think about that now. More pressing is working out what Barbara was trying to imply in that email. I stand for a moment, my hands resting on the kitchen counter, and then a horrible realization creeps up my spine. I may still have no idea why I put Elspeth into the back of the car and drove her to her death on the 12th May but someone does and that someone is Barbara Cosgrove.

41

Dear Mummy,

*Zoe has been really ill for the last few weeks though at first I
didn't know quite what was wrong with her. She refused to
go to school and just lay on her bed staring at the ceiling. She
stopped listening to her music, stopped smoking; she wouldn't
even come down to dinner. I got really worried about her
because she was getting so skinny and pale. Weasel Face
said she needed to snap out of it but she didn't do anything to
help, she just left her there. After dinner I would come up to
see if she was okay but when I tried to talk she'd just turn
on her side and make this horrible noise, like a really long
sigh. I smuggled food out of the dining room and left it by the
bed but in the morning it would still be there.*

*Then last night she asked me if I would find a CD for
her. I asked which one and she said it was in her top drawer.
I was going to ask why it wasn't on the shelf like her other
CDs but when I opened the drawer and saw it I realized
why. Most of the music she plays is by American rappers,
especially Tupac, who I'd never heard of before I came here.
Now I know every word of that album because Zoe has
played it so much. Anyway, the CD in the drawer was*

Elton John's Greatest Hits. I took it out and showed it to Zoe, asked if this was the one she wanted. She nodded her head then lay back on the bed and told me to play it. 'Put track five on,' she said.

I did as I was told then went and sat on my bunk. The song started. It was 'Goodbye Yellowbrick Road'. I'd heard it on the radio back at home. I sat there and listened to the first few lines and then Zoe started singing, really quietly. It was nice. She had a really lovely voice. I closed my eyes for a bit and listened to her singing. Then the song ended and she asked me to turn it on again. When I sat back down I asked her why she liked the song so much and she said that her mum used to play it all the time when she was little. They used to dance around the kitchen singing into cardboard tubes and pretending they were on Top of the Pops. I asked her where her mum was now and she said that she'd died of an overdose when Zoe was five. I tried to ask her some more questions then, about how she ended up here, but she just started singing again. After a while I joined in too, though I can't sing as well as Zoe. When it finished she said, 'That was really nice. Thanks.' And we went to sleep.

When I woke up this morning her bed was empty. She wasn't in the dining room at breakfast and she wasn't in the entrance waiting for me as I left the house. I guessed she must have gone to school early but then at hometime this afternoon she wasn't waiting for me at the gate. I felt something weird in the pit of my stomach as I walked back; like freezing cold *air was blowing right through me. And then I saw two police cars parked outside the house. When I got inside Weasel Face was standing with a policeman. She told me to go to my room but I sat on the landing and listened to what they were saying. I heard the policeman say that a body had been found on the railway track. And then he said her full name: Zoe Maria Mathers. I wanted to scream but I knew I'd get in trouble for snooping if I made a sound. So I went back to my room, lay on Zoe's bed and played that song over and over until I fell asleep.*

I've just woken up and the first thing I thought about was you and how much I need you.

Please answer this letter Mummy.

Please come and get me.

I love you.
Your lovely daughter xxx

42

Wednesday 9 August

As I make my way across the farmyard towards the house I'm struck by how neglected it looks. The tarmac is covered in potholes and weeds; the door of the barn is broken and hanging off its hinges. It's like I'm walking through a ghost estate. How could Barbara have let Ketton House Farm fall into such disrepair.

My stomach twists as I approach the farmhouse. The thought of confronting Barbara terrifies me but I know I have to do it.

Unlike the yard, the house appears to be in good order. The windows are gleaming and the doorstep looks like it's been freshly painted. There's a basket of geraniums hanging above the door. The ground is damp beneath as though someone has just watered them. I imagine Barbara behind the door, watering can in hand, ready to pounce.

Come on, Maggie, I think to myself as I stand on the step, you have to do this. I take a deep breath, then knock three times on the door. I'm not even sure what I'm going to say. My head has turned to fudge. I wait a few moments then knock again. There's still no answer, though I'm sure I can hear the muffled sound of voices behind the door. Maybe she left the radio on before she went out. I knock one more time just in case before turning and walking back across the farmyard.

I head for the gate, but as I do, something on the far left of the yard catches my eye. I turn and see a dilapidated round building with moss and ivy trailing over it.

The playhouse. Where most kids would have been content with a plastic Wendy house, Ben got his very own outbuilding, a roundhouse built in the late 1800s. We used to play for hours in here when I was a kid. I remember thinking it was like the turret of a castle that had fallen to the ground. But then it had become something else; something darker.

I stand looking at it, willing myself not to go there, to just turn round and get the hell out of here. But curiosity gradually gets the better of me and I slowly make my way towards it.

The windows are filthy and cracked; the tiles on the roof are broken, the stone exterior crumbling. I think back to the last time I was here. It was the night of Barbara's party. When we arrived Barbara had swept my parents into the house, thrusting glasses of champagne into their hands. 'Oh, Margaret,' she called over her shoulder as I stood awkwardly on the step. 'You don't want to be in here with the old fogeys. Why don't you go and see Ben and his friends? They're in the playhouse.'

Though Ben and I had been friends as kids we'd drifted apart as we got older. After all, there was a four-year age gap between us and though we had loved playing games of hide and seek and swimming in the river when we were five and nine, the older Ben had decided it was rather uncool to be hanging around with an awkward child. That night, despite my glamorous dress, I still felt like a little kid, and as I walked towards the playhouse my hands were sweating with nerves.

Loud music was coming from inside: 'How Soon is Now?' by the Smiths. To this day I can't listen to that song. I'd stood on the step, practising what I would say. I had to seem cool, like I didn't really care. After all, this party was full of Ben's friends from Oxford, clever people with money and the right clothes, and I was just some kid Ben used to play hide and seek with. When I'd finally plucked up the courage to knock on the door it had been opened by a beautiful girl with black bobbed hair, flawless olive skin and pouty scarlet lips.

'Yeah?' she'd said, looking me up and down.

I'd tried to speak but I was so nervous I just started stuttering. Then Ben appeared in the door with a weird smirk on his face. I discovered later that this was because he was stoned out of his head.

'Zoshi, are you scaring little Maggie?' he laughed.

Every part of me wanted to run away but I didn't. Instead I followed him inside and sealed my fate.

Enough, I tell myself, this isn't what you came here for. Just leave it alone. But then, before I know what I'm doing, I'm pushing the door open.

The damp hits me as I enter and I start to cough. I grab my inhaler and take a good few puffs. When I've composed myself I look around and am met with a sight so startling I'm almost knocked off my feet.

It's like I've stepped inside a time capsule. The whole room is exactly as it was in 1988. The walls are covered in posters of the Smiths and the Waterboys – Ben's favourite bands. Used joss sticks are dotted around the stone fireplace and the sofas are draped in the Aztec throws that Ben brought back from his volunteering trip to Mexico. I can still hear the sounds of the party that night, the high-pitched laughter and smash of glass when Ben dropped the tray of munchies on to the stone floor, the way the music seemed to warp as the evening wore on though only later would I find out why. As I stand in the middle of the room it seems like the last thirty years have never happened; that the world stopped in 1988.

I step over the piles of vinyl records that are scattered across the floor. The air is thick with dust and I put my hand over my mouth. Then I see it, a small wooden door almost hidden in a little alcove on the far side of the room. Don't do it, Maggie, I tell myself, but my feet are leading the way.

Slowly, slowly, I push open the door. I'd forgotten how tiny this room was. In my memories it had taken on epic proportions, become a monster of a thing. The reality is a small, round bedroom with a curved window looking out on to the farmland and the Downs beyond. I stand at the door, not daring to enter. The single bed still has the red and black quilt cover on it. The walls are bare now though I remember there being a huge black-and-white print of Marilyn Monroe leaning over a balcony. I remember because I had fixed my eyes on her all the time it was happening.

I step inside the room, keeping my hands clasped to my mouth. I don't want to breathe this air because I know what it contains. I step towards the bed and place my hand on the pillow, checking to see if it's real. When I bring my hand back it is sticky with cobweb.

I turn from the bed and slowly walk across the room. The bulky oak wardrobe stands by the window. I remember that. When we were kids and this was simply a playhouse, Ben used to make us stand in there with our eyes closed. 'When you open them, we'll be in Narnia,' he'd tell me.

But we never were.

I open the door of the wardrobe and a waft of dust and mothballs hits me. It's empty save for some wire coat hangers and a sticker on the inside door showing a smiley face and the name Benjamin spelled out in stars.

I close the wardrobe and turn to the chest of drawers wedged against the wall on the other side of the window. I pull out the top drawer. It's stuffed with papers. I pick one out. It's a cardboard certificate. I read the words across the top of it: 'Awarded to Benjamin Cosgrove for excellence in spelling 13/09/1980'. Why the hell have they kept all this junk, I think to myself as I put the certificate back and close the drawer.

I pull out the middle one, expecting to see more rubbish, but this drawer is full of photograph albums. The top one has a Union Jack cover. I lift it out and open the first page. It's full of baby photos of Ben. The first shows him, chubby-cheeked and grinning, on a rocking horse in the drawing room of Ketton House. The next one is a photograph of Ben's father, Harry, sitting on a horse.

As I look at his kind face I remember him coming to see me in the psychiatric unit. Nobody else had bothered to visit. My parents had said it was best if they left me alone; Barbara was still furious. And Ben, well, he'd returned to university and cut me out of his life completely. As time went on it felt like what had happened between us was some strange dream, so much so that I began to doubt that Ben Cosgrove had even existed. The only person who had any concern for me was Harry. I remember how I sobbed when I saw him standing in the waiting room. He had worn a suit. For a countryman who spent most of his days in a waxed jacket and wellies, this was a poignant touch. He stayed with me the whole afternoon. We made small talk mostly. I told him how bad the food was and he said if he'd known he'd have packed a couple of Cornish pasties for me. He knew how much I used to like them. I didn't have the heart to tell him I wasn't really eating anything. Talking to Harry, I felt like a child again. I was still only fourteen, a baby, and yet I'd been forced to become an adult overnight. When the time came for Harry to leave I gripped hold of him, terrified of being left alone in that place. But Harry was so kind. He told me that everything was going to be fine, that I just had to be there for a few more months to get myself better and then life could begin again. But it was his parting words that stayed with me, that helped me get through those next few months without losing my mind. As we stood at the door of the visitors' room he took my hand and squeezed it tightly. 'You're a good person, Maggie Carrington,' he said as tears cascaded down my face. 'Don't ever forget that.'

And he said it so sincerely that I believed it.

I turn the page and flick through image after image of Ben at various ages and then suddenly there I am. I must be about four years old and I'm sitting on the front step of Ketton House. I beam up at the camera with a gappy-toothed smile. I stare at the photo for a few moments wondering what it is about it that is making me feel strange. And then I realize it's because I look so much like Elspeth. When the bad thing happened, my mother, in a fit of rage, had thrown away all her photos of me so I never quite remembered what I looked like. I always thought Elspeth was more like Sean, but looking at this photo the likeness is startling.

I don't want to see any more, I think to myself, as I close the album and shove it back in the drawer. And yet, I can't resist opening the bottom drawer. This one is lined with flowery scented paper. Drawer liners. My mother always used them. On top of the liners are piles of notebooks. I pick one up and flick through pages of notes on *Macbeth*. They must be Ben's notebooks from Oxford. I rummage through the pile and then I see something that makes my blood go cold. There, at the bottom of the drawer, is a yellowing newspaper cutting with the words DRAMA AT THE

RIVERBANK emblazoned across the top. It's dated 15th January 1989. I pick it up and see, below the headline, a black-and-white photograph of me.

'No,' I gasp, dropping the cutting on the floor and running out of the room. 'No, no, no.'

43

Dear Mummy,

What does it take to be your daughter?
 Do I have to be pretty?
 Do I have to be smart?
 Do I have to be popular?
 I'm trying so hard to be all these things, so that when you see me you won't be disappointed. But I just can't understand why you wouldn't reply to my letters. You can see in them how sad and scared I've been and then there was all the stuff about Zoe. It's like you have no heart, like you've just thrown me away and washed your hands of it all.

 I've never had a sister before though Zoe was the closest thing. She was the only person who cared for me these last few months, the only one who listened to me, who stuck up for me when those boys were bullying me. Every night when I go to sleep I hear that song in my head, the one we listened to the night before she died, and now I know the words off by heart I can see what they meant to her. She wanted to go home, back to that kitchen where she was dancing with her mum. But she never got there, she just ended up on that railway track.

Zoe and I were more alike than I realized. We both wanted our mums to come and get us. We both just wanted to go home. Zoe wasn't the cleverest or the prettiest but she had a kind heart and she looked after me. I wish I'd been able to do the same for her; wish I could have stopped her doing what she did.

I don't know what you want from me Mummy but I'll keep on trying my best to be good. I don't know why I was sent away but I can't let myself believe that it was because you didn't want me any more. Freya says you just need to get better and maybe that's what it's all about. I hope so.

Please write back Mummy.

Please don't give up on me.

I need you.
Your lovely daughter xxx

44

I'm still trembling when I get back to the flat an hour later. The smell inside the playhouse lingers around me. How could Barbara have left it undisturbed all these years? And the old newspaper cutting in the bottom of the drawer: why would Ben have kept that? Why would he need a reminder of that terrible day? I take my keys out of my pocket and fumble with the lock. Why won't it work? Then I turn the handle and it yields. Did I forget to lock it?

I step inside, my heart thudding inside my chest. I close the door behind me, then as I go towards the living room I hear a noise. There's someone in the kitchen. Just turn round and get help, I say to myself, but I'm so scared I can't move. Then I hear footsteps. They are coming this way. Please don't let them hurt me.

'Maggie?'

Relief floods through me as I hear a familiar voice.

'Sonia,' I gasp. 'What are you doing? You almost gave me a heart attack.'

'I'm sorry,' she says, as she comes towards me, her face flushed. 'I was already on my way over here when

I got your text saying you were popping out. I thought I may as well let myself in and get on with some cleaning. I hope you don't mind.'

'Sorry?' I say, still feeling shaken. 'What . . . what did you say?'

'I said I hope you don't mind that I let myself in,' she says, looking embarrassed. 'I mean, I had the key and, well, it's not like I'm breaking in or anything.'

'Of course not,' I say, composing myself. 'You just gave me a bit of a fright, that's all.'

'I'm so sorry,' she says, her eyes widening. 'I really didn't mean to . . .'

'It's fine, Sonia. Honestly,' I say, as I follow her into the kitchen.

'Well, I've done the bathroom,' she says, wiping her forehead with the back of her hand. 'And I was just about to make a start on the vacuuming when I got it into my head to make some bread. I thought it would go nicely with the soup.'

She lifts a tea towel from the freshly baked loaf and brings it over to me.

'What do you think? It's a bit burnt on the bottom but it should be okay.'

'It's wonderful, Sonia,' I say, my eyes twitching with exhaustion. 'Just wonderful.'

I feel faint suddenly and put my hands out on to the counter to steady myself.

'Are you okay, Maggie?' says Sonia, placing the

bread on the table. 'God, I'm so stupid. Here I am wittering on about bread and I haven't even asked you how it went today. You said you were going to see an old friend?'

I exhale slowly and as the dizziness subsides I raise my head. Sonia puts her hand on my shoulder.

'Do you want to talk about it?' she says gently.

'I'm very, very tired,' I say. 'I think I might just go and have a lie-down.'

'Of course,' she says. 'Can I get you anything? A glass of water? A warm drink?'

'No thanks, I'm fine. I just . . . I just want to go to sleep.'

When I reach the privacy of my room I slump down on the bed and let the shock of the last few hours sink in. Being back in that playhouse felt like walking through a nightmare. Every little detail of that night came back to me magnified. The dizziness, the blood. It just won't end, will it, I tell myself as I close my eyes and drift off to sleep. It will never end.

All is quiet now. Sonia has just put her head round the door to tell me that she is going home and that there's some soup and bread in the kitchen if I feel hungry. I thanked her but the last thing I can face right now is food.

I feel very peculiar, as though I'm floating above

myself. Perhaps it's the shock of everything. I turn on my side and try to go back to sleep but as I close my eyes the doorbell rings.

I take my phone from the bedside table and look at the time. It's 8.30 p.m. Who could be at the door at this hour? Maybe if I ignore them whoever it is will go away. But then it rings again and I hear a voice calling through the letter box.

'Maggie. Are you in there? It's Julia.'

Julia? I think to myself as I make my way down the corridor. What does she want?

I take a quick look in the living-room mirror as I pass. I look dreadful. It's been days since I last washed my hair and my face is pale and blotchy. I run my fingers through my hair so I look a little more presentable then I take the chain off the door and open it.

'Hi, Maggie,' says Julia. 'I just wanted to pop round and see how you were getting on with the new medication. May I come in?'

As always, she looks a vision of elegance. Today's trouser suit is deep purple velvet with a pretty lilac lace camisole underneath.

'Of course,' I say. 'Come through.'

'Something smells nice,' she says as she steps inside. 'Have you been cooking?'

'No, that was Sonia,' I say as I lead her into the living room. 'She's been baking bread.'

'Well, I hope you've been eating it,' says Julia. 'Good nutrition is vital when you're healing, mentally as well as physically.'

'I've been trying,' I say. 'Though I've never had much of an appetite.'

'Listen, Maggie, I was hoping we could have a little chat,' she says, her voice softening. 'Would that be okay?'

'A chat? What about?'

'Don't look so alarmed,' she says, smiling. 'Listen, why don't you sit down and I'll put the kettle on. What would you like?'

'Er, I don't mind really,' I say. 'There's some camomile tea in the cupboard.'

'Okay,' she says as she disappears into the kitchen. 'I won't be a sec.'

I sit on the sofa and close my eyes. As I listen to Julia preparing the tea in the kitchen I suddenly feel very calm. I like that she's here.

'Here we go.'

I look up as she comes in with the tea. She places a cup in front of me.

'Are you not having one?' I say, picking up the cup.

'No,' she says, sitting down on the armchair opposite me. 'Water's fine for me.'

She reaches into her bag and pulls out a bottle of

mineral water, an expensive brand. She unscrews the top, takes a sip then puts it back in the bag.

'So, Maggie,' she says, sitting up straight. 'It's been a few days since I prescribed the new medication. How are you managing with the tablets?'

I roll the question over and over but my mind is blank.

'Maggie?'

'Oh, they're fine,' I say. 'I've been feeling a little floaty today but I'm not sure whether that's the tablets or just me.'

'When did you last take one?'

'About an hour ago.'

Julia narrows her eyes.

'And are you still feeling floaty?'

'I'm just very tired,' I say, leaning back into the sofa. 'But I don't know if it's the tablets or the shock.'

'Shock?' says Julia, frowning.

'I went to see someone I used to know,' I tell her, my voice slow and laboured. 'And it just brought back some painful memories, that's all.'

'Okay,' says Julia, her features softening.

'There's something else that's been troubling me,' I say. 'Something I found.'

'Oh? What was it?'

'I'll show you.'

I put my tea down on the table next to me then

stand up and go to the bedroom. The letter is where I left it, on the radiator. It got so wet the other night I was worried it was ruined but the heat has dried it and the writing can still be made out. I carefully lift it off and bring it back into the living room.

'Sean, or someone close to him, had put all of my things in a storage unit,' I say to Julia. 'When I went there the other day I found this.'

I hand her the letter.

'It was underneath one of the boxes.'

'What is it?' she says, holding the paper tentatively.

'Read it,' I say, returning to the sofa.

I watch as she unfolds the paper. As she reads she lets out a little gasp, then drops the letter on to her lap. When she looks up her eyes are watery. Tiredness or tears? I can't be sure.

'It's from Elspeth,' I say. 'Though I have no idea when she wrote it.'

'Elspeth,' she repeats, nodding her head.

'Yes. She must have written it before she . . . My little girl wrote me a beautiful poem and I didn't even know.'

'What do you mean, you didn't know?'

'Well, she was always writing things and coming to show me but more often than not I'd be so engrossed in my own stuff I didn't notice. I can't remember ever reading this poem. Or else I did and then forgot all about it.'

Julia reads the poem again then looks up at me

with a strange expression on her face. She's judging me. I know she is. She's thinking, what kind of mother forgets something like that?

'And it was on the floor of the storage unit?' says Julia, folding the note.

'Yes,' I say. 'I was just about to leave when I saw it. It was wedged between two boxes.'

'How strange,' she says, wiping her eyes with the tip of her manicured finger. 'That you don't remember it.'

'Like I said, Elspeth would always be flitting about when I was working in my study but half the time I was so preoccupied with my work I didn't pay any attention.'

Julia looks at me and nods.

'I know what you're thinking,' I say. 'You're thinking I neglected her; that I'm a bad mother.'

'I'm not thinking that at all, Maggie,' says Julia. 'On the contrary, it sounds like you loved her very much.'

'Yes,' I say. 'And I should have loved her more. I should have read this poem when she gave it to me and I should have told her it was beautiful and that I loved her with all my heart, but I didn't and now it's too late.'

'At least you had that time together,' says Julia. 'It might have been short but some mothers and daughters don't even have that.'

I remember then that Julia's mother died when she was a baby and I realize how insensitive I've been.

'A child is the most precious thing in the world,' she says, wiping her eyes quickly as though embarrassed.

'Yes,' I say, quietly.

'You should keep this safe,' she says, handing the letter back to me.

'Do you know what hurts the most,' I say, placing the letter on my lap. 'The fact that I couldn't keep her safe . . . that I actually put her in danger that night.'

'I'm sure that wasn't the case,' says Julia. 'It was just a tragic accident. Nobody is suggesting you had anything to do with it, are they?'

I shake my head.

'I should go now,' says Julia, standing up. 'You look exhausted.'

She is right. My eyes are so tired I can barely keep them open.

I walk Julia to the door. The porch is dark so I turn the light on.

'Oh, you've got some post,' says Julia, bending down to pick something up from the mat.

She hands me it. It's a piece of folded-up paper. Probably a flyer.

'Thanks,' I say, tucking it under my arm as I unlock the door. 'Listen, thanks again for popping over, Julia, I really appreciate it.'

'Not a problem,' she says as she steps out on to the dark street. 'Now get yourself inside and try to rest, okay?'

'I will. Bye, Julia.'

'Bye, Maggie.'

I close the door and bolt it. When I come back into the living room the flyer falls on to the floor. I pick it up and make my way to the kitchen. I'm about to throw it in the bin when something catches my eye. The paper is thin and semi-transparent. I can see handwriting through it. This isn't a flyer.

I sit down at the kitchen table and unfold the paper. What I see chills me to the bone. It's a letter written in Elspeth's distinctive handwriting. I lay it out on the table and read:

Dear Mummy,

I'm so scared. I don't know why I have been sent here. Did I do something wrong? If I was naughty then I can make up for it. I promise I won't be naughty again. This place is very cold and dark. The walls are bare and white and nobody smiles. I miss my old room. I miss the smell of the countryside. All I see when I look out of the window is concrete and glass. It's like a prison. When can I come home? They have told me that you and Daddy are not coming back but that can't be true, you love me more than anything in this world, I know you do. I think about you all the time and wonder what you are doing. There are some books here. They're old and the pages are ripped but I don't want to read them anyway because stories and books just remind me of you and then I get upset.

Mummy you can't forget about me, even if you're angry with me I'm still your daughter.

Please don't leave me here. I need to be with you.

I promise I'll be a good girl and I won't make you cross.

I love you Mummy and I just want to come home.

Your lovely daughter xxx

45

Thursday 10 August

It's just coming up to 7 a.m. and the streets are deserted. I sat up through the night, reading and rereading Elspeth's letter, trying to work out what was going on. It seems she is trapped in some place along with 'others' and she is waiting for me to come and collect her. But there is no address on the letter, and it was hand-delivered without an envelope, so I have no way of tracking her down. I'm terrified that she is being held somewhere against her will, but where and by whom?

I push open the door of the police station and make my way across the now-familiar reception area to the main desk. An older woman with short grey hair sits behind it. She looks up as I approach. Her face is lined and she has a sour expression that deepens when she sees me. It is then, when I look down, that I see I am still in my pyjamas. I'd flung my coat over them and pulled on some trainers in my rush to get out of the house this morning. Still, I don't care, I just want to find out what's happened to Elspeth.

'Hello, can I help you?' says the woman.

'Er, yes,' I say, taking the letter out of my coat pocket. 'I'd like to speak to DS Grayling.'

'DS Grayling?'

'Yes,' I reply.

'DS Grayling's not here at the moment,' she says. 'Can I be of any help?'

I look at her. She's wearing a uniform and Grayling isn't here. I have no choice.

'This was put through my letter box last night,' I say, placing the letter on the desk.

The woman takes the letter and reads it. She frowns then looks up at me.

'Okay,' she says, sighing. 'And why is this a police matter?'

'This letter is from my daughter,' I say, my chest tightening with anxiety.

'Right,' says the woman. 'And that is a problem because . . .'

'It's a problem because my daughter is dead,' I say. 'She was killed in a car accident three months ago.'

The woman's expression changes. She picks up the letter and reads it again then she picks up the phone.

'One moment,' she says. 'I'll get one of the officers to come and see you.'

Ten minutes later I'm sitting in a small, stuffy interview room. The officer who 'came to see me' is PC Kitson, a short, stocky man in his late thirties.

He has made me a cup of tea and is now busy reading the letter for the second time.

'And you're sure you didn't see who delivered it?' he says, looking up at me from the other side of the table.

'I'm positive,' I reply. 'It was quite late, around nine thirty, and I was seeing my friend out. The letter was lying on the mat in the porch.'

He nods his head.

'From what you've told me, Mrs Allan, it sounds like some kind of prank.'

'No,' I say, my voice trembling. 'No, it's definitely her. It's Elspeth. Nobody else writes like this and the tone of it, the voice, it's her. My little girl is in danger. I just know it. She's being held somewhere against her will and whoever delivered this must know something. Can you not check it for fingerprints?'

He smiles awkwardly.

'Mrs Allan,' he says gently, 'we know that's impossible because your daughter passed away. She was identified by your husband at Lewes Victoria Hospital on the twelfth of May, and her funeral took place three weeks later. There is no doubt that she's dead.'

'But mistakes are made all the time,' I say, wiping my forehead which is damp with sweat. 'Morgues get bodies mixed up. I've read about it. God, I swear to you, this is Elspeth. It's her handwriting.'

'Your husband identified the body, Mrs Allan,'

he says firmly. 'And as your daughter only had minor facial injuries, it would have been a straightforward ID.'

I flinch. How can he say that so callously?

He has a file of notes sitting next to him; the details of Elspeth's death all neatly explained within. But this can't be explained. This is beyond reason. My instinct tells me the letter is from my daughter because as her mother I know; I just know.

'Actually,' I say, suddenly remembering something. 'My husband was in a state of shock when he identified her. He said so in the ICU diary. He was only in there for a few minutes, how could he have been one hundred per cent certain it was her?'

Kitson looks at me, confused.

'I can bring it in if you like, the diary,' I say, trying to remember where I left it. 'You can see for yourself.'

'Mrs Allan, your husband formally identified the body as being that of your daughter, Elspeth.'

I go to speak but then, noticing his expression, decide that it's not worth pursuing.

'My hunch is that this is some idiot's idea of a joke,' says PC Kitson, looking at the letter again. 'It's sick and insensitive but that's how some of these morons get their kicks. Honestly, I thought these trolls were all on the internet these days but it seems not.'

'But why would someone do that?' I say, my eyes

raw from crying. 'Why would someone pretend to be my daughter?'

'I don't know. As I said, there are some sick people out there. They hear about these accidents on the news and they want to get involved. It makes them feel significant though they're anything but.'

'I understand what you're saying,' I reply. 'And I've heard of people like the ones you're describing, internet trolls and what have you, but they are usually threatening or insulting. This letter doesn't seem like it was written by someone like that. And how could they replicate my daughter's handwriting?'

PC Kitson sighs and shakes his head.

'I don't know, could it be one of your daughter's school friends?' he says. 'In my experience children deal with grief in a variety of ways, some pretty strange.'

'If that was the case then it would mean a ten-year-old child had snuck out last thing at night to post it. That doesn't add up.'

'Didn't you say the letter was on the mat at nine thirty?' says Kitson. 'And you and your friend had been sitting in the front room for quite a while and not heard anything being put through the letter box?'

I nod my head.

'Well then, it could have been posted at any time during the evening,' he says. 'It's summer. Light nights. Kids are playing out for longer.'

'Some kids,' I say, glaring at him.

'I'm sorry,' he says, his face flushing. 'I didn't mean to be insensitive.'

'It's okay,' I say. 'I just want to find her.'

'Mrs Allan,' he says, getting to his feet, 'I'm sorry you've had to be exposed to this. It's the last thing a grieving parent should have to deal with.'

I nod my head and slowly stand up, feeling dizzy with the heat. I know he's never going to help me. I'm on my own.

'But if any more of these come through, let us know,' he says, opening the door.

'I will,' I say as we step out into the corridor. 'Oh and could I ask you to let DS Grayling know about the letter too? She's been working on this case.'

'DS Grayling's not here today,' he says, leading me back along the corridor towards reception. 'But I'll let her know what's happened.'

'Thank you.'

When we reach the main doors he leans over me to open them. It's then I see that he is still holding the letter in his hand.

'May I please keep that?' I say, turning to face him.

He looks down at the letter and frowns.

'I'm not sure if that's a good idea.'

'Please,' I say. 'I want to hold on to it.'

He looks at me with pity and who can blame him? Here I am standing in a pair of old pyjamas, insisting my dead daughter is alive somewhere. Still, despite what he thinks, I need that letter.

'Please?' I say.

He relents and hands me the letter.

'Thank you,' I say, then slip it into my coat pocket.

As I lie here on my bed, the letter still in my hands, I think back to the events of the morning. The police officer seemed convinced that the letter was just a silly prank and yet it is Elspeth's handwriting, tall and spidery. How could a random prankster replicate that?

None of it makes sense and the lack of support from the police just makes it all the more frustrating. I try to order my thoughts. What do I know? That Sean thinks I killed Elspeth; that on the day of the accident I put Elspeth into the car in her dressing gown and drove to the Plough Inn; that there may or may not have been someone standing on the riverbank dressed in red; that actually Elspeth might not even be dead but be trapped somewhere; that Barbara Cosgrove thinks I was planning to do something evil at the riverbank.

And then there is Freya Nielssen. Who is she?

My eyes grow heavy. I shouldn't be able to sleep after all that's happened, but something is dragging me down. I'm helpless, sucked in. I dream I'm at the river. I feel numb with fear but I know I have to go through with this; that there is no alternative. She's there in the water, she wants me to stop but I can't. Her eyes are full of panic. She screams and I push down hard on her shoulders. I feel her wriggling beneath the water. I know I should stop but some powerful force is guiding me; voices inside my head screaming at me to do it. Then, at the last moment, the voices fall silent and I come to my senses. I let go my grip and lift her to the surface.

But it's too late.

46

Dear Mummy,

I think Zoe was right. Parents just let you down. Why aren't you answering my letters? I know you've received them because Freya sent me a card the other week and she said she'd passed them on to you.

What is it Mummy? Why are you ignoring me? Is this it? I just get left here?

Weasel Face has moved me into another bedroom. The old one had too many memories of Zoe. I couldn't sleep in there. Every time I closed my eyes I saw her lying on the train tracks. The new room is better though I still have nightmares.

School is just as bad, worse actually because now I don't have Zoe to talk to when I get home. The other girls are being really horrible to me. There's a big group of them, led by this girl called Jade who sits on my table. It started with them stealing my pencil case, then hiding my coat, stupid things, but then since Zoe died it's just got worse and worse.

Last week I was sitting in the library reading my science book and I felt a jolt. I turned round and Jade was standing there grinning at me. She had a pair of scissors in one hand and a clump of hair in the other. It took me a couple of moments to realize that it was my hair. I could hear her laughing behind me as I ran to the toilets. I shut the door and went over to the mirror. When I saw what she had done I screamed. She'd cut off a chunk of my hair. I looked like a freak.

And that is what they started calling me. Freak. Every time I walked into the classroom I heard it and it was just low enough for the adults not to hear. Freak. Freak. That word hammered at my head. I heard it every moment of the day, from the time I woke up until I went to sleep at night. Sometimes I heard it in my dreams, a horrible chorus of girls repeating it over and over again, freak, freak, freak.

Anyway, a couple of days ago things changed. I became more like Zoe.

Jade thinks she's safe as long as she has that big group of friends around. Everywhere she goes they go with her. There are two who are her best friends – a short, fat girl called Heidi and a tall, spotty one called Paula – and they are the worst. While they are there to egg her on she can do what she likes. But then a couple of days ago Paula and Heidi were both off sick and Jade was by herself. At break, I saw her standing by the boiler room at the far end of the playground. She was bouncing a tennis ball against the wall. Up and down. Up and down. It had been raining and I wanted to look for snails. Since the trip to the museum I've been collecting specimens to examine. I don't know why I'm telling you this. Why would you be bothered? You can't even reply to my letters. Still, it makes me feel better to write it all down. Anyway, as I walked across the playground with my new specimen jar in my hand I felt Jade's eyes on me. There were no snails but I saw a fat brown slug on the path. I was just bending down to pick it up when I heard it.

'Freak.'

I looked up. She was still standing by the wall but she had stopped bouncing the tennis ball. She had her arms folded across her chest and her pug face was screwed up with hatred. I put the slug in the jar and walked up the path. I just wanted to go inside to the school library and concentrate on my experiment. But as I drew level with her she kicked my ankle and I fell over. The jar smashed to the ground. I jumped up to try and rescue the slug but she got there before I did or at least her foot did. I heard a horrible squishing noise as she ground the slug with her shoe.

I asked her why she did it and she said I was a freak, a weirdo who puts dead things in jars. She said that I was a loser whose parents had dumped me and that no wonder Zoe killed herself, having to put up with me.

And when she said that, my brain went all hot and fuzzy and I couldn't think straight. All I could see was her disgusting smile. It was horrible, like an evil clown. I wanted to wipe the smile off her face so I grabbed her hair and smashed her head against the wall, again and again and again. She started screaming but I didn't stop. I liked the fact that she was scared of me and I wanted her to learn a lesson. I wanted to smash all the horrible things that she had said about me out of her brain.

She started screaming then some teachers came out and pulled me off her. They started fussing over Jade and I was sent to the Head's office. I've been put in detention for a week and I have to see the school counsellor again to deal with my anger.

I don't care about any of it. I'm just glad I stood up to that witch. Whenever she sees me now she backs away. I've scared her and I'm glad.

47

I wake up sweating. I breathe out slowly, relieved that it was just a dream.

And then I hear it. Voices. I lie on the bed for a moment, fear gripping my insides. Someone is in the flat. Slowly, I haul myself up and walk to the door, opening it a fraction. 'Hello,' I call, but my voice is croaky from sleep and the word comes out as a whimper.

I hear footsteps on the wooden floor in the living room.

What if the person, I think to myself as I shrink back against the wall in the corridor, the person holding Elspeth, what if they have come to get me?

The footsteps draw closer. I lean back into the wall and close my eyes. Any moment now they're going to grab me and . . .

'Maggie. What are you doing?'

I open my eyes and see Sonia standing there with a sweeping brush in her hands.

'Oh, thank God,' I gasp. 'I thought you were an intruder.'

'Don't be silly,' she says with a smile. 'What kind of intruder does the housework?'

She turns and heads back into the living room. I follow, my heart still thudding with fright.

'Why didn't you tell me you were here?' I say, slumping down on to the sofa.

'I looked in on you when I arrived but you were sound asleep,' she says, kneeling down to pick up the overflowing dustpan. 'So I thought I'd do a bit of cleaning before you got up.'

'What time is it?' I ask, feeling disorientated.

'1.45,' she says. 'We should get a wriggle on. You've got your physio session at the hospital at 3 p.m. Shall I fix you some lunch?'

All that information makes my head spin. 1.45? I got home from the police station at 10. Then I lay on the bed, read Elspeth's letter and then . . . then that dream. It was horrifying.

'Maggie?'

'Sorry, what?'

'I said shall I fix you some lunch?'

'I'm not hungry,' I say distractedly. Part of me is still inside the dream.

'Maggie, you have to eat,' says Sonia. 'Even if it's just a little bit.'

'Okay, thanks,' I say, sighing. 'Just something small.'

Sonia smiles and heads back into the kitchen. I sit,

motionless, running the dream over and over in my head. Was it just a nightmare, my worst fears coming out through my subconscious, or . . .?

I can't bring myself to contemplate the alternative.

'Are you sure you're okay, Maggie? You're awfully quiet.'

Sonia looks across at me as we sit in the hospital waiting room.

'I'm fine, Sonia,' I reply. 'I'm just a bit tired, that's all.'

The truth is I'm not feeling fine. This is the first time I have been back to the hospital since I came out. Every so often I hear sirens outside and it makes me jump up in my seat. I look along the corridor as a man in scrubs and a mask hurries along. Is he responding to whatever is in the ambulance? Is it an adult or a child? Will he save them? And then it comes again, the dream, and I start to wheeze.

'You okay, Maggie?' says Sonia, beside me. 'It's so hot in here. Do you need your inhaler?'

I nod my head and she reaches down and retrieves it from my bag.

'Here you go.'

I'm just taking a long inhalation when I hear my name being called. I look up and see a man standing in the doorway of the consulting room opposite. He is wearing a navy-blue polo shirt and pale trousers.

'This is us,' says Sonia, taking my arm and helping me to my feet.

'Hello, Maggie. My name's Adil. Please come through.'

He ushers us into the consulting room. The walls are painted bright yellow and there are bits and pieces of apparatus dotted around. On the far wall is a large poster on which is written: THE BIGGEST OF JOURNEYS STARTS WITH ONE SMALL STEP.

'Do sit down,' says Adil, pulling out two chairs.

We do as he says and I sit there trying to keep the panic that is rising up inside me at bay by tapping my fingers on my knee.

'Okay, welcome,' says Adil, smiling. 'Now as this is your first appointment I wanted to spend some time asking a few questions about your health and your lifestyle so we can go on to formulate a treatment plan that will work best for you. Does that sound okay?'

'Yes,' I say. I touch my forehead. It's damp with sweat.

'Great,' he says. 'Now I have your medical notes here.'

He looks at his computer then blinks awkwardly.

'I understand that you have been through an incredibly traumatic ordeal,' he says, turning to me. 'I'm very sorry about your daughter.'

I nod my head then look down at the floor. Thankfully he takes the hint and changes the subject.

'Okay,' he says, clearing his throat. 'Now I just

want to gauge what kind of physical demands you have in your day-to-day life. May I ask if your job requires any kind of physical exertion?'

'I don't have a job,' I reply, too drained to even begin to make excuses. 'I was a full-time mother.'

'Oh,' he says, his face twitching slightly. 'Erm, right, and how about your house? Do you have stairs?'

I shake my head.

'Would you say that you were an active person?'

'Active?'

'Did you like jogging for instance? Or were you a keen swimmer? Before the accident, of course.'

He smiles then. It's a perfectly innocent smile but something inside me snaps.

'Why are you asking me that?' I cry, jumping to my feet. 'I didn't do it.'

'Mrs Allan?'

'Maggie. It's okay.'

I turn to Sonia. 'I didn't do it,' I say.

I look at her and she starts to blur in front of my eyes. I'm back inside the dream. My heart is beating so fast it feels like it will burst out of my chest.

'I . . . can't . . . breathe,' I say as I sink to my knees. 'Help . . . me.'

Adil is beside me in seconds. He grabs my shoulders and brings me to a standing position.

'Maggie, I need you to breathe really slowly out,' he says. 'Like this.'

He makes an 'o' with his mouth and I can feel his breath on my face as he slowly exhales. I try to do as he asks but my chest is tightening. I'm going to pass out. I grab Adil's arm. His face is the last thing I see before I hit the ground.

'Maggie.'

I can smell river water. It is everywhere. In my eyes, my nose, my hair. I am sinking but I need to keep afloat. I need to find Elspeth.

'Maggie, can you hear me?'

I try to keep hold of the car but it's slipping. Pain rips through my fingers, so intense that I have no choice but to let go. I feel myself rising up, up, to the surface of the river. Water fills my lungs and I start to choke, gasping huge gulps of air in.

'Oh, Maggie, thank goodness.'

I surface, coughing and spluttering. Sonia and Adil are standing over me.

'What happened?' I say.

'You fainted,' says Adil, gently guiding me into a sitting position. 'It looked like a panic attack.'

'I need to get out of here,' I whisper, trying to get to my feet.

'Mrs Allan, slow down,' says Adil, holding me by the arms. 'You need to take a few moments before you try to stand up.'

'No,' I cry. 'I'm fine. I just want to go.'

*

It's raining when we reach Western Road, light summer rain that falls like faint mist. The air smells like fresh soil as I step out of the car and I take great gulps of it. The panic attack has left me feeling weak and drowsy, like my body has just endured some great battle. I hold Sonia's arm and wait while she unlocks the door.

'That's strange,' she says as she tries to push the door open.

'What?' I reply impatiently, wanting my bed.

'There's something jamming the door,' says Sonia, leaning her body sideways at the wooden frame. 'On the other side.'

She manages to get it open a fraction then she slides her hand inside.

'Oh, I can see now,' she says, her voice muffled as she grabs whatever it is from the other side of the door. 'You must have dropped it on your way out.'

She opens the door fully and as I step towards her my knees buckle. She is holding a tiny purple cardigan. Elspeth's school cardigan.

'It was just this blocking the door,' says Sonia breezily. 'As I said, you must have –'

'Give it to me,' I say, yanking it from her hands.

I press the cardigan to my face but there is no trace of Elspeth. The cardigan smells of an unfamiliar fabric softener, one I don't use. Someone has washed it. Some stranger.

'Maggie, what's the matter?' asks Sonia, closing the door behind us as I walk into the living room.

I sit down on the sofa and spread the cardigan out on my knee. I look at the label: Marks & Spencer. Age 8–9. Elspeth always wore the next size down. She was small for her age. I pull the label up and look on the other side. Her name will be here. I remember writing it in black pen on the first day of term: *Elspeth Allan. Year 5*. But her name is not there. It has been washed away.

'Maggie?'

Sonia sits down next to me and places her hand on my arm.

'It's Elspeth's,' I say, turning to her. 'Her school cardigan. Someone's posted it through the letter box.'

Sonia looks at me then at the cardigan.

'Why would they do that?' she says.

'Because they're holding her hostage,' I reply, pressing the cardigan to my chest. 'She said so in her letter.'

'What letter?' says Sonia.

I put my hand in my pocket and give her the letter. She opens it up and starts to read.

'How did you get this?' she says, handing it back to me.

'It was posted through the door last night,' I tell her. 'I went to the police this morning and they seem to think it's some sick practical joke. Elspeth is

304

officially dead, they tell me. Sean identified her so it's obviously true.'

'Maggie, they're right,' says Sonia gently. 'Elspeth is . . . she's gone. And as for this, well, if it's someone playing a joke then they need serious help. I mean, what kind of scumbag . . .'

'She needs me,' I say, cradling the cardigan in my arms. 'This just confirms it.'

'Maggie,' says Sonia tentatively. 'You've been so tired today. Maybe you took it out of one of Elspeth's boxes.'

'Then why would it be on the doormat?' I snap.

'Maybe you were holding it when we were heading out,' says Sonia. 'We were in a bit of a rush. You could have dropped it . . .'

'I'm not crazy, Sonia,' I say, exasperated now. 'Yes, I'm tired and grief-stricken and stuffed to my eyeballs with medication but I know I didn't take that cardigan out of the box and I know something is not right here. Elspeth is alive. I'm certain of it.'

'Maggie, you've got to stop this. You'll make yourself ill. Do you want me to call Dr Mathers?'

'No, I don't want you to call Dr Mathers,' I snap. 'I just want to be left alone.'

'Maggie?'

I get up off the sofa, clutching the cardigan to me.

'Can you please just go, Sonia?' I say, making my way to the bedroom. 'I want to be with Elspeth now.'

I stop outside the bedroom door and listen as Sonia opens the porch door and lets herself out. Then I go into the room and lie down on the bed, holding the cardigan in my arms like a sleeping baby, and I start to cry so hard it feels like my heart is snapping in two.

48

Dear Mummy,

Here are some psychological terms for you:

— *Mentally unstable*
— *Lack of emotion*
— *Obsessive*
— *Delusional*
— *Socially awkward*
— *Prone to violent outbursts*
— *Inability to form friendships with others*

The school counsellor has referred me to a child psychologist and this is how she described me in her notes. She is so stupid she didn't know that I could read what she was writing on her crummy notebook even if it was upside down.

So because some girl, who had bullied me for months, finally got what she deserved I get psychologically assessed. Me! I'm the victim here. I told the psychologist this but she wouldn't listen. She kept on going on about my anger issues and said that I needed to let go of the idea of you and Daddy coming back for me, that it wasn't going to happen.

Well that was it. I didn't care what she said about my mental state or any of the things that I listed above, but to say that I had to let you go! My parents! The two people that are supposed to love me more than anything in the world? Is she totally stupid? If I'm incapable of feeling emotion then how come I love you and Daddy so much it hurts? And what about Zoe? I loved her like a sister. She was the only one who knew what it felt like to be abandoned.

But I didn't bring Zoe into the conversation and neither did the psychologist. She was too busy going on and on about you and Daddy and how I needed to let go of the 'idea' of you.

I told her that she didn't understand the concept of ideas and then I told her about Charles at the museum and the picture of the woman with no legs. I told her about my specimen jars and how science is stepping out of the darkness into the light. I told her how Charles had told me that ideas are there to be made manifest so in that case my 'idea' of you and Daddy had every chance of becoming a reality.

But she didn't listen. She just sighed and shook her head. Then she wrote something down in her book but I wasn't finished.

I told her there was no way I was giving up on you and Daddy, that you were both just sorting your lives out and then you'd be coming back for me. And then, you know what she did? She shook her head and said, 'You have to stop this fantasy now. You have to start living in the real world. It's not doing you any good to be telling yourself something is going to happen when it isn't. Your parents are not coming back for you. You have to accept that.'

And then she smiled. She bloody smiled – sorry for the swear word Mummy but as you'll understand sometimes it's the only way – with her jagged yellow teeth. And that was it. I jumped out of my chair, grabbed her grubby little notebook and ripped it to pieces. That list she'd written had already been committed to memory. Did I tell you I have perfect recall?

Anyway she got all fussed and pressed some button then they all came running, the people who work at the clinic. There were two women and a man. They ran towards me, put me on the floor and held my arms. I don't know why they had to be so dramatic. It's not like I was going to kill the stupid cow. I just didn't like what she said to me and I didn't like her smile.

I don't know why I'm putting all this in a letter to you. It's not like you're going to write back is it?

I told that woman that I believed in you and that I loved you because I didn't want to prove her right. I wanted her to think that I was strong. But you know what? As time goes on I'm starting to wish that it was you who died instead of Zoe. She was more like a mother to me than you've ever been. She looked after me, made sure I ate properly. She was a real live person in my life who cared; not an idea, not a fantasy. But I'm beginning to realize that's what happens when you love someone. They leave you.

49

Friday 11 August

Golden light trickles through the open curtains. It's morning now and I'm still holding Elspeth's cardigan. Though it no longer has her smell, it still retains her shape. I spread it out on the bed in front of me and as I lie looking at it I see her, standing in the driveway at Larkfields. She has her hair tied back in a plait and she's holding a Hello Kitty lunch box in her hands.

'Come on, Mummy,' she says impatiently. 'We can't be late. Not on the first day.'

'I just want to take a photograph of you so we can text it to Daddy,' I say, holding my phone out in front of me. 'I want to show him how grown up you look now you're Year Five.'

'Okay,' she says.

Then she holds up her hands and jumps in the air and I press the red button.

'Let me see. Let me see,' she says, running to my side and looking over my shoulder as I get the image on the screen. 'Oh wow, I look like I'm flying.'

And she's right. The picture shows a beaming girl, her arms skywards, her legs curled up beneath her, floating in the air like some gappy-toothed angel.

'Send it to Daddy. See what he thinks,' she says excitedly as we make our way to the car.

I open the back door for her and help her secure the seat belt. Then I get in the driver's seat and type a hurried text to Sean with the photo attached:

Look at our big girl flying off to Year 5.

Within a minute he texts back:

Go get 'em Elspeth! Daddy loves you very much xxx

'What did he say?'

I pass her the phone and hear her giggling. Then she kisses the screen and says, 'Love you too, Daddy.'

'He can't hear you, Elspeth,' I say as I start the car and pull out of the drive.

'Oh, he can,' she says. 'Daddy has special powers. Mummy, isn't it great that my uniform is purple? How did they know that it was my favourite colour?'

I look down at the cardigan and run my fingers over the fabric, willing it to take shape.

'Where are you, baby?' I whisper. 'Where are you?'

And then I think about those words: 'Daddy has special powers.' I need to hear Sean's voice. I need him to assure me that our little girl is definitely dead.

I sit up in bed and take the ICU diary from the bed-side table where I left it last night. I turn to his first entry and read it closely, looking for any small detail that might prove that the child he identified wasn't Elspeth.

'. . . every part of me wanted to say, "No, that's not my daughter. My daughter's at home, safe and well."'

But the next sentence, the one I have memorized word for word, confirms what I've always known.

'. . . when I looked down there was no question who it was.'

I slam the diary shut and put it down on the bed. If Elspeth is dead then where did the cardigan come from? And how to explain the letter, written in her hand? Did she write it before the accident? Was she play acting? My head begins to throb. None of it makes any kind of sense.

I look down at the diary, remembering what Amanda had said when she gave it to me: some patients find it helps. I take the diary in my hands. No matter how painful, I want to read Sean's last entry again, try and work out what he was talking about. I flick through the pages impatiently and then something drops out on to the bed: a small square photograph.

I look at it in disbelief. How did that get there?

Taking the photograph in my hands, I look down at my fourteen-year-old self. I'm lying on my back, my arms stretched out behind me. My eyes are glazed and drooping and a chain of pink flowers has been placed precariously on my head. Ben is beside me. His bare arms are wrapped round me, his lips touching my face.

'No,' I cry, dropping the photograph on to the bed. 'God, no.'

We're in the playhouse. Ben's unofficial party. I've spent most of the evening standing in the corner of the room, watching as Ben's friends get more and more drunk. Ben, ever the social butterfly, flutters about, topping up people's glasses and dancing with the girls. By nine o'clock I've had enough of being a wallflower and decide to leave, but as I reach the door I feel a hand on my shoulder.

'Where do you think you're going, party pooper?'

I turn round and see Ben. His hair is wet with sweat; all that dancing has taken its toll. But his eyes are sparkling. He looks radiant and happy; like the Ben I'd known as a child.

I tell him that my parents will be expecting me to meet them at the gate soon but he takes my hand and puts it against his chest.

'I've been waiting to see you all night,' he says. 'You know what parties are like. You have to go round everyone, make sure they're having fun. It's such a bore. And you were the only person I wanted to be here.'

'Really?' I say. Clichéd as it may sound, this is one of those moments when the room seems to stand still; the kind of moment you want to capture and bottle for ever.

'Really,' he replies. 'Now, come with me. It's far too noisy out here.'

He takes my hand and leads me through the crowded room. Bobbed-hair girl is slow-dancing to a Sade song with some floppy-haired guy. She smirks when she sees Ben holding my hand. As we walk past I hear her mutter 'cradle snatcher'.

But I don't care. All that matters is Ben and me, and the way my hand feels in his.

He opens the bedroom door and we step inside. The lights are off and we begin to kiss. I've wanted to do this for so long. He tastes of alcohol but his lips are soft and it feels like I'm dissolving into him. Then he puts his tongue inside my mouth. It shocks me, but then I get used to it, and I use mine too, running it up and down his. It is the most beautiful feeling.

'Come here,' he whispers, and my body begins to tingle as he leads me further into the room.

The moon is shining through the window, casting a silvery glow so that Ben's face looks spectral. He sits down on the bed then beckons me to join him. We curl up next to each other and I feel his hands move down my body. He lifts my dress and before I know it his fingers are inside me. It's a sharp, rather unpleasant feeling, but then as he continues it starts to feel almost good. I lie back and close my eyes, feeling Ben's warm breath on my face. Then the door opens and someone turns the light on.

'Shit, sorry, folks,' says a girl in a red dress. 'I was looking for the loo.'

'Other way,' hisses Ben. 'By the front door.'

'Where's that?' she slurs.

As Ben is talking to the girl I sit up and notice a red stain on the duvet. My first thought is that my period has come. I'm utterly mortified.

'Out there, you idiot,' Ben snaps at the girl.

'Charming,' she mutters, backing out of the room clumsily.

'Now where were we,' says Ben, turning back to me.

I put my hand over the stain, try to hide it from him, but he has seen. He smiles at me.

'That's normal,' he says, stroking my face gently. 'When you do it for the first time.'

'Are you sure?' I say, feeling my cheeks redden.

He nods his head.

'Listen,' he says. 'We're not going to get any kind of privacy here and I really wanted this to be special. Are you up for an adventure?'

I look at him quizzically.

'Well, I promised my parents I'd meet them at the gate at eleven.'

'We can make it back for eleven,' he says, standing up. 'We're not going far. Just to the river.'

The night air smells of meadowsweet and wood-smoke as we walk across the barley field towards the little stretch of river. Ben is holding my hand. The evening is peachy ripe, succulent and warm, and my skin tingles with excitement.

When we get to the river, Ben takes his jacket off and lays it on the ground between two alder trees. I sit down while he stands and rolls a joint. I watch as he lights it then takes a hit. The weed smells foul but I nod my head all the same when Ben passes it to me. I don't want him to think that I'm a stupid little girl. When we finish smoking I lie back on the ground, my head fuzzy. Then Ben comes and lies beside me. He strokes my hair and kisses me gently on my nose.

'God, you're beautiful,' he says. And I feel it. I truly feel it.

We start to kiss, soft at first and then harder. Ben shifts position and I feel something sharp digging into my stomach.

'Ow,' I cry out.

Ben stops then fiddles with his trousers.

'Shit, sorry about that,' he says, holding up a square black camera. 'It was still in my pocket from the party.'

We look at each other and start to laugh.

'Talk about ruining the mood,' he says, rolling his eyes. 'Nice one, Ben.'

316

And then I don't know whether it's the weed or whether Ben's flattery has emboldened me but I begin to take my clothes off. Ben's eyes widen then he smiles mischievously and undresses too.

He lies down next to me and we kiss.

'Ben,' I whisper. 'May I ask you something?'

He stops and looks at me.

'I haven't got anything with me,' he says. 'But I'll be really careful, I promise.'

I laugh then, stoned and oblivious to any kind of risk.

'Not that,' I giggle. 'Something else.'

'What?' says Ben. He is giggling too now. It's contagious.

'Would you take a picture of us?' I slur. 'For austerity.'

'It's posterity, you noodle,' he laughs. 'But sure, why not?'

I smile and watch as he gets up to retrieve the camera that is lying on the ground by our clothes.

'You need flowers,' he says, stumbling around by the river's edge. 'Look, these are pretty. These pink ones.'

He comes over to me with a handful of pink clover and starts threading it through my hair. When he's finished he looks at me and smiles.

'That's perfect,' he whispers. Then he kisses me, long and sensuously, on the mouth.

'Come on,' I say, pushing him away playfully. 'Go set up the camera.'

'God, you're such a tease,' he groans as he gets to his feet.

I watch as he places the camera on a stone just in front of us.

'Right, we've got ten seconds,' he shouts as he runs towards me.

'One, two, three, four . . .'

I grab his shoulders and pull him down on top of me, wrapping my arms round his neck. When the camera clicks I throw my head back. I have never felt so free.

I put the photograph down and my hands begin to shake so badly I have to squeeze them together to make them stop. It is all clear now, every little bit of it.

The details I have spent the last few weeks desperately trying to hide from myself suddenly come tumbling forth. The day of the accident. I was sitting at my desk writing the next chapter of my novel. My phone buzzed. I picked it up and read the text. It was Ben.

Are you free to meet tonight? It would be great to say hi. For old time's sake . . .

I'd held the phone in my hands for a couple of moments, trying to assemble my thoughts. I'd assumed his phone call the previous day had been a one off. I never imagined he'd want to meet up. I couldn't do it, I told myself, I couldn't rake up all those feelings again. Best to tell him thanks but no thanks. But then I thought about the last few months, about Sean's late nights, his trip to Stockholm, Christmas Eve. I thought about my novel – the story of a woman having imaginary conversations with a long-dead author – and the loneliness that made me want to write it.

Now I know why I have chosen to block out the events of that day. It's because they confirm what I am: a selfish person; a disloyal wife; a terrible mother.

But as I typed out my reply to Ben I didn't feel any of those things. Instead I felt excited, alive. Even after what he'd done to me.

Ben had texted back immediately, suggesting we meet at the pub by the river. The Plough Inn. I told him that I'd have to bring Elspeth and that I didn't want to be too late as it was a school night. He'd replied that it would be lovely to see her, that one late night wouldn't hurt.

And then I bundled Elspeth into the car and drove towards the river.

Her cardigan lies on the bed next to me. I take it in my hands and rub the coarse material between my finger and thumb. It all makes sense now. Sean sent it. He is the only person, aside from me, who would have access to Elspeth's things. This is Sean's way of punishing me, of making me feel the pain he has felt these last few months. It's his way of telling me that he knows.

I made a huge mistake and Elspeth paid for it with her life. There is nothing more to find out. I know the truth now and there is only one solution.

I get up from the sofa and go into the bedroom. I take a notebook out of my bag and rip out two pages. Then, returning to the living room, I spread them on the coffee table and write two identical notes: one for Sonia and one for Julia. In it, I thank them both for all they have done for me these last few weeks. I tell them that I don't deserve that kindness because I am a bad person. I tell them that I have discovered the truth about the day of the accident and that I am to blame for Elspeth's death.

But what I don't tell them is that I am going back to the place where this all began, the place where I committed an act of violence against my child; the place that knows my secrets.

I am going back to the river.

50

Dear Mother

How do I hate you? Let me count the ways.

    I thought you'd appreciate the literary reference. After all, you love words, don't you? That's what Freya told me. She said that you were never without a book. Oh yes, how happy you must have been, lost in your dream world, surrounded by your precious books while your little girl was sent away, scared and confused.

    I've been sent to a new place now. It's much the same as the other one though I have changed. I'm tougher now. I can handle myself. If one of the other kids tries to give me trouble I can see them off. Zoe taught me that. She taught me a lot of things, such as not to trust parents. They just mess with your head, she told me, and she was right. You have messed with my head, Mother, to the point where I thought I was going mad but I'm not the mad one. I know that now.

    Before I left the other place, Freya came to see me. She sat me down and told me what I had always known, deep in my gut, that you were not coming to find me; that you never would. She said that my father had gone somewhere far away for work reasons and also because he needed to clear his head and start afresh. I asked her again if she had given you my letters and she said she had, she promised she had. Your mother is a very complicated person, she told me, she is troubled and troubled people can think only of themselves. Some people aren't meant to be mothers, she said, some people can only cause hurt.

At that point I thought she was being harsh. Yes, you hadn't replied to my letters but that didn't mean you were a bad person. I said to Freya that maybe you needed more time; maybe you weren't completely better yet. I told her that you were my mother and that you must love me, you had to love me. Mothers don't just send their children away like that and never come back.

Freya listened to me going on like this for about ten minutes and then she shouted 'Enough!' in this really angry voice. I'd never heard her like that before. Her face was all red and her eyes were bulging. I sat back in the chair and waited for her to calm down. It took a couple of minutes then she took a deep breath, turned to me and told me something so horrifying I almost passed out.

She told me about you, Mother; about what you did that night by the river. I tried to take it in but it was just too much and I started to scream. Freya tried to hug me but I pushed her away. I didn't want anyone to touch me. In the end the people from the new place intervened and told Freya to leave. I went and sat on my bed. For a second I thought about doing what Zoe did. About ending it all. But then I *thought that would make it too easy for you. So, instead, I'm going to make sure I become a success. I'm going to work so hard that nothing and no one can ever hurt me again. I'm stepping out of the darkness into the light. You were my darkness, Mother; I know that now. It's time I left you behind.*

So, there it is: my final letter. I hope the life you have led since that night has been worth it. I hope that you dream about me every night. I hope that you never find peace as long as you live.

51

It is a perfect late-summer morning. The sun hangs lazily beside a white cloud as though trying to make up its mind whether to hide or shine. I lay my blanket down on the ground beneath the alder trees and watch as a heron pokes its beak into the water on the other side of the river. Elspeth loved herons. She said they were her spirit animal; whenever she'd had a bad day one would appear and make everything better.

The heron is a sign that I'm doing the right thing. Elspeth is near and in a short while I will be with her again.

I sit down on the ground and open my bag, taking out the boxes of painkillers. I lift out the bottle of cheap vodka that I bought on the way here. Hopefully, if I drink enough, I should be knocked out before the drugs take effect.

I remember the last time. It was winter, so different to now. The river was frozen solid and the two alder trees were stripped bare. I was fourteen years old and seven months pregnant with the baby Ben and I had conceived in this very spot the night of the party. At first I'd refused to acknowledge it, hidden my growing bump with baggy clothing, but by seven months it was getting too big to hide and I had to tell my parents. My mother reacted in her usual way: silence. For days, after I'd told her, she walked around the house like a ghost, refusing to speak to me. Dad, as always, tried to be helpful and pragmatic, talked about 'doing the right thing'. Mum found her voice when she heard that. 'Do the right thing? It's far too late for that. She'll have to go through with it and look at her, she's only a kid herself.' Ben had returned to Oxford a few days after the party and I'd found out from my mother via Barbara that he was now in a relationship with Zosha, the young woman from the party. 'She's a very bright girl,' Barbara had said. 'Her father's in the Cabinet, you know. Very high up. And they have the most amazing house in Holland Park.' At that point my mother had no idea what had gone on with Ben and she told me all this as a piece of gossip. I remember sitting there listening, my heart breaking silently. I hadn't wanted to tell Ben but my mother was so angry she marched round to Ketton House and confronted him. He denied all knowledge, saying that I'd been obsessed with him; that he'd politely turned me down and I was telling lies in order to get revenge on him. Barbara had backed him up. She called me a little slut who had tried to destroy her son's life. He has a beautiful girlfriend, she'd yelled. Why on earth would he be interested in Margaret?

Bit by bit, everyone I loved, everyone I had trusted, pulled away from me. Ben, my mother. Even my dad. I overheard him talking to Mum one evening when they thought I was in bed. 'What a mess,' he said. 'What a bloody mess. This will ruin her life, you know. It will ruin all our lives. I mean, what prospects will she have, a teenage mother? God help her, Marion, God help her.'

And in that moment I knew there was only one way to go.

So I came here that January morning with a bottle of vodka and the contents of my mother's pill drawer. Before I took the pills I left Ben a note, telling him what I was doing and also telling him how much I loved him because back then I believed that what had existed between the two of us was love. I knew I was going to kill our baby too, but what choice did I have?

It was Harry, Ben's dad, who found me. He was taking their big old Labrador, Tilly, for a walk, and saw me lying unconscious on the riverbank. He called an ambulance and I was taken to hospital. What happened there – I still can't bear to think about it.

Barbara came to visit and told me to keep my mouth shut for the sake of my reputation and Ben's.

Though really she meant *her* reputation. But I nodded my head and told her that I wouldn't cause any trouble; that I was out of her life for good.

When I went home to Larkfields, everything fell apart. I fell behind at school; I stopped eating. I shut myself away in my bedroom and tried to read but the books I'd loved so much no longer soothed me. Instead, they reminded me of everything I had lost. I had nothing. When I tried to kill myself for the second time, with my father's razor blades, Mum said she couldn't cope any more and booked me into the psychiatric hospital, where I stayed for three years. I emerged at the age of eighteen to a world that had passed me by. My school friends were all at university; Ben was working for a fashion magazine in the US; my parents had sold Larkfields. Nothing would be the same again.

As I open the box of painkillers I know this is my only option. I deserve to die. I take a handful of pills and swallow them down with the vodka. The river ripples in front of my eyes, its surface glistening in the heat. I stare at the water as I summon the courage to take the next lot of pills and as I do I feel myself getting lighter.

It's different this time. My body is older, weaker. All the fight in me is gone. I take another long slug of vodka. It tastes disgusting but I need it if I'm to carry this out properly. As I knock it back my head begins to spin. I try to focus on the water in front of me but it has turned into a whirlpool, the ripples twisting into grotesque shapes; demons dancing on the surface of the river. It's time. I fumble about for the box of pills but I can't locate them. Everything is a blur. I try to get to my feet but I lose my balance and fall on to my back. And then the most extraordinary thing happens: I feel myself rising out of my body.

I'm airborne now and the sky above me is no longer golden but black, deep and heavy and utterly impenetrable. I feel it wrap around me, tighter and tighter. I'm completely detached from my body and for a moment I feel euphoric, like a great weight has been lifted from me. All the pain, all the sadness has been removed as I hang suspended in the air like a feather caught in the breeze. Then I look down and see the riverbank. There's a car, my red Nissan. It's starting to roll. I see a figure running towards it. The feeling of euphoria is replaced with one of panic and horror. I scream and yell at her, then I realize the figure is me. I'm trying to stop it, but the car gains speed. Then I hear a voice, a woman's voice. It is muffled and distant, like it's coming through a wire. I follow the direction of the voice and see a flash of red in the trees. Then the person looks up and we lock eyes.

I'm falling. Down, down towards the ground. As I

do I hear the voice again, loaded with venom, calling my name.

I get to my feet, my head spinning. A huge wave of nausea comes over me and I throw up on the grass. The vodka and pills come out in a disgusting chalky bile which burns my throat.

My body trembles as I pick up my bag and stagger away from the riverbank.

PART THREE

52

I stand outside the house, rigid with fear. I raise my hand and knock on the door three times. Behind the glass a shadow crosses the hallway and it's all I can do to stop myself from running away. Stay strong, I tell myself as someone turns the key on the other side of the door, you're not a scared child any more.

She is dressed for winter in a dove-grey jacket and long silver skirt.

'Hello, Barbara,' I say, staring her straight in the eye. 'May I come in?'

The colour drains from her face so that she becomes as pale as her attire. She tries to shut the door, but I put my foot in the way.

'What are you doing?' she cries as I step past her. 'You can't just barge in here like this.'

'Like you barged into my life?' I hiss, spinning on my heels to face her. 'Like you appeared at the scene of the accident and then ran away, leaving my daughter to drown? I know you were there that night, Barbara, so perhaps now you can stop lying to me.'

She goes to speak and then her eyes widen, like she's seen a ghost.

'Barbara,' says a voice from behind me. 'Is everything all right?'

I turn round and see a tall, familiar figure walking down the hallway towards us.

'Julia?' I gasp. 'What . . . are you doing here?'

'That's none of your business, Margaret,' Barbara hisses behind me.

I look at Julia. She folds her arms across her chest defensively.

'What is going on?' I say, looking from one to the other. 'Why are you here?'

'I was here to discuss some work that needs doing on the house,' says Julia, but she's avoiding eye contact.

'On Larkfields?' I exclaim. 'What's that got to do with Barbara?'

'She's my . . . well, my landlady, I guess,' says Julia.

'Your what?' I cry, turning to face Barbara. 'What's she talking about?'

'I'm afraid it's true,' says Barbara, a sick smile appearing on her face. 'Julia is my tenant. I really never intended for you to find out like this, Margaret, but as you've barged in here throwing accusations at me you've left me no choice.'

'Your tenant?' I repeat incredulously. 'You mean you –'

'Own Larkfields,' says Barbara. 'That's correct, I do.'

I stand for a moment, unable to move, the smell of flowery air freshener clogging my lungs.

'Listen, I should go,' says Julia awkwardly. 'You two have a lot to discuss.'

'No,' I cry, running after her as she makes her way to the door. 'You can't just go like that. I want to talk to you.'

'I'm sorry,' says Julia, her face flushing. 'I really do have to go. I'm due at the surgery.'

She glances at Barbara and something passes between them.

'I'll see you out, dear.'

I watch as Barbara opens the door and ushers Julia out. Closing it behind her, she turns to me with a grave expression.

'I think we should go to the kitchen,' she says. 'I don't know about you but I need a drink.'

She leads the way down a set of narrow stone steps to the large basement kitchen. It's a dark cavernous room with only a small window above the sink to let in light. The walls are exposed brick and are covered with oil paintings of pastoral scenes. Barbara's 'other' kitchen, the one she uses to entertain, is on the ground floor if I remember correctly. My mother had been so envious of it. This basement kitchen had been the staff quarters, though now it looks rather neglected. I suppose, with Harry gone, the days of Barbara's elaborate entertaining are over. I haven't been here since I was a child. I grimace as I recall hiding in the pantry down here during the games of hide and seek Ben and I used to play. I'd found the place oppressive back then and it feels even more so now as I sit down at the large wooden table.

'You'll have a cup of tea, Margaret,' says Barbara as she lights the stove.

It's more a statement than a question. I don't respond. Instead I think about Julia. How can she have kept this from me, knowing the distress I was in? And her body language with Barbara just now was very strange; it was like she was scared of her.

'Here,' says Barbara, placing a tray of cups and a teapot on to the table. 'Help yourself. I'm afraid I only have plain biscuits.'

'Oh for God's sake, Barbara,' I cry, slamming my hand on the table. 'I don't care about bloody biscuits. Will you just tell me what is going on.'

Barbara's face hardens. 'What do you want to know?' she says, sitting down on a chair at the far end of the table.

'Well, I came here to confront you about the night of the accident and the fact that you were there,' I say, my voice shaking with anger. 'But then I arrive to find my doctor here, a person I thought was my friend, saying that you're her landlord. I want to know what the hell is going on.'

'As Julia told you, I am the owner of Larkfields,' says Barbara, her voice measured.

'But how?' I cry. 'When?'

'We purchased it in 2009,' says Barbara, raising her eyebrow. 'And as for the reason why, I'm afraid it was Harry who dragged me into it.'

'Harry?'

'Yes,' says Barbara. 'He and your husband concocted the whole thing.'

'But Sean didn't know Harry,' I say incredulously. 'This doesn't make any sort of sense.'

'You're right, he didn't know him,' says Barbara, narrowing her eyes. 'In all the time you lived there neither you nor he made any effort to re-acquaint with your neighbours.'

'Are you serious?' I exclaim. 'After everything that happened to me when I was a teenager you think I was going to be friends with you?'

'Do you want me to tell you or not?' she says, glaring at me.

I nod my head and she continues.

'The thing is, Margaret,' she says, twisting her diamond ring between her finger and thumb, 'you are more like your mother than you realize.'

'What are you talking about?'

'I'm talking about living in a fantasy world,' she says. 'Living beyond your means. Your poor father mortgaged himself up to the hilt so his darling Marion could live her "Country Life" dream and it seems the apple didn't fall far from the tree.'

'How dare you bring my parents into this,' I say,

anger burning through me. 'They were worth a thousand of you. All this, the Sussex country set, the parties, the etiquette, it's just bullshit.'

'Oh, really?' says Barbara. 'If that's the case then why did you force your poor husband to saddle himself with crippling debt so you could live in your childhood home? If it's all "bullshit" as you put it then why did you move back here?'

'Debt?' I say. 'What debt?'

'Sean was up to his eyeballs,' cries Barbara, throwing her arms in the air. 'He had a good income but not enough to pay that huge mortgage. After the financial crash his wages were capped and he started to take out loans. Loans he couldn't afford.'

'How do you know all this?' I say, my head spinning.

'Just let me finish,' she says. 'He couldn't afford the repayment on those loans so he turned to credit cards. The debts mounted up. He tried to remortgage Larkfields but he was seen as high risk by the bank.'

'No,' I say, shaking my head. 'You're lying. If Sean was in this kind of trouble I would have known. He would have told me.'

'Oh for God's sake, snap out of your bloody fantasy world,' says Barbara. 'He didn't tell you because he was scared. You were happy to be a full-time mother living the country-house dream and faffing about with bits of writing. Sean knew you were mentally unstable. He was terrified that if he told you the house was under threat you'd have some sort of relapse.'

I try to speak but no words will come out. I feel like I've entered some parallel world.

'Anyway, poor chap was at his wits' end,' continues Barbara, oblivious to my distress. 'Bills and final demands were coming in left, right and centre. He'd just found out that the bank had turned down his request to remortgage when he and Harry got talking in the pub. Harry asked if he was okay and out it all poured. As soon as he mentioned you and the little one and how you could be made homeless Harry stepped in and offered to buy Larkfields.'

'Why would he do that?'

'I know what my husband was like,' she says bitterly. 'He was a sucker for a sob story and despite the unpleasantness that you'd brought into our family he always had a soft spot for you. He told Sean that the whole thing would be done discreetly, with the minimum disruption. You could stay in the house and pay a minimal rent as and when Sean got back on his feet financially.'

My eyes fill with tears as I remember Harry sitting in the visitor's room at the psychiatric unit. All those years later he had helped me again.

'The estate agent told me that a company called BH2 Properties had bought Larkfields,' I say, my brain rebooting. 'So who are they?'

'The name is made up of mine and Harry's initials,' says Barbara, watching me stealthily from the other side of the table. 'We thought the buyer needed to remain anonymous.'

'Well, I can understand Harry wanting to help,' I say. 'But what about you? You've always hated me. Surely you would have been glad to see the back of me.'

'That's true,' she says, her lip curling. 'Though to be honest I rather liked the idea of owning the place. Of course, after the accident there was no way I was going to help you any more. I told Sean he'd need to give notice. Though it turned out he was only too happy to leave after what you did to him.'

What is she getting at? Is she accusing me of harming Elspeth? I feel scared and fragile, just like I did when I was fourteen and my mother marched round to Ketton House to confront Ben.

'Do you know where he is?' I say, my voice trembling. 'Sean.'

'No, I don't,' she says. 'As far away as possible from you I'd imagine.'

'You know he was having an affair, don't you? With a woman called Freya Nielssen.'

Barbara stares at me for a moment then her face breaks into a horrible smile.

'Why are you smiling?' I cry. 'For God's sake, do you think this is funny?'

She leans forward, her hands clasped on the table in front of her.

'*I* am Freya Nielssen,' she says, her glassy green eyes hardening.

'What?'

'That is my official name, Freya Barbara Nielssen,' she says with a flourish. 'Though I always preferred Barbara. I never took Harry's name when we married as I didn't much care for it. Cosgrove is such an ugly English name.'

'So it was your name on the estate agent's papers,' I say. '*You* sent my things to the storage facility?'

Now the words on the boxes make sense. There is only one person who sees me as a bitch round here and she is sitting right opposite me, her face distorted with hatred.

'I had no choice,' she says. 'I knew that we'd never get another tenant with all that piled up inside. So I arranged for everything to be collected and I made sure that your name was recorded as a key holder. I suppose I could have just got rid of the lot but I knew there was a lot of the child's stuff there and . . . well, I thought it might give me some leverage should I need to make you leave.'

'Leverage?' I cry. 'What are you . . .'

I stop speaking and look at Barbara. Now it all makes sense.

'It was you,' I say. 'You sent Elspeth's cardigan, didn't you?'

'Oh, what are you talking about now, Margaret?' says Barbara, shaking her head condescendingly. 'You really are quite deranged, aren't you?'

'I'm not mad,' I yell, pushing the chair back so hard it falls over. 'Even though you've tried to drive me to it. I know exactly what you've been doing.'

'For goodness' sake, calm down, girl,' she says, slamming her hand on the table. 'You're talking nonsense.'

'No,' I say. 'That's what you'd like to think, but my mind is very clear. You sent me Elspeth's cardigan and you were there the night of the accident. You were wearing red.'

'Was I indeed?' says Barbara. 'And was there a pink elephant there too and little green men?'

I can see I've shaken her though. She coughs out a hollow laugh and the scared fourteen-year-old cowering inside me suddenly gets angry. I rush at her, sending the delicate tea set flying.

'You evil witch,' I cry, grabbing her arm. 'You think it's funny, eh? You think it's funny to stand and watch a child die? To watch her mother in the water trying to save her and just do nothing?'

Barbara wrenches away from me and strides towards the door.

'Come back,' I yell. 'You don't get to walk away without telling me the truth.'

She stops and looks round, her face contorted with hatred.

'Truth?' she hisses, her face inches from mine. 'You don't deserve the truth.'

She turns and opens the door. I hear her footsteps on the stone steps.

'Come back here!' I yell as I follow her up the steps, back towards the hallway.

It's dark and I can't see. But I can feel the steps beneath my feet. My chest is tightening and I don't have my inhaler with me. Just count, I tell myself, and take one at a time. Then I hear someone at the top of the steps. I turn and stagger towards them but as I reach the top step they push me hard in the chest. I scream as my legs give way and I feel myself falling. I try to grab the railings but there is nothing there.

53

When I open my eyes I am back in the kitchen. My head is burning with pain. I try to touch it but my arms won't move. I look down and see that they have been bound.

'Hello?' I say, my voice raw and cracking. 'Help me!'

I hear footsteps. I look up. Barbara is standing in the doorway.

'Untie me,' I say as she comes towards me. 'This is insane. Just untie me and let me go.'

Barbara ignores me and sits down at the table opposite. She leans forward and clasps her hands tightly.

'I told you to stop and look what's happened. Why didn't you just stay away?'

'Why have you tied me up, you mad woman?' I yell.

'She didn't,' says a voice. 'I did.'

I turn round. Julia is standing at the sink. Her hands are covered in blood.

'Julia?' I say. 'What are you . . .'

And then I see it. The knife. A simple kitchen knife, but the way she is clasping it in her right hand fills me with fear. The blade glints in the light.

'Please,' I say, trying to keep my voice calm and

steady. 'I don't know what is happening here. I don't know what I've done.'

I look at Barbara. The colour has drained from her face. It's then I realize: she's scared too.

'Julia,' she says shakily. 'Why don't you put that down? There really isn't any need for –'

'I'll decide what there's a need for,' Julia snaps, her eyes blazing.

She comes towards me then and instinctively I flinch.

'Don't be so jumpy,' she says, pulling a chair out next to me. 'I just want to talk.'

She sits down, still holding the knife.

'What do you want to talk about?' I say, keeping my eyes on the knife.

'I want to talk about me,' she says, leaning forward. 'I want to tell you about my life.'

'Julia, come now, stop this,' says Barbara. 'You're doing yourself no favours.'

'I don't want favours,' she says, spitting the words out. 'I just want to let this bitch know what she's done to me.'

'Done to you?' I say. 'I've done nothing to you. I barely even know you.'

'That's right, you don't know me,' she cries, leaping to her feet. 'You don't know anything about me.'

'Julia, calm down,' says Barbara. 'Or someone's going to get hurt.'

'I think it's too late for that,' Julia says quietly.

Then she kneels down in front of me and holds the knife to my throat. I can feel it there, pressing against my skin. I don't dare to breathe.

'Please,' I whisper. 'Please, I'm begging you. Don't hurt me. Whatever it is. Whatever you think I've done to you. We can sort it out. I'm sure.'

'You're scared, aren't you?' she says. I can feel the knife, feel the shake in her hand through it. 'You're really scared.'

'Julia, that's enough,' shouts Barbara. 'Just put the knife down.'

'I was scared once,' she says, ignoring the old woman's pleas. 'But then I learned to look after myself. You have to, when you're all alone in the world.'

'I'm sorry,' I say, remembering her dead mother. 'It must have been very tough for you.'

She stares at me and for a moment her expression softens; she's changing her mind. But then her face twists again and she slides the knife across my cheek.

'No,' cries Barbara. 'Julia, stop.'

'It's nothing more than a paper cut,' she says, putting her fingers to it. It stings. 'You forget, I'm a doctor.'

'Why are you doing this to me, Julia?' I say. 'I don't understand.'

'Neither did I,' she says, taking the knife away. 'I didn't understand why I'd been abandoned. I was a little girl, a scared little girl who just wanted her mummy. I was trapped in hell hole after hell hole waiting patiently for the day when she would walk through the door and rescue me. But she never did so I got on with my life without her. Well, guess what? I found her.'

'What?'

'You heard me.'

And then I look at her. The straight blonde hair, the pale-green eyes, her clear-sighted intelligence. I see myself, Elspeth and Ben all rolled into one.

'You mean . . . you're . . .'

'I'm your daughter?' says Julia. 'Yes. I am. The daughter you tried to kill.'

54

As I sit looking into Julia's hate-filled eyes, the event I have spent my life blocking out comes back to me. I try but I can't stop it. When I attempted suicide that first time they managed to save the baby I was carrying. I was pumped so full of drugs that I remember very little about it, only what my mother told me afterwards. That the baby was born by caesarean section; that she was a girl weighing three pounds six ounces; that she was taken straight to the special care baby unit where she was handed over to the care of Social Services, which, my mother told me, 'was for the best'. Since then I've tried so hard not to think about that baby, and what became of her. I tried to put her to the back of my mind, but it was no use; she was always there. My missing piece.

'How . . . how did you find me?'

'That's not important,' says Julia, picking up the knife again.

'Look, let's talk,' I say, my voice high-pitched with fear. 'I'll tell you whatever you want to know.'

Julia stares at me for a moment and then starts to laugh.

'God, you're deluded,' she says, shaking her head. 'You see, *Mother*, I know everything about you. I know what happened, what you did. And I also know what you didn't do. You don't seem to realize that for all these years you've been my obsession, my specialist subject.'

Acidic bile rises up my throat. I try to swallow it down but it burns and I start to cough. Barbara gets up and goes to the sink. She pours a glass of water then comes over and holds it to my mouth. As she comes closer I can smell her perfume. Must de Cartier: a cloying, musky scent. My mother had bought bottles of it back in the eighties in an attempt to be more like Barbara.

'So you see,' continues Julia, who had paused in her ranting while I drank the water, 'I have no interest in what you have to say. Instead I want you to listen.'

My body is in so much pain I can barely breathe, let alone make sense of what is happening, but I nod my head and Julia seems to take this as a sign of acquiescence.

'I assume that as a good parent you would want to know that your child is safe, wouldn't you?' she says, leaning back in her chair.

I look at her warily. I don't know where she is going with this.

'Wouldn't you?' she yells.

'Yes,' I whisper. 'Yes, of course.'

'Like your precious Elspeth,' she says. 'I mean, she was always safe, wasn't she?'

She smirks and looks across to Barbara, who has now poured herself a glass of brandy.

'Leave Elspeth out of this,' I say, wincing as the tendons in my arms pull against whatever it is she has tied my hands with. 'This has nothing to do with her.'

'Oh, I think you'll find it does,' she says, turning back to me. 'I think you'll find it has everything to do with her. Because, you see, Mother, you are the common factor here. Two daughters. Both neglected. One sent away to be abused and bullied, the other drowned in your charge.'

'Stop,' I cry, pulling myself forward in the chair. 'Stop it now.'

'Why? The truth too painful for you, is it? Go on then, show me how good a mother you were. Tell me the name of the first place I was sent to.'

My brain is closing down, the room is hot and everything is out of focus. Why won't she just stop?

'That's right, you don't know,' she says. 'Well, I'll tell you. It was the Elmfield Children's Centre in Southampton. I spent ten years there, until it closed down and I was moved on.'

She continues talking but I can hardly take in what she is saying.

'Where was it next?' says Julia. 'Oh, yeah. The Fallow

Mill Home in Eastleigh. That's where they shipped me off to next; the place where I got bullied to within an inch of my life. When I fought back they told me I had psychological problems. Told me I was delusional for thinking you would one day come and get me. The only good thing that ever happened to me was meeting a surrogate sister, a person who stood up for me and made sure I was okay. Her name was Zoe and she was my family. I even took her surname because it meant more to me than yours. But she died, Mother, she threw herself under a train because she thought that without proper parents to love and cherish her she had nothing to live for.'

'I'm sorry,' I say, my voice trembling. 'I'm sorry you had to go through that. It must have been so hard.'

'It was,' she says. 'But I stood up for myself because by then I was getting tougher. I was discovering that nobody else was going to do it for me. And then I started to work hard. I passed all my exams and I got the fuck out of there and I made something of my life.'

The pain subsides a little and I look up at her. The similarity to Elspeth is striking. The colour of her eyes, the shape of her mouth, even her defensiveness: they are so alike, it's scary. How could I not have seen it before? But then, as I know only too well, the brain chooses what it wants to see.

'I am proud,' I say. 'Very much so.'

'You have no right to be,' she says. 'Not after what you did; where you sent me.'

'But I didn't know what had happened to you,' I cry. 'My mother wouldn't tell me where you were. I was only a child myself.'

She looks deep into my eyes and it seems for a moment as though she is softening but then she clenches her fists and slams them on the table.

'You were a child who had known nothing but love and happiness and care,' she yells. 'Your parents didn't just throw you away.'

'Yes they did,' I say, angry now at this onslaught. 'And you know they did because it was all there in my notes. I was sent away and, like that, my life was ruined. I failed my exams, I had nothing.'

'Failed your exams?' she cries, jumping to her feet. 'You call that having nothing? You were sent to a private psychiatric unit where your every whim was catered to. You had your own room, your own things, people visiting you. What did I have? Nothing. I used to cry myself to sleep at night, willing you to come and get me, willing you to be my mother.'

'Come now, Julia,' says Barbara, putting her hand on Julia's arm. 'Don't upset yourself. You'll be ill.'

Julia looks at her and smiles. It is a warm, genuine smile.

'Freya was the only person who cared,' she says. 'Do you know that? You call her all these names, accuse her of being this bitch, and yet where were you when I was being called a freak and a weirdo,

352

when I was being attacked by the other kids? You weren't there but Freya was.'

'What?' I say, looking at Barbara, whose face is flushed with alcohol. 'You visited her? After everything you said to me about keeping quiet for the sake of your reputation. You kept in touch with the baby I was forced to give away.'

'She was my granddaughter,' says Barbara. 'She *is* my granddaughter. She was part of Ben. How could I just walk away?'

'How did you know where she was?'

'I spoke to Social Services,' she says, her eyes pooling with tears. 'I was in the special care baby unit, looking at her in that tiny incubator, when they arrived to take her. I was devastated. She looked so vulnerable, so tiny, though the doctors said she was ready to go.'

She stops then and rubs Julia's hand. I've never seen Barbara look so tender.

'I begged Harry to keep her but he said we had to let her go, that it was for the best. That it would be cruel for you to have to see us bring your baby up. That was Harry all over, always thinking about you and your wellbeing. Anyway, the director of Lewes Social Services was an old family friend. He pulled some strings, made sure I was kept informed of where the baby ended up. I gave them my other name just in case it got back to anyone.'

'So you've known her since she was a baby?' I say, guilt and envy needling my stomach.

'Unfortunately, no,' says Barbara, glancing at Julia. 'I first made contact when she was ten years old. 1998 had been a tough year. I'd had a breast cancer scare, Harry and I were going through a bad patch. Benjamin had moved to the US and barely visited us. I felt utterly alone. I'd go and sit in the playhouse for hours on end, thinking about what had happened and how it had destroyed my poor Ben.'

'I saw the playhouse,' I say. 'You left it unchanged all these years.'

'After what happened I couldn't bring myself to go near it,' says Barbara, her face stricken. 'I locked the door and let the whole thing gather dust. But then, I suppose part of me derived some comfort from knowing Ben's things were there just as they had been. It felt like a little part of him had remained here at Ketton House.'

She smiles a strange half-smile and her eyes grow misty. Her beloved Ben: the boy who could do no wrong.

'Anyway,' she says briskly. 'The cancer scare proved to be a benign cyst but at that point I thought I was dying and I wanted to put my affairs in order. I needed to see my granddaughter.'

'Barbara visited me as often as she could,' says Julia. 'She brought me dolls and books and coloured pens.'

'I tried my best,' says Barbara. 'But then Harry found out what I was doing and put a stop to it. He said I had to leave it well alone. Those were his words. And so, with a heavy heart, I did just that and I've never forgiven myself. I just wanted to do the right thing.'

'Do the right thing?' I say. 'You stood back and said nothing when your son got me pregnant. You made me think I'd done something wrong.'

'Shut up,' cries Julia, squeezing the handle of the knife tighter and stepping towards me. 'It wasn't Barbara's fault. She'd tried her best. And anyway, she wasn't my mother, you were. And you knew exactly where I was, you knew the name and address of every damned place I was sent to, you knew that I needed you and you just left me to rot.'

'What are you talking about, Julia?' I say, trying to keep up with her bullet-fast accusations. 'I had no idea where you were. I didn't even get to see you after the birth. They just took you away.'

'Don't lie to me,' Julia yells, waving the knife in my direction. 'Don't fucking lie to me. You knew where I was because I told you repeatedly. You knew and you chose to ignore me, even when I was begging for you to come and rescue me. So when I heard you'd been in an accident I was glad because I wanted you to feel the pain that I had felt. I wanted you to know what it's like to be scared and alone.'

'You were there for me,' I say, gulping down the sick feeling that is rising up through my body. 'You wanted to be my GP. You helped me. Why would you do all that?'

'I admit at first I wanted to see you for myself. Get inside your head. But then I realized you didn't feel bad at all. You had forgotten me. Then I saw how weak you were,' she says, leaning closer to me. 'I realized how easy it would be for you to try it again.'

'What – what do you mean?'

'I'm saying, Mother, that I wanted to get you back for everything you'd put me through,' she says, her face inches from mine. 'I wanted to play with your head the way you played with my life and I wanted you to feel like you had no other option but to . . .'

She stops then to catch her breath.

'No option but to what, Julia?' I say, my voice shaking.

She looks up at me and smiles and warmth filters through me because it's Elspeth's face and I just want to get out of this damned chair and hug her. But then her expression changes. Her eyes glaze and her lip curls. She leans in to me and whispers in my ear.

'No option but to die. I wanted you to die.'

55

Barbara stands up and pours herself another large brandy. Her hair has come undone and her mascara has smudged. I watch as she haltingly makes her way back to the top of the table.

'Barbara, please. Let me go,' I say as she takes a large glug of brandy. 'Whatever I might have done, however much both of you think I deserve this, you can't just keep me here. Sonia will come.'

'Sonia thinks you're dead,' says Julia, rolling her eyes. 'You left her a suicide note, remember?'

I do remember. I also know that my phone is in my back pocket. With my hands tied there is no way I can get to it to make a call.

'Please,' I beg her. 'Just stop it. This isn't you. You're not evil.'

'How do you know?' she says indignantly. 'You know nothing about me.'

'I've spent enough time around you to know that you're a good person, Julia,' I say. 'That you have a heart. You're not a killer. You're a hurt and scared little girl.'

When I say this her face turns red and she jumps to her feet and comes at me.

'Don't you dare call me that,' she yells, waving the knife in my face. I can almost feel its cruel cut. 'I used to be a hurt and scared little girl but I've grown up now. You had every chance to be my mother, every chance, and you just chose to act like I didn't exist.'

'That's not true,' I cry, tears blurring my eyes. 'I loved you. I loved you so much. I never stopped. The thought of you and everything you could be haunted me for years. I tried to talk about you but my parents told me to move on, to forget you, but I couldn't, I wouldn't.'

'You're lying.'

'I swear to you, I'm not,' I say as the cold blade presses harder into my skin. 'I saw you everywhere I went. On buses and tube trains. Every little girl was you. You were the empty space that I could never fill. Don't you understand? They took you from me. They ripped you out and sent you away. I had no choice.'

'You tried to kill me,' she says, her voice low and brooding.

'I tried to kill *myself*,' I say, choking back my tears. 'Because I thought I had no choice. Your father didn't want to know; Barbara thought I was bringing shame on her family; my parents were clueless. I was all alone and I needed help but there was no one around to give it. Surely you can understand that?'

The pressure of the knife eases a little. Her eyes are red. I try to show her with my eyes how much I care. I want to comfort her, to be her mum.

'Julia?' I whisper. 'Julia, it's okay.'

'What about the letters?' she says, her expression hardening.

'Letters?' I say, shaking my head. 'What letters?'

'I wrote letters to you almost every week from the care home,' she says, glancing across to Barbara, whose head is slumped on the table.

'Julia, I never received any letters,' I say. 'If I had it would have been the greatest thing, but I didn't. And anyway, how would you have known where to send them?'

She looks across at Barbara again and then turns to me.

'I sent them to her,' she says, pointing at Barbara. 'She promised she would pass them on to you.'

'I promise, Julia, I never saw them.'

'Of course I sent her the letters,' says Barbara. 'She's lying to you.'

Julia looks at me. If I can just get through to her . . .

'Julia, please,' I cry. 'You have to believe me. I didn't receive any letters.'

'I know you did. I saw the poem that I wrote to you. It's in your flat.'

Then I remember. The poem I thought was Elspeth's.

'That was yours?' I say, aghast.

'You know it was mine,' she cries. 'How else would you have it?'

'I told you. I found it in the lock-up.'

'Yeah. Amongst your things.'

'But I'd never seen it before,' I say. 'Please, Julia, you have to believe me.'

Julia doesn't respond. She stands deathly still, her hands clasped round the knife. I look at Barbara.

'Actually, Julia,' I say, keeping my eyes firmly on Barbara, 'I did receive one of the letters. It was posted through my letter box a couple of days ago, wasn't it, Barbara?'

The older woman looks up at me, her eyes blazing with venom.

'I don't know what you're talking about,' she says, taking a long slug of brandy.

'Oh, I think you do,' I say.

Barbara doesn't answer. Instead she stares down at her glass.

'Just like you sent Elspeth's cardigan,' I continue. 'How did you describe having access to her things: leverage?'

'Barbara, what is she talking about?' says Julia shakily.

'Nonsense, that's what,' says Barbara, running her finger round the rim of her brandy glass. 'Don't listen to her, Julia, she's a very disturbed woman.'

'*I'm* a very disturbed woman?' I cry. 'You used the death of my child to taunt me, to scare me off, and you call me disturbed.'

'You have no idea,' says Barbara. 'No idea at all.'

'Oh, I do, Barbara,' I reply, holding her gaze. 'I have a very good idea. You have always wanted to control people. Harry, Ben, now Julia, and when people can't be controlled, when they get in the way of your perfect order, you get angry, don't you?'

'Barbara, tell me she's lying,' says Julia, her eyes bulging. 'Tell me you sent her those letters when I asked you to. You promised me.'

Barbara doesn't answer. Instead she stares at me.

'What were you doing at the river the night of the accident?' I say, my voice steady though my heart is pounding with rage. 'Why did you run away?'

'You're a fantasist, Margaret,' she says. But she looks scared. 'Always have been, always will be. Your poor mother had her hands full with you, no wonder she killed herself.'

'Tell me the truth,' I say. 'What were you doing at the river that night? Did you follow Ben, is that it? You were keeping tabs.'

'Oh, for God's sake, Ben had nothing to do with it,' she cries, slamming her fist on the table. 'He wasn't even there.'

'What did you say?'

'Look, just untie her, Julia, and get her out of this house.'

Julia doesn't move. Instead, like me, she sits watching Barbara.

'I'll ask again,' I say. 'What were you doing there?'

She stares back at me, her eyes glazed with alcohol, then she leans forward and takes another sip of brandy.

'I wanted to stop you,' she says, putting the glass down on the table. 'I knew he'd been in touch and I couldn't let it happen again; couldn't let you ruin his life.'

'So, what? You read his texts? You followed him. Is that it?'

Barbara shakes her head.

'Then what, Barbara? For God's sake, just tell me.'

'It wasn't Ben who wrote that text asking you to meet,' she says. 'It was me.'

56

I sit in silence for a few moments, trying to take in what she has just said. Beside me, Julia has put her head in her hands. I can hear her quietly sobbing.

'You texted me from Ben's phone?' I say, unable to conceal the hatred in my voice. 'And then you watched as my little girl drowned? You fucking *watched*?'

'I didn't watch,' she says, placing her hands on the table in front of her. 'I was . . . I was terrified. I didn't know what to do.'

'You watched her die,' I say bitterly. 'You did nothing.'

'I called the emergency services,' cries Barbara.

'Not till it was too late. She only had a couple of minutes, Barbara. You were just scared of them implicating you.'

A sob slips from her throat and she puts her head in her hands. 'I'm sorry, Margaret. I'm truly sorry. I didn't know what to do.'

'"Sorry". You don't know the meaning of the word,' I say. 'How can you have been sorry when you sat down and wrote that poisonous email? When you told me I was to blame for my daughter's death?'

I look at Julia. She has tightened her grip on the knife.

'They told me you would be placed with a good family,' I say, trying to make her look into my eyes. 'They told me that you would go to someone who would give you everything I couldn't.'

'They say a lot of things, social workers,' says Julia. 'And in my experience it's usually lies.'

'You have to believe me,' I say. 'If I'd known for a second that you were being mistreated I would have been there like a shot. I loved you with all my heart, Julia. I wanted you so much.'

'I don't believe you,' she says. 'How can that be true when you gave me away the moment I was born?'

'On the day of the accident,' I say, speaking as steadily as I can through the rising pain in my chest, 'I was going . . . I was going to meet your father, or at least I thought I was. But the only reason I agreed is because I wanted to talk about you. He was the only person who could possibly have understood what it felt like to lose you.'

'I thought you said he wanted nothing to do with it?'

'No, not at the time,' I say. 'But he was an eighteen-year-old boy who just wanted to get back to university and have fun. I thought that with age and experience he might have changed. I thought the fact that he wanted to meet must mean that he wanted to talk about it too. But I was wrong, wasn't I, Barbara?'

I turn round. Barbara is busy pouring herself another brandy. She looks up and then I see it again: Barbara running away from the scene, her red coat disappearing into the trees.

'Tell me why you did it, Barbara.'

'Harry was dying and Ben had come home to visit him,' she says, looking down into her half-empty glass. 'But I knew something was up. He was permanently glued to that bloody phone. That morning, Ben was up in the bedroom talking to Harry. I noticed he'd left the phone on the kitchen table. It wasn't locked so I had a look through his call history. I wanted to see what was preoccupying him. And that's when I saw your name.'

She looks up at me and shakes her head. 'You,' she cries. 'The girl who had done so much damage to our family; the girl who had ruined Ben's life, opened a rift between my husband and me that would never be fully healed. I couldn't believe it. It couldn't be happening. Anyway, I saw that it had been just one call but that call had lasted an hour. I knew it would escalate and I knew that if you wormed your way back in then our Ben would stand no chance so I sent you a message and asked if you would meet that evening.'

'Why would you want to meet me?'

'I wanted to put a stop to whatever was about to unfold between the two of you,' she says. 'I knew what that poor chap of yours was going through, having to sell his house and work all the hours God sends just to keep you, and I wanted to talk some sense into you.'

'But why would you pretend to be Ben?'

'Oh, Margaret,' she says. 'I hardly think you'd have agreed to meet me. What choice did I have?'

I sit for a moment, letting her words sink in.

'You were wearing red,' I say. 'A red coat.'

'Yes, I think I was.'

Then the final piece comes back to me.

'I locked the door because I didn't want Elspeth to hear what you had to say,' I continue. 'I knew you'd be spouting poison and I didn't want her to get scared.'

'That was your choice, and a rather foolish one at that,' she says.

And I realize, with a sickening feeling, that she's right. I think back to the text message, the prickle of excitement I'd felt when I saw Ben's name. Why hadn't I just left it alone?

'That poor child,' says Barbara, dabbing her eyes with a tissue. 'As far as I am aware, Margaret, it was you who caused your child's death. You got out of the car on a steep bank and left your handbrake off.'

'Don't you dare accuse me of killing my child,' I yell, tears flooding down my face. 'You ran, while I did everything I could to save her. I was a good mother to her. I was. And I would have been a good mother to Julia too. You're a monster.'

'Oh, am I?' she says, folding her arms across her chest. 'Well, you can think that if you wish but I like to think that I'm just a mother and a mother will do anything to protect her child, won't she, Margaret?'

'Protect your child?' I say, shaking my head. 'Ben's a forty-seven-year-old man. What did he need protecting from?'

'From you,' Barbara cries, jumping to her feet. 'From the pain that you caused him. You have no idea, have you? No idea what your sordid little fumble cost him. It messed up his life for years.'

I go to speak but she shouts over me.

'You have built your life around being a victim,' she spits. 'Poor little Maggie, the kid who had no friends because she talked to herself, the kid who set her sights on my son, dropped her knickers and to hell with the consequences.'

I shake my head, anger rising through my chest.

'Ben was distraught about the baby,' she says, eyes blazing. 'Utterly distraught. He kept asking to speak to you and we had to tell him you refused to see him.'

'You did what?'

'We did what was best for our son,' she says. 'But he still ended up dropping out of Oxford before the end of his second year. It took him years to get back on track. He's still never met anyone else. No grandchildren. You destroyed him. And he was so bright, so clever.'

'So,' I say, my hands shaking with anger, 'you think that because Ben dropped out of Oxford it excuses the fact that you watched my child screaming for help and did nothing?'

'It was your fault she was there. Your fault you didn't put the handbrake on,' Barbara yells.

'You think it excuses the fact that you played with your granddaughter's head and let her believe that you'd passed her letters on to me?'

'I was not playing with her head, I was protecting her from you,' she screams. 'What good would it have done to give you the letters? You were in no fit state to be a mother to anyone, let alone a damaged child.'

Behind me, Julia gasps. 'What did you say?'

She stands frozen to the spot, her eyes on Barbara.

'Julia, please, you don't know what kind of a person your mother was,' says Barbara, her voice shaking. 'She was – is – highly disturbed. I was protecting you. I –'

'No,' says Julia. 'No.'

'Julia, calm down,' says Barbara. 'Let me explain this to you.'

'There is nothing to explain,' says Julia.

'You were in that awful place,' says Barbara, her voice growing high-pitched with fear and agitation. 'I just wanted to give you a bit of hope.'

Julia nods her head ominously.

'You promised me,' she says, her voice low and menacing. 'You looked me in the eye and promised me. Why would you do that?'

'I wanted to help,' says Barbara pleadingly. 'After all, what light did you have in there, you needed *something*.'

'I had Zoe,' says Julia. 'She was always there for me.'

'Oh, please,' says Barbara, rolling her eyes. 'That little pikey? She wasn't like you, dear. She was a mess. The child of drug dealers if I remember correctly. And such a bad influence on you. You were so much better off when she was gone.'

'You bitch,' screams Julia. 'You fucking bitch.'

She lurches towards Barbara. I see the glint of the blade in her hand.

'Julia, no!' I cry.

But I'm too late. It's over in a second. A flash as the blade moves in the air. A sickening squishing sound as the knife meets flesh. Barbara tries to scream but instead a horrifying gurgle comes out of her mouth. She staggers for a couple of moments, her hand at her throat. Then she looks at me, an expression of utter bewilderment. I watch as she struggles for breath then falls on the stone floor, her silver skirt rippling like moonlight across the surface of a river.

57

A low wail fills the room, so loud that at first I fear it's some sort of alarm but then I see where it is coming from. Julia is standing above Barbara's body, the knife still in her hands, and the sound is coming from her mouth.

'Untie me, Julia,' I say, trying to keep calm.

She doesn't respond, though the noise continues.

'Julia,' I say, raising my voice. 'Untie me. Now.'

The tone of my voice seems to have an effect. She stops and turns towards me. Her face is parchment white.

'I . . . I didn't mean to . . .' she says, her eyes wide with fear.

'We don't need to think about that just yet,' I say, trying to keep my own breathing steady. 'Untie me and we can sort this out.'

She looks at me then nods her head briskly. For a moment I see the child she once was, lost and bewildered, and I know that I must be strong for her now.

'Good girl,' I say as she drops the knife on to the ground and slowly walks towards me. 'That's it. Just untie me. It's all going to be fine.'

But her hands are shaking so badly that at first she can't get a grip on the knotted wires.

'I can't do it,' she cries.

'Keep calm,' I say as I feel them loosening. 'You're almost there.'

When she finally unknots them I slump forward in my chair as the reality of what has happened sinks in. Then my chest begins to tighten. I can feel my breathing grow shallow. But I have no inhaler. I'm going to have to focus, try to keep calm.

'I . . . don't know what to do.' Julia is sobbing. 'She's dead. She's definitely dead.'

She is next to the body, staring down at the silvery mess.

'I should check her pulse,' she says.

'Don't touch her,' I cry as I stagger to my feet. The room starts to spin and I clutch the edge of the table for support. 'Just don't touch her.'

Then Julia's shoulders begin to shake violently.

'I'm scared,' she says, looking towards me. 'I didn't mean to do it. They'll send me to prison. I can't go there.'

I let go of the table and slowly make my way towards her. Holding her shoulders with my hands so that she is facing me, I look into her eyes and my heart crumbles. Prison would kill her. Just like the home nearly did. I can't do that to her again.

'Listen to me,' I say firmly. 'You are not going to prison.'

Julia's lip starts to quiver. Her body is shaking so badly I'm scared she will have a panic attack. It is Elspeth's face looking back at me the night of the accident, her big green eyes pleading: 'No, Mummy, no.'

'You are not going to prison, Julia,' I say, rubbing her arms to warm her up. 'But you have to do as I say, do you understand?'

She nods.

'Good girl,' I say. 'I let you down, I know I did, but I am going to make it up to you. I promise you that, Julia. I'm here now and I'm not going to let anyone or anything harm you ever again.'

She looks at me, her face flushed from crying.

'I thought you'd . . . I thought you didn't want me. I'm so sorry . . .'

'You have nothing to be sorry for, do you hear me? Nothing. But you're going to have to be strong for the next hour or so, okay? We both are.'

She looks across at Barbara's body and nods her head.

'Okay,' she says, wiping her eyes. 'What should I do?'

'Go over there and wash your hands,' I say, gesturing to the sink. 'Scrub them.'

She looks down at her hands. They are splattered with blood. But like an obedient child, she does as she is told.

While she is washing her hands I tidy the chairs and place the wire Julia had used to bind my arms in a drawer. Once all that is finished I go and stand beside Barbara's body. I look at the perfectly styled blonde hair now stained with blood, the bejewelled hands balled into fists, and I remember the panic that had filled my entire body as I waded into the river that night. I'd looked back at her as she stood on the riverbank, her red coat a beacon in the twilight, and begged her to help me. Elspeth's screams ring in my head as I think of how Barbara calmly walked away. She destroyed one daughter; she's not going to destroy another.

'Julia, can I use your phone please?' I say, my eyes fixed on the body.

'Why?' she says, wiping her hands on a tea towel.

'I'm going to call the police.'

'No,' she cries, dropping the towel. 'No, you can't . . .'

'You're not going to prison,' I say. 'I told you that. Now give me your phone.'

'How can you be so sure?'

'You have to trust me,' I say. 'Can you do that?'

She starts to cry again.

'Julia, you need be strong now, okay?' I say. 'You need a clear head and you need to believe me when I say you're not going to prison. Now give me the phone.'

Shakily, she puts her hand inside her pocket and pulls out the phone.

'I'm scared,' she says, holding it to her chest. 'I'm so scared.'

'You don't have to be scared,' I say, taking the phone from her hands. 'I'm going to sort this.'

I turn towards Barbara's body. The knife is lying on the ground by her feet. I bend over and pick it up, running my hands up and down the blade and the handle. Then I lift the phone and press 'emergency call'.

'Police, please.'

I wait to be connected. Behind me I can hear Julia sobbing.

'Hello,' I say as a female voice comes on the line. 'My name is Maggie Allan. I'm calling from Ketton House Farm. The owner, Barbara Cosgrove, has been stabbed.'

The woman asks me if she is breathing. I look down at the lifeless body at my feet and shake my head.

'No, she's not breathing,' I say, my heart somersaulting in my chest. 'She's dead. I killed her.'

58

'No,' cries Julia as I end the call. 'You can't do this.'

I turn. She is standing by the kitchen counter, her hands clasped to her mouth.

'It's the only way,' I tell her.

'I can't breathe. I need air,' she says, running to the back door. She unbolts it and runs out into the night.

'Julia, wait!' I cry, stumbling behind.

I step outside. The farmyard is bathed in moonlight. Up ahead I see the shadowy outline of the playhouse, the door swinging off its hinges. Then I see Julia crouched outside it. I walk towards her across the gravel. When she sees me approach she looks up.

'I shouldn't have come back,' she says, getting to her feet. 'I should have just left it all in the past.'

'No,' I say, putting my hand on her shoulder. 'I'm glad you came. You're the best thing to have come out of all this horror.'

She turns to me, her face flushed from crying.

'Do you mean that?'

I nod my head.

'I was so angry with you,' she says, looking down at her feet. 'For years I was angry. Frey— Barbara told me to stop sending the letters after a while. She said that you didn't want to know me, that you were a bad person, that you'd tried to kill me.'

'Oh, Julia,' I say, squeezing her hand in mine. 'That wasn't how it happened. I was trying to kill myself, not you. I was so young and confused. I needed help but there was no one around to give it.'

'After that, she stopped visiting,' says Julia. 'Though she wrote to me from time to time. When I graduated from Cambridge she sent me a card.'

'You went to Cambridge?' I say, suddenly realizing there is so much I don't know about my daughter. 'That's amazing.'

'It was the happiest time of my life,' she says. 'The only place I'd ever lived where I didn't feel like a freak.'

'You're not a freak,' I say. 'You're an exceptionally gifted young woman.'

She manages a small smile.

'I've waited so long to hear that,' she says. 'For you to be proud of me. You know, in a weird way, what I thought was your rejection actually spurred me on. I forced myself to be the best so that I could show you I was worth something.'

My eyes fill with tears. There is so much I want to say and yet it's just so big, so fundamental, where do I even begin?

'Why did you come to find me?' I say, remembering the first time I saw her, standing in the doorway of Larkfields, glaring at me. 'It can't have been a co-incidence that you were living in that house.'

'I got the job in Lewes,' she says. 'Until then I'd been living in London but when I saw the role advertised it just seemed like fate. I think part of me thought it might help me put my demons to rest. I got in touch with Barbara again to see if she might help me make the move. But then she called to say that there'd been an accident.'

'My accident?'

Julia nods her head.

'She said that you were fighting for your life in hospital,' she continues. 'And that your little girl had been killed. I was upset and told her that I wanted to visit you. That's when she started to lie.'

'What did she tell you?'

'She said that you were responsible,' she says. 'That you'd killed her, like you'd tried to kill me. She said you had a history of mental illness and violence and that you were dangerous.'

I see Barbara standing on that riverbank, watching, and I shake my head.

'I wasn't going to come back at all, but then she was so nice. She apologized for stopping her visits,' continues Julia. 'She let me stay in Larkfields, came shopping with me, cooked me meals. Basically she became the loving grandmother I'd always wanted. But then you came out of the coma and it all changed; she changed.'

'In what way?'

'I don't know,' she says, shaking her head. 'It was like she was on this mission and no one was going to stand in her way. She wanted to destroy you, to get you back for all the things you'd done.'

'I had no idea. I just thought I was going mad.'

'I'm sorry, I really am,' she says, tears filling her eyes. 'But I was so angry at you. In my head you were this monster who had tried to kill me and then killed your own kid.'

'Julia, none of those things are true,' I say. 'You must believe me. And those letters – well, you saw how I reacted when I read the poem. It was the most beautiful thing.'

'I do believe you,' says Julia, wiping her eyes with the back of her sleeve. 'It was so hard . . . not having anyone. I wanted a mother so badly, it hurt.'

'God, I'm sorry,' I say. 'If I could turn back the clock . . . I just wish you'd told me who you were, that first day when I came to Larkfields. If you'd told me then I could have explained.'

'It's okay,' says Julia softly. 'You don't need to explain.'

'I want to make it up to you,' I say, my voice trembling. 'I want to get to know you and, if you'll let me, I want to be your mum.'

I hear a distant whine. At first it sounds like the wind in the trees. Then I realize it's the sound of sirens.

I wipe my eyes with the back of my sleeve. 'Right, you need to listen to me now, my love.'

'I can't let you do this,' says Julia. 'I can't let you take the blame for what I did to Barbara.'

'Shh,' I say, putting my hand to her mouth. 'That's the last time you say that, okay? I killed Barbara. She came at me with a knife, then I wrestled it off her and stabbed her. You tried to stop me. That's what happened, Julia.'

'But –'

'No buts,' I say firmly. 'This is what happened, are you clear?'

She looks at me for a moment then she nods.

'And I'll always be here for you,' I say gently. 'However long it takes, I'm going to make it up to you – everything that happened before you were born, for the letters, what you went through in those places. When all this is over we're going to start again, you and me.'

She looks up at me then and her eyes brighten. She looks like a little girl; *my* little girl.

'Everything is going to be okay,' I tell her, putting my hand on hers. 'I promise you.'

Julia goes to speak but before she can get her words out the yard is filled with lights and ear-piercing sirens.

'Oh God,' she mutters beside me. 'Oh God.'

'Be strong,' I whisper, clutching her arm in mine. 'And remember what I told you.'

She nods and we stand and watch as the police car doors open and uniformed officers run towards us. I step forward into the lights. Someone calls my name. I see a familiar face.

'Mrs Allan?'

I watch as DS Grayling approaches me.

They bundle me into the car. I am placed in the middle with an officer on either side. The engine starts up and I strain my neck to see if Julia is still talking to the policewoman. I hope to God that she is sticking to our plan. As the car pulls away, I close my eyes and pray that she will be okay, that she will stay strong and do as I asked. When she looked up at me, the knife dangling by her side, fear and confusion etched on her face, I knew then that I would take the blame for her. It was an instinct, deep inside me, ancient and raw, the same instinct that made me cling on to that car with my fingernails and, perversely, the same instinct that made Barbara pursue her repellent plan in Ben's name. It's the instinct that comes with motherhood, a wild, savage, sometimes violent compulsion.

Like Barbara said, a mother will do anything to protect her child.

Epilogue

I see him before he sees me. He is sitting at the far end of the room. His elbows rest on the table in front of him; his head is bowed. As I walk to the table I take in his new appearance. His hair, always neat and cut close to his head, has grown long, and his face is smattered with salt-and-pepper stubble. It's not him, I think to myself, it's his ghost.

And then he looks up. His pale-blue eyes are brittle, his mouth taut.

'Maggie,' he says, remaining seated.

'Hello, Sean.'

I pull the chair out and sit down. He leans back and folds his arms across his chest defensively.

'It's so good to see you,' I say, my voice cracking. 'I couldn't believe it when I got your letter.'

'Shall we cut the small talk?' he says, his voice hard. 'I came here because I want answers.'

I nod my head. 'Ask me anything.'

He takes a deep breath. 'How long was it going on?' he says. 'The affair with Ben Cosgrove?'

'There wasn't an affair,' I say. 'I mean, I'd been in touch with him. And there was a part of me that always wondered what had happened to him. But his text on the day of the accident, the one you saw on my phone, was actually from Barbara pretending to be Ben.'

'Why would she do that?'

'I don't really know, Sean,' I say. 'I guess because she hated me.'

'I read about it in the papers,' he says, leaning forward in his seat. 'Ben. The baby. Why didn't you tell me, Maggie? All those years we were together and you never once mentioned it. You knew I'd have understood, just like I understood about the unit. I just don't get it.'

'I know you would have listened,' I say, flinching as someone scrapes a chair across the floor behind me. 'But I couldn't bring myself to talk about it. I was so young, I . . . Sean, some things are just too big, too painful to talk about. The baby was one of them.'

His face remains stony. I put my head in my hands. This wasn't how I imagined it would be.

'And what about you?' I say, looking up. 'Why didn't you tell me about the house and the debts?'

'Because I didn't want to hurt you,' he says, his tone softening. 'For fuck's sake, Maggie, I loved you so much.'

'Then why the hell did you disappear?' I cry. 'I had

no idea what had happened to you. At first I thought you'd harmed yourself, then I thought you'd run off with another woman.'

'I needed to start again,' he says, sighing. 'My life had just imploded. My little girl was dead. You . . . you'd betrayed me, or so I thought. The only way I could deal with it was to run as far away as possible. You and . . . and Elspeth were my world.'

'Ditto,' I say, my eyes filling with the tears I've been trying to repress.

'Ditto?' he says, his eyes flaring. 'You locked our child in a car then let it roll into the fucking river. You took her out at night to meet your ex when she should have been safely tucked up in bed.'

'And you think I don't blame myself every day?' I cry, slamming my fists on the table.

He looks at me for a moment then puts his head down.

'You should have told me,' he said. 'When you got the text. If you had nothing to hide then why all the secrecy?'

'You were working all hours,' I say. 'I barely saw you in the months leading up to the accident. I actually thought you were having an affair, though now I know you were trying to pay off the debts. So if we're talking about secrecy, Sean, you're hardly blameless.'

'What happened, Maggie?' he says, lowering his voice. 'With Barbara? I mean, I've read about it and not one bit of it rings true. You're not capable of something like that.'

'Barbara was there that night,' I say, looking down so I don't have to meet his eye. 'When the car started to roll I ran after it but I couldn't get to Elspeth. I screamed to Barbara to help but she just stood and watched. She watched our little girl drown.'

I look up. His face is crumpled. I want to reach out and take his hand but I know I can't.

'That night at Ketton House she tried to do it again,' I say. 'She had a knife and she was coming for Julia. She would have killed her. I'm convinced of that. I stepped in between them and . . . it all happened so fast. I didn't know what I was doing.'

He's not fooled for a moment. I know that. Sean has always been the one person who can read me, who can understand me. But he doesn't press the matter and it's in that moment I remember why I fell in love with him all those years ago.

'So how long will you be in here for?'

'Four years,' I say. 'It could have been longer but because I pleaded guilty to the manslaughter charge I was given a lighter sentence.'

'Four years,' says Sean, putting his hand to his mouth. 'Jesus, Maggie.'

'My solicitor says I could be out in eighteen months,' I say. 'And it's not as bad as I thought it would be. I've got a little job in the prison library and –'

'This Julia,' he says, pronouncing the name as though it, too, is a lie. 'What kind of person is she? I read that she'd been in care.'

'Yes,' I say. 'She had a terrible childhood but she came good. She went to Cambridge and now she's a GP.'

Sean looks at me for a moment.

'What?' I say. 'What are you thinking?'

'It's nothing,' he says. 'Just, well, I hope she realizes what you've done for her.'

I look at him. Just as I suspected, he's seen right through me.

He goes to stand up. I want to grab his hand but the guard is looking at me. No touching allowed.

'Please don't go,' I say, leaning forward. 'Not yet.

'I have to,' he says, pushing the chair back. 'I've a flight to catch.'

He stands up and it's then that the wall I've spent the last few months building comes crashing down.

'I'm sorry,' I say, blinking through my tears. 'I'm so so sorry.'

'Maggie, don't.'

'I loved you both so much,' I say. 'But I always knew it was too good to be true, that I didn't deserve it; that one day it would all be ripped away from me.'

'You've spent your life punishing yourself,' he says. 'Maybe now it's time to stop.'

'Will you write to me again?' I say.

'I don't think that's a good idea, Maggie.'

'Okay,' I say, my heart shredding inside my chest.

'You know I've never been very good with words. Not like you.'

I go to speak but my throat tightens. I nod my head instead, and as I watch the prison officer escort him out of the room I see a troubled young woman sitting behind a reception desk drowning in words; I see Waterloo Station at twilight and a young couple heading out for a drink that will change both their lives; I see a little girl smiling up at me as she prepares to make her May procession. I see love and death and life and sadness beaming back at me like light through a prism and I know, deep in my heart, that this is the last time I will ever see him.

'Goodbye, Sean,' I whisper as the door closes behind him.

Two years later

This morning I was released from prison. I carried a bag containing my scant possessions, among them the finished manuscript for my novel. I don't know if anything will come of it, but it's something I had to do. Prison gave me the time to reflect on my life, my choices and mistakes, and writing the novel was my way of making sense of it all. When I finished writing it I felt like something had departed, some heavy stone that had sat in the pit of my stomach for years. I know now that it is impossible to live your life through your children or try to rewrite the past through them. Maybe now, I'll be able to move on with my life. Maybe there will be another book. A new start.

As I emerge from the prison gates I see that Sonia is waiting for me in her car. I smile, remembering those early days when I'd just come out of hospital and how she had helped me navigate my way through the fog. Even when I was sent to prison she stuck by me; coming to visit and keeping me updated on her progress at university. She's a good person and I will always be grateful to her.

As we drive away I hold on tight to the bouquet of peonies that arrived at the prison this morning: from Julia. There's a little card attached.

Dear Mum

I am not ready yet. But maybe soon.

Stay in touch,
Your daughter x

When we reach the crossroads I ask Sonia if she will take a detour. There is somewhere I need to go; someone I have to see.

Sonia stays in the car. She knows I have to do this

on my own. The air is still and cool as I make my way across the churchyard, weaving in and out of the stones. Up ahead I see a collared dove sitting on an old lichen-covered stone.

And then I see her. Elspeth Catherine Allan. Born on a crisp February morning in Chelsea and Westminster Hospital weighing eight pounds six ounces. A fair-haired girl with green eyes and beautiful soft pink skin. A healthy baby, according to the midwife, strong and thriving. When they laid her on my chest the heat of her body warmed mine. She'd curled her little hand into a fist and I had wrapped my hand around it. 'Hello, beautiful girl,' I'd whispered. 'I'm your mummy.'

My legs feel stiff as I kneel by the stone. I stretch them out then turn and lie on my side. I close my eyes and imagine that I'm lying next to her on the bed. We've just finished reading the latest chapter of her book and we're both so tired we can barely keep our eyes open. I hear her breath rising and falling next to me, feel the soft skin of her arm as it wraps round mine. 'Mummy, will you sing to me until I go to sleep?' And so I sing our song about the moon shining bright until I feel her body grow heavy.

The dove regards me for a moment with its beady eye then spreads its wings and takes flight. My eyes follow it as it rises into the winter sky, so alive and vital, like it's about to embark on the greatest adventure of its life.

'Goodnight, beautiful girl,' I whisper. 'Sleep tight.'

Acknowledgements

My deepest thanks and appreciation to Katy Loftus, the best editor a writer could wish for! It has been a dream to work with you and the amazing team at Viking Penguin.

Thank you to my agent Madeleine Milburn for all your help and support and for believing in my writing from the very start. Also to Hayley Steed, Alice Sutherland-Hawes, Giles Milburn and Anna Hogarty at the MMLA Agency. You're a super team and I appreciate your support so much.

A big thank you goes to the immensely talented Carolyn Jess-Cooke who invited me to be a part of her Writing Motherhood project back in 2015. The project hoped to dispel the Cyril Connolly quote that 'there is no more sombre enemy of good art than the pram in the hall' and I think it succeeded in showing that parenthood and the creation of art need not be mutually exclusive. The women I met through the workshops we led, and the stories they shared, inspired and moved me a great deal. One conversation particularly resonated with me. It was with a young mother who told me that she wrote in secret as she felt guilty for taking time out from her young baby to work on something that could be seen as indulgent. This idea that creative work is an indulgence or guilty pleasure, particularly for mothers, was something I wanted to explore in this novel and it really helped shape the character of Maggie.

Heartfelt thanks go to Tamsin for sharing your experiences of foster care – the good and the bad. Your stories will stay with me for ever.

My love and thanks also to my wonderful family for your endless patience, cups of coffee, glasses of wine, 'mad half hours' and words of encouragement. I couldn't have done any of this without you and I love you all very much!

Finally, I'd like to acknowledge the beautiful village of Rodmell in Sussex. Though Larkfields, Ketton House Farm and the Plough Inn are purely fictional, my affinity and fascination with this beautiful corner of Sussex are very much real. I rediscovered Virginia Woolf, and the watery landscape where she spent much of her life, eleven years ago when I was heavily pregnant with my son Luke. We'd moved to Sussex from London and, desperate for fresh air, I headed out on long walks across the Downs. The river Ouse was my constant companion. It snaked alongside me as I walked, listening to my hopes and fears of life and impending motherhood and sometimes giving away secrets of its own. Many years later when I sat down at my desk, in a house that overlooks another

River Ouse, and began to write *The Day of the Accident*, I thought about those few months of solitary river-walking. Like the young woman I'd met during the Writing Motherhood Project, back then I had concealed my desire to write and wondered what the future would hold. Little did I know that becoming a mother would reignite my creativity and give me the strength to pursue my dream of writing novels.

And it all began with a walk by the river near Rodmell . . .

THE NEXT THRILLER BY NUALA ELLWOOD

THE HOUSE ON THE LAKE

A mother and child run away . . .

Lisa needs to disappear for a while. So Rowan Isle House, an old holiday home set on a lake in the wilds of Yorkshire, seems like the perfect place for her and her son to hide. All she wants is to start again, to be left alone with the son she so nearly lost.

But when a man from the local village tells her about a woman called Grace, who died there in mysterious circumstances, Lisa realizes that the house may not be the sanctuary she thought.

What secret is the house on the lake hiding?

And how can Lisa keep her son safe from the danger that surrounds them?

COMING SOON

PRE-ORDER NOW